Praise for the
Bridal Bouquet Shop Mysteries

Bloom and Doom

"*Bloom and Doom* captivated my attention from the very first page. With the meanings of flowers skillfully woven throughout the story, it was as delightful as a freshly cut bouquet of ranunculus (radiant charm) and tarragon (lasting interest). . . . A thoroughly entertaining and engaging mystery! I can't wait for the next one!"
—Jenn McKinlay, *New York Times* bestselling author

"It's an engaging bouquet of mayhem and murder. What a delight for cozy readers!"
—Erika Chase, national bestselling author of the Ashton Corners Book Club Mysteries

"Allen's upbeat series debut reads smoothly and easily, with excellent dialogue and an immensely likable cast. . . . The flower business really stars in this cozy." —*Library Journal*

"A highly entertaining, fun, and snappy mystery . . . *Bloom and Doom* has everything to keep you engaged: a compelling murder to be solved, great humor, warm friendship, and the language of flowers." —CriminalElement.com

"Provides readers with a fresh twist on the amateur-sleuth story." —*Booklist*

"A terrific start to a new series." —*Suspense Magazine*

"Has all the ingredients that make up a charming cozy mystery—likable characters, good mystery, and a little fun and romance thrown in." —*Fresh Fiction*

D1051999

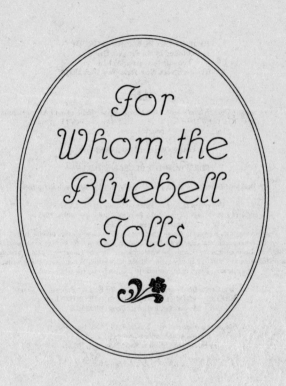

For Whom the Bluebell Tolls

Beverly Allen

BERKLEY PRIME CRIME, NEW YORK

THE BERKLEY PUBLISHING GROUP
Published by the Penguin Group
Penguin Group (USA) LLC
375 Hudson Street, New York, New York 10014

USA • Canada • UK • Ireland • Australia • New Zealand • India • South Africa • China

penguin.com

A Penguin Random House Company

FOR WHOM THE BLUEBELL TOLLS

A Berkley Prime Crime Book / published by arrangement with the author

For information, address: The Berkley Publishing Group,
a division of Penguin Group (USA) LLC,
375 Hudson Street, New York, New York 10014.

ISBN: 978-0-425-26498-0

PUBLISHING HISTORY
Berkley Prime Crime mass-market edition / January 2015

PRINTED IN THE UNITED STATES OF AMERICA

10 9 8 7 6 5 4 3 2 1

Cover illustration by Ben Perini.
Cover design by Diana Kolsky.
Interior text design by Kelly Lipovich.

Dedicated to Him whose words bring life.

Acknowledgments

In the language of flowers, the larkspur can stand for *brightness*, *lightness*, or *levity*. And I have a bouquet to distribute to my very bright critique partners and readers: Christine Bress (who also reviewed Audrey's flower designs), Janice Cline, Anita Mae Draper, Aric Gaughan, Kathy Hurst, Debra Marvin, Niki Turner, and Lynne Wallace-Lee. Together, they have kept me from turning in a manuscript featuring a man with a tick in his face (tic), concealing cheese (congealing), and taught muscles (taut). Hence the levity.

I also have double daffodils of *regard* for my agent, Kim Lionetti, and my fantastic editor, Katherine Pelz, and all the other wonderful folks at Berkley.

For the readers who have told me how much you enjoyed *Bloom and Doom*, small white bellflowers to show my *gratitude*.

Purple violets for my family. *You occupy my thoughts.*

Chapter 1

❧

"Audrey, I . . ."

I stood on my front stoop, hand-in-hand with Nick Maxwell after one of our sporadic dinner dates. The moon cooperated, already aglow in the dusky sky, and a gentle breeze stirred the leaves in the trees—very welcome after the heat of the day. I closed my eyes, waiting for our good-night kiss.

Chester interrupted our romantic moment, scratching on the glass window and yowling for me to get inside and serve his every whim. (Did I mention Chester is my cat?) My neighbor Tom added percussion to the feline chorus, using the last remaining moments of daylight to tack up a Fourth of July banner a few feet away. Ah, the joys of apartment living. Then my phone started ringing in my living room.

"I should let you get that. Good night, Audrey." Nick planted a chaste kiss on my forehead and gave my hand a squeeze before sending Tom a wave and walking back to his truck.

I leaned against the door frame for a moment and watched him go. I knew Nick was encouraged by the growth of the bakery, which now supplied fresh baked goods and breads to local restaurants. But his early hours had really taken a toll on our date time.

Meanwhile, my phone had stopped ringing. I opened my door as the answering machine picked up. A click showed that the caller declined to leave a message.

I bumped my behemoth of a window air conditioner up to the max, then made my way to the kitchen with Chester nipping at my ankles and weaving around my legs. I spooned out a half can of something labeled "Fresh Seafood," but which smelled more like the Dumpster behind a sushi restaurant. He didn't seem to mind. I managed to refill his water dish before the phone rang again.

I carried the receiver so I could stand in front of the roaring air conditioner, then lifted my ponytail so the chilled air hit the back of my neck. "Hello?"

"Audrey, where have you been? I've been calling all night."

Letting my hair fall, I jerked into my full and upright position. "Hey, Brad." Where I'd been was none of his business. Not anymore. Brad the Cad had blown his chance with me. I really needed to get caller ID.

"Listen, Audrey, I'm coming back to Ramble."

Well, let's call the town band and organize a parade, why don't we? But instead of saying that, I sank onto the sofa. "Coming back?"

"Just for a visit. Well, work, really."

"How nice for you."

"Aw, come on, Audrey. I know you're upset with me, but I hoped we could talk. Clear the air. There might be a job in it for you. A huge wedding."

"Are you getting married?" A logical question, considering I made my living as a florist specializing in wedding bouquets at the Rose in Bloom, the shop that my cousin Liv and I owned.

A long pause was followed by a slow inhalation and exhalation. "No, Audrey. I'm not getting married. You were right. New York isn't exactly what I thought it would be. I really messed up when I left you behind."

I swallowed hard. For a long time I'd dreamed of hearing those words. And I'd rehearsed all kinds of reactions, ranging from running into his arms—hard to do over the phone—and stomping on his foot with my highest and spikiest pair of heels—equally hard to do over the phone.

"Yeah?" Okay, so that wasn't one of the reactions I'd practiced.

"Look, I'm coming back with the whole film crew."

"I thought the show you were working on was canceled."

"It was. Who knew *The Lumberjack Logs* would turn out to be such a yawn? But a friend hooked me up with *Fix My Wedding*. I'm the production assistant. Might even make associate producer, with a little more experience."

"And they're coming to Ramble?" My ears perked up. *Fix My Wedding* had become one of my favorite guilty pleasures. Gigi Welch's snarky treatment of brides brought them to tears as she mocked their original—and usually tacky— plans. Then her cohort, Gary Davoll, would sweep in like a fairy godfather and whisk the bride away, spoiling her like a princess. I won't say the elaborate weddings they staged were much less tacky than the bride's original plans, but the show had chemistry. And I could justify the hours I spent watching it by labeling the time as work—research for anyone in the bridal industry.

"Yep. And I might have had something to do with that." Pride rang in his voice. "The original venue fell through. The bride in question is nuts—"

"Aren't they usually?"

"Same old Audrey. Quick-witted and never letting me finish a sentence." The tone in his voice was teasing and cheerful. It belonged to the old charming Brad I had dated, not the monster I'd recast him as since the breakup. I shifted my emotions to defensive mode. I would not fall for him again. I would not . . .

"Anyway," he continued, "The bride is nutty about bells, and I told her about the hand-rung bell in the old First Baptist. I showed Gary and Gigi pictures of some of the other local assets, so they're going to hold the wedding at the church and the reception at the Ashbury."

Oh, lovely. The Ashbury. The restaurant where Brad dumped me. This was getting better by the minute. "And you said there might be a job for me?"

"Yes, I showed Gigi and Gary the article about you in the paper, and they thought the whole language-of-flowers thing was cute. Said a local florist with that kind of reputation might make the episode more interesting. Well, 'quaint,' they said, but you know Gigi."

"And the bride's crazy about bells?" My brain started turning. I'd seen bell-shaped vases that might work. Maybe campanula, also known as bellflowers, or any of the other flower varieties that resembled bells. Or was that too literal?

The meanings were suitable. Bellflowers signified *constancy*, a great meaning for a marriage, and the small white ones meant *gratitude*. Of course, the bluebell also could signify *sorrowful regret*, but maybe I could steer her away from that color. Not all of the bellflowers are commonly used by many florists, but I was sure I could get my hands on them if needed. And if I couldn't, Liv was a whiz at acquisition.

"Yes, some fetish with bells," he continued. "We're busing in a bell choir to perform at the ceremony. Guests are ringing little silver bells instead of throwing rice. I think Gary is even arranging to have bells woven into her dress. Crazy, huh? But that's why people watch the show. I hope you're not overbooked and can squeeze in the wedding. Mom said the shop has been real busy."

"When is the wedding?"

"Um, we're coming next week. Like I said, the other venue canceled at the last minute. Can you do it? I know it's the middle of summer. It has to be a busy time for weddings."

Proving once again that Brad never paid attention. July might be a prime time for a wedding in many parts of the country. But in Ramble, Virginia, where most weddings were held at the old First Baptist, which lacked air conditioning, or outside in the gardens of the Ashbury, local brides tended to opt for late spring or early fall, when the temperatures were more manageable.

"I should be free. I'll have to see if Liv can source the flowers for a quick delivery. It may cost a bit more."

"No problem," he said. "The show has deep pockets. We'll make sure the cost of anything you need is written into the contract. Should be some nice publicity for your shop, too."

"Of course, I'll have to talk it over with Liv."

"Last time I called Mom, she told me that Liv and Eric are going to have a baby. They must be tickled pink."

"Or blue," I said. "They want to be surprised."

"That's great. Give them my best. Or I can do it when I get into town. Oh, Audrey, I've missed you. I'm looking forward to seeing you."

My stomach twisted. He sounded like the same old Brad that I had dated for a year. But did I really want to see him again? And where would that leave my budding relationship (pardon the floral pun) with Nick Maxwell?

"Yes, Brad, I'm looking forward to seeing you again, too."

I inserted the mouthpiece into my tuba and drummed my fingers across the valves. Leaning back against the creaky wood chair only reminded me of the sweat running down my back. It was bad enough that Mayor Watkins decided the arriving film crew needed a formal welcome from the town band. That he'd decreed we be in our military-style uniforms—wool pants, wool coats with leather overlays and epaulets, and leather hats—on one of the hottest days of the year was more than I could take. At least we could play in the shade of the gazebo and not march down Main Street.

Welcome home, Brad, I thought. You almost got your parade after all.

Liv hopped up onto the special pedestal constructed to accommodate her petite frame (not a family trait I inherited), adjusted the music stand above her burgeoning belly, and tapped the stand with her baton. As the conductor, she hadn't had to dress in the stifling uniform. Not that they came in maternity sizes, anyway.

"The film crew has been spotted about ten miles out of town," she said, "so let's get warmed up."

A couple of groans from the clarinet section were followed by an anonymous, "We're warm enough already."

Liv smiled. "Sorry. I know those uniforms are torture. Tell you what, lemonade for everybody after this little shindig is over. My treat." Liv nodded to Nick Maxwell's cupcake truck stationed just off the town square, where the folk of Ramble were lined up to buy their sweet treats. Today they mainly walked away from the food truck with cold drinks.

A cacophony of woodwinds, brass, and percussion ensued as we tuned our instruments and the bassoonist tried to make a move on our newest piccolo player. When the band played a note to Liv's satisfaction, we started cycling through the book of marches that we normally reserved for patriotic concerts. Knowing Brad, he'd arrive in town to the opening chords of "Hail to the Chief." At least the music required enough focus that it took my attention away from the stifling heat.

It could not, however, still the butterflies doing aerobatics in my stomach over the prospect of seeing Brad. I was over him, surely, but the rational part of me decided it was a good idea to meet with him, put the past behind me, and let go of some of the bitterness I'd heaped over my heart as a bandage. Grandma Mae always said to never flog a dead horse. Since we never owned horses, dead or otherwise, I always assumed she meant we needed to let things go. So I'd determined to be cool, professional, and maybe even friendly to Brad. The cad.

We turned the page and started Sousa's "Liberty Bell March" as the first truck crawled down Main Street and passed under the banner, which read, "Ramble Welcomes *Fix My Wedding*." A handful of vans and cars followed, some with vinyl placards announcing the show. One, a giant recreational vehicle wrapped with Gary's and Gigi's over-sized faces and the show's logo, stopped in front of the town square.

The residents of Ramble rose from the sea of lawn chairs that circled the white gazebo.

Out of the corner of my eye, I saw two people exit the RV. A yell erupted that overpowered our music. We were right at a section where the tuba part had only a repetitive line on the downbeats, so I watched as Gary and Gigi held hands and ran toward the gazebo.

Only this was not the sleek cosmopolitan pair that I'd come to . . . I wasn't sure what my emotions were toward Gigi and Gary. "Love" would be overstating it. I supposed I was merely entertained and amused.

But when they climbed out of their RV in Ramble, they looked like they'd dressed for an evening of line dancing in some country-western bar. Gigi had slithered into a pair of low-slung, skintight, faded jeans and wore a plaid shirt, tight to her bosom, unbuttoned to show considerable cleavage and tied up to expose a flat, tanned midriff. She popped a cow-boy hat onto her loose-flowing black hair.

If she was a little bit country, Gary looked like he had just stepped off the stage of the Grand Ole Opry. Fringe dangled from the sleeves of a sequined and embroidered pink cowboy shirt, accented with a wide Western belt, bolo tie, skinny jeans, and elaborately engraved boots. He doffed a ten-gallon—or maybe twenty-gallon—white hat, revealing his short ginger hair, and waved at the crowd as he climbed the gazebo steps.

Mayor Watkins, dressed in his conservative designer suit and tie, reached out and shook Gary's hand, then gave Gigi a brief hug.

Then I found myself *oomp*-ing when nobody was *pah*-ing. Liv must have cut the band when I wasn't paying attention, giving me an awkward solo. I avoided her eyes and rested my tuba on the floor.

The mayor held up his hands to mute the applause Gary and Gigi seemed to revel in. He then tapped the microphone.

"Please be seated," he said to the crowd, amid a pulse of feedback.

He paused while the townsfolk lowered themselves into their squeaky and creaky lawn chairs.

"As mayor, it gives me great pleasure to award, this day, the key to the Town of Ramble to our most distinguished guests, Gigi Welch and Gary Davoll, hosts of the reality television show *Fix My Wedding*." He handed the wood key to Gary and a small bouquet Liv had made for the occasion to Gigi. White lilies (*purity* and *sweetness*), pink roses (*secret love*), and alstroemeria. Some say the flower, also known as the Peruvian lily, symbolizes *friendship* and *devotion*. Others insist it's a symbol of *prosperity* and *good fortune*. In either case, the bouquet was stunning. The photographer from the *Ramble On*, the town's local paper, flashed a picture of Gigi holding it.

While the audience applauded, Gigi grabbed hold of the other end of the key and Gary took possession of the flowers, hoisting them up like the Statue of Liberty bearing her torch. The audience laughed and the photographer snapped another picture.

When the applause died down again, Gigi and Gary stepped to the microphone.

"Hey, y'all," Gigi said. "We've been so looking forward to this visit." Although her back was turned to me, I could hear the broad smile in her voice. "My thanks to all the citizens . . . here. We're looking forward to some good ole Southern hospitality. And hopefully some fried chicken and cornbread."

Yeah, like that body ever actually consumed fried chicken. And I wasn't sure they'd find it on the menu at the Ashbury, which boasted gourmet fare featuring locally grown organic produce, lamb and veal from local farms, and wine bottled by monks at a monastery in the surrounding hills.

I wasn't sure if, even if this were fifty or sixty years ago, Ramble was ever the Hicksville they'd apparently expected to find. With the cultivation and grace the area derived from founding fathers such as Jefferson and Washington, and the influx of a more cosmopolitan influence from the DC transplants who built second homes and sprawling estates among the hills of the area, I can assure you that we all had indoor plumbing, wore shoes, kept most of our own teeth well into our thirties, never married our cousins, and didn't subsist on possum, squirrel, or polecat.

A long, uncomfortable pause ensued, perhaps as the two scanned the audience and saw no sign of Ma and Pa Kettle or cows and horses loping down Main Street. Gigi looked to Gary.

"Anyway . . . " Gary cleared his throat and fingered his bolo tie. "We look forward to spending time in Ramble while we film and getting to know you folks better. Thanks for watching the show." He blew the crowd a few kisses, sending loud smacking sounds into the microphone.

For this we'd sweated for hours in the sun?

Liv raised her baton to start another march when tires squealed on Main Street.

"He's a fraud!" A familiar-looking, buxom blonde hopped out of the driver's seat of a decrepit van, then three other young women piled out of the same vehicle.

"Fraud, fraud, fraud," they chanted while hoisting

crumpled poster-board signs. At first I thought the signs read "Gigi and Gary fixed my wedding." Only they'd crossed out *"fixed"* and substituted another word—one Grandma Mae had told us should never leave a lady's mouth, or a gentleman's, either.

Chief Bixby made his way over to the disrupting interlopers, followed by Ken Lafferty, Ramble's youngest and most inexperienced officer. The rookie's eyes were wide and he looked panicked.

He should be. I recognized the blonde. She'd been one of the first brides to have her wedding "fixed" on the reality show, and it had been a humdinger. The episode was still my favorite. As I recalled, the bride's name was Jackie. Gigi had dubbed her "Tacky Jackie," which was also the name of the episode. And she'd been a nervous wreck. Gigi and Gary "calmed her" with dinner and drinks, a spa day and drinks, cocktail testing, a quick belt after her fitting, followed by a wine-tasting with more drinks after. Jackie had spent most of the episode, including the wedding, sloshed out of her gourd.

The final scene of the show was generally reserved for couples gushing about the wonderful job Gigi and Gary had done. Instead, Jackie had taken a wild swing at Gary with a champagne bottle. He'd ducked and the bottle connected with the groom's head instead. As the credits rolled, EMTs were trying to bring the groom back to consciousness while Jackie, her face a blob of mucus, was being restrained by the police. That one episode made *Fix My Wedding* an overnight sensation. I know it found a permanent place on my DVR.

While Chief Bixby worked at quieting the four women, another cluster of unfamiliar people carrying signs had made their way from the street to the perimeter of the gathering. What they lacked in numbers, they made up for with noise. One of them, a rather rotund young man in gray sweatpants and a sweat-soaked blue T-shirt, carried a bullhorn.

"We love Gigi. We love Gary," he started, and his small group parroted his chant.

The two groups continued their contrary shouting, while the amused residents of Ramble looked back and forth between the two as if they were watching a tennis match.

The mayor whispered something to Liv, and she raised her baton. We quickly turned our eyes to the next march in the book. Coincidentally, it was "The Victors," the march Sousa had acclaimed as the greatest fight song ever written.

I was grateful the music was so familiar. While we played, I was able to follow the action. A private security team marched up, dressed in black and wearing reflective sunglasses. They held their arms out as if ready to take a bullet as they escorted Gary and Gigi back into their RV. As they drove off, the police led Jackie and her cohorts back to their double-parked van and sent them on their way. The fan with the bullhorn set it down, and he and his crew took to swaying and clapping to the beat of the march, as if they were in some college pep rally.

Liv then led us in two more marches while the crowd settled and dispersed back to their homes and businesses.

I packed away my tuba before peeling off the sticky hat and fluffing my damp hair. "How bad is it?" I asked Liv.

"Not too bad. Kind of like you just stepped out of the shower. With everything else going on, I doubt anyone will even notice your hair."

"Plenty for Ramble folks to yammer about. I don't know what will get more attention: those outlandish hootenanny outfits or Jackie's appearance."

"Jackie?"

I had forgotten Liv didn't watch the show. She was currently addicted to *A Baby Story*, but I wasn't sure if it was easing her fears about her upcoming delivery or fueling them.

"Tacky Jackie was one of the first brides on *Fix My Wedding*," I said. "The episode has a cult following."

"And that blonde was Jackie? Who were the women with her?"

"Bridesmaids, I think." I peeled off the leather overlay and shimmied out of the jacket, draping it over the back of my chair. The uniform would need a good airing out. I'm sure it didn't look pretty, but at least my sweat-drenched tee felt cool by comparison. "We'd better get over to the food truck to pay for that lemonade you promised."

"Nick will give me credit, I think. I have an in with him. He's dating my cousin." She paused and fixed me with her most penetrating gaze. Sometimes I think Liv has superpowers that allow her to follow which synapses are firing deep inside a person's frontal lobe. "He still is dating my cousin, right? You don't have any plans to reconcile with a former boyfriend or anything, do you? With Brad Simmons back in town . . ."

"No, but I did promise to meet Brad for dinner, just to clear the air. But only dinner."

"Oh, boy."

"No, nothing more," I said, with perhaps a bit too much force. "Things ended so badly. I figured it would be a good idea to meet again, to part on a friendlier basis. Don't you agree?"

"Maybe. As long as that's what Brad has in mind, too, I guess it couldn't hurt. Especially since you're going to be working together. But make sure you get the scoop on Jackie. I imagine her presence here is going to make the filming more difficult."

"It's a reality show. I'm sure they'll spin whatever happens into more ratings. It seems to me the controversy could only help them. But yes, I'll get the scoop."

We'd just stepped down from the gazebo when Brad's mother waddled over from the small group of Ramblers still seated around the gazebo, probably talking about the recent excitement.

"Oh, Audrey . . ." Mrs. Simmons dropped her lawn chair, reached up, and planted her hands on my cheeks. "I told you he would come home. It will be so good to have you in the house again tonight."

"I thought Brad was taking me out to eat." I bent down to pick up her fallen chair for her.

"And I told him that was stuff and nonsense. Why go out when I can cook a perfectly good meal for both of you? Put a little meat on those bones. But don't you worry. Right after supper I can sneak out. I know when two young folks want to be alone." She winked at me.

"Mrs. Simmons, I—"

"Now, none of that, my dear. You know what I like to be called."

"But it hardly seems appropriate to call you 'Mom' under the circumstances."

"Circumstances change, hon. You'll see. We eat at six. Oh, it'll be so nice to see the both of you across the table. We're having roast beef."

I think she sang that last part about the beef. Then Mrs. Simmons pinched my cheek and practically floated away.

"Well, if Brad thinks this is just a friendly dinner," Liv said, putting her arm around my shoulder and leading me toward the food truck, "he didn't clue his mother in."

The line was short by the time we arrived at the converted bakery truck. Nick stood behind the counter. He had draped a white apron over his baker's whites, and sweat beaded on his face. A bandana tied around his forehead was damp. At least I wasn't going to be the only one walking around with hat hair.

"Lemonade for two?" Nick said.

"Yes, and I need to settle my bill," Liv said. "I hope you've been keeping track of the band members I sent over for lemonade."

"No need." Nick slid two frosty plastic glasses to the front of the counter, each with a twist of lemon on the side and a straw. "I'll consider it my donation in the spirit of community service. I might even be able to deduct it."

I took a sip. The sweet citrus washed away the vestiges of tuba-mouth. Before I knew it, I'd gulped half of the glass.

"Easy there," Nick said. "And I saved you each a cupcake, too. Last ones. Key lime."

"My favorite," I said.

"They're all your favorite." Liv quickly peeled back the paper wrapper on hers.

"You should talk."

I immediately regretted needling her. Liv had been exceptionally hungry since the beginning of her pregnancy. The weight was starting to stack up on her petite frame, and I suspected the post-pregnancy weight loss was going to be difficult.

"Hey, Audrey," Nick said. "Now that the rally is over, I think I can manage some time off. You up for dinner tonight?"

"Tonight?" I searched my brain for an excuse. Nick and I had never discussed having an exclusive relationship, so it wasn't like I had something to hide. But I wasn't sure I wanted to tell him I was meeting my ex-boyfriend. "I'm sorry. I have . . . plans."

"Oh." His sad eyes reminded me of a puppy dog some ogre had kicked in the belly.

"I'll have to take a rain check. It's just that you've been so busy at the bakery that I didn't expect . . ."

"I understand." He forced a smile.

"I'm . . ."

"No, really, I do. But I will take you up on that rain check." He smiled, and his eyes twinkled, sending a shiver down my sweat-drenched back.

Chapter 2

ॐ

"So how are we going to do this?" Amber Lee asked. Amber Lee was the first employee Liv and I had taken on at the Rose in Bloom. A retired schoolteacher and lifelong resident of Ramble, she was our connection to the town's current gossip. Technically, she was my assistant, but her skill and dedication had proven she was ready for more responsibility. She had become our girl Friday and had made huge inroads into Monday, Thursday, and Saturday as well.

"The designated florist—that's us," I said, "shows the bride three possible bridal bouquets."

"And she picks one." Liv crossed her arms and leaned against one of the worktables in the back room of the shop. The space was cluttered, but in a cheerful and familiar way, each wall lined with shelves that exploded with colorful ribbon, vases, and every accessory needed to help the town of Ramble celebrate births and birthdays, young love, weddings, and anniversaries. And, unfortunately, to cheer sickbeds and honor the recently departed. But such was the flower business.

Shelby, one of our part-time employees, snickered. "The bride *never* gets a choice," he said. "Gary always picks the bridal bouquets."

"I see I'm not the only one hooked on the show," I said. "That will come in handy."

"Then how do they decide on the rest of the flowers?" Liv asked.

"They never get into that on the show," Shelby said.

"But it was all covered in the paperwork Brad sent." I plopped a large manila folder onto the work table. "Basically, after Gary picks the bridal bouquet, we construct coordinating sample bridesmaid bouquets, church flowers, and reception centerpieces, and Gary and Gigi will either okay or nix them. Hopefully they won't nix them."

"But that means we can't nail down the designs until he picks the bride's bouquet," Amber Lee said. "How will we get the flowers delivered on time when we don't know what we need?"

"That was the tricky part," Liv said. "But I basically ordered everything we might need. Twice over."

Amber Lee whistled. "That must have cost a pretty penny."

Liv turned almost ashen, then she swung panicked eyes in my direction.

"Brad did say the show had deep pockets," I assured her. "I'm holding him to that."

"Anyway," Liv said, "I ordered every flower that I could think of that resembled a bell and made sure we were well-stocked with roses, lilies, and all our staples."

"So I think"—I paced the back room with my hands clasped behind my back, feeling suddenly like a schoolteacher—"if we give them three very different bouquets to choose from, that should satisfy the camera. I thought I'd construct a very traditional, almost Victorian bouquet. Liv, could you do something clean and modern? And I thought maybe . . . Shelby."

Shelby's eyes lit up at the mention of his name. The young man was a natural-born floral designer, even if he was still only partway through his horticulture studies at Nathaniel Bacon University.

"Shelby's designs are artistic and innovative," I said to the rest of our staff, before turning to him. "I hoped you could come up with something novel and maybe a bit edgy."

"For the show? For real?" He clapped his hands gleefully.

"I have to approve it first." Shelby's designs often teetered on the border of genius, but sometimes took a left turn at practicality. "But yes, for the show." I couldn't help a small sigh. I would never stand in the young man's way, but he had a bright future ahead of him—one that was sure to lead him away from Ramble.

"And, Amber Lee," I said, "you have a very important role to play as well."

"Let me guess. While all this other work is going on, you need me to run the shop."

I caught my breath. Would she feel like she was missing out on all the glamour of the TV show? I hadn't meant to exclude her, but I felt that I'd picked the best people to make three distinctive bouquets. "Do you mind?" I watched her face for the answer.

She smiled a broad smile. "I'm glad you have the faith in me. And I'm much happier behind the scenes. I may look like a diva, but I have no desire to play one on TV." She fluffed her hair with one hand, pursed her lips, and struck a Hollywood glamour pose—almost an impossibility in the dowdy black Rose in Bloom aprons we all wore.

"But there's more I'd like you to do," I said. "The nasty part of this filming business is that the privacy rules mean we're not allowed to discuss our plans with any of the other wedding vendors."

Shelby raised his eyebrows about two feet. "Then how do we coordinate designs?"

"We keep our eyes and ears open." I gave a careful nod

to Amber Lee. "There's nothing in the rules about information we might happen to overhear . . ."

She erupted into a full-throated laugh. "You're making me a spy. You want me to exploit my connections in Ramble's gossip network for the good of the company. Your grandmother would be . . ."

I inhaled quickly. What would Grandma Mae think of the plan? She was sweet, but also savvy and coy.

"Proud, I think," Liv said. And in that instant, I knew it to be true.

"I'll be happy to listen for clues on the wedding," Amber Lee said. "I don't think Ramble is going to be talking about much else, anyway."

The bell above the front door jingled.

Amber Lee saluted. "Agent double-oh six and three-quarters reporting for duty. Licensed to grill." She swooped out to greet the customer.

"And each of you is also deputized." I nodded to Liv, Shelby, and then Darnell, our other part-timer. "You never know where information will come from. Just make sure we don't give it out."

"Uh, Audrey?" Amber Lee peeked her head back in the door. "Gary Davoll and Brad Simmons are here."

"Game time!" I wiped a sweaty palm on my pant leg. "Show them back, please."

I greeted them both with a smile and an offered hand, hopefully dry.

Brad, of course, had been in the back room any number of times when we were dating. He took my hand with a brief but tender shake, letting his fingers graze against my palm. I'd have to do something about that boy.

Gary had stopped mid-stride, placed his hands on his hips, and stared at the cacophony of colors and shapes lining the walls. "I'm glad we decided to film the floral segment at the Ashbury." He poked at some green floral foam soaking in the utility sink. "This place is a mess."

"It's a working flower shop," I said. "Unfortunately they tend to be a little more cluttered than the quaint sets used by Martha Stewart." I offered my hand again. "I'm Audrey Bloom. We talked on the phone."

"Ah, yes." He stared at my hand for a moment before he gave it a brief shake. "I wanted to talk about the shooting schedule."

"I was about to tell my staff that the bridal bouquets needed to be ready by Tuesday morning."

"We've upped it to Monday." Gary crossed his arms in front of him. "Some snag with the fashions not being shipped on time. Can't be helped."

"But that's the day after tomorrow." I have a special talent for stating the obvious.

"Will that be a problem?" He turned to Brad. "You said the local florist could be counted on, but I didn't know it would be such a small operation. Maybe we should call in—"

"We can do it," I insisted, surveying my staff. Liv dipped her chin in firm resolve. And Shelby bobbed his head enthusiastically.

"They're really quite good," Brad said.

"Tell me what you have in mind." Gary hoisted himself onto a worktable and sat cross-legged.

"Three designs," I explained, "each using bell-shaped flowers. One inspired by the Victorian language of flowers. Very traditional. The second design clean and modern. The third a little on the edgier side."

"Audrey is known in the whole region for her designs based on the language of flowers." Brad's voice carried a smidgen of pride. "If you recall, a feature article that was carried by quite a few papers called her the botanical Dr. Dolittle."

I resisted the urge to cringe at the mention of that unfortunate nickname. Made me sound like a nut who talked to flowers and fancied that they talked back. Rather, I liked discussing the meanings of flowers with prospective brides. Many had enjoyed creating their own personalized bouquets with flowers that held meanings that matched their personalities or characterized their relationships with their future spouses.

I scrutinized Brad's face, wondering if he was poking a little fun at me with the Dr. Dolittle reference, but his expression bore no trace that he was teasing. I remembered his mother had told me she was going to send him the article written for the *On*. The story was later picked up by a news service and had generated a little business for us at the time, but things like that are quickly forgotten.

"Make sure you don't 'do little' this time." Gary snorted. "And tell me a little more about this flower language of yours."

"The Victorians associated meanings with most flowers common to them at the time," I began. "Bouquets often communicated messages, sometimes secret ones. Some of my brides find it interesting. If you think viewers would like it, I could explain what each of the flowers in the bouquets mean."

"Maybe for the Victorian one." Gary pulled out his smartphone and started scrolling through messages. "I don't want to get bogged down with that jazz, but it could be an interesting side note. We're shooting at eight on Monday. Be there an hour before. Three bouquets, but two identical versions of each one. Sure you can do that?"

"Absolutely! We'll be there." I resisted the urge to add "with bells on."

Gary slid off the worktable and took one step toward the door, then stopped. He turned back to face me. "*You'll* be there. One person."

"But—"

He shook his head. "Too many people clutter the shot and take the attention away from the flowers. Just you." And then he was out the door with Brad in his wake.

"See you later, Audrey," Brad called, as the door jingled once more.

I turned to Liv and Shelby. "I'm so sorry. I thought you'd each be on camera."

"It's okay." Liv patted her belly. "Not the most flattering time for me to be on television, anyway. You know, the whole adding-ten-pounds thing."

"I disagree." I put an arm around her shoulder. "You're rocking that baby bump."

Liv smiled, but Shelby was silent for a moment. He finally shrugged his shoulders. "It's okay with me, too."

"I'll try to mention your names, at least," I added.

That drew a smile from Shelby.

"But now we've got to hurry." Liv glanced at the wall clock. "That's less than forty-eight hours away."

"Hurry is what we do best," I said.

Choosing what to wear for dinner with my ex and his mother turned out to be harder than picking the flowers for my Victorian-inspired bouquet. I vacillated between dressing up and dressing down. Part of me wanted to show Brad the Cad, the one who dumped me, that he wasn't worth the effort, so I pulled out a comfortable pair of yoga pants and a tee. Then again, if I pulled out all the stops and slithered into a slinky dress, I could show him what he missed out on. In the end, I split the difference and left the tee and the drop-dead dress draped over my bed and opted for black pants and a flattering purple V-necked top. I took a quick shower to wash off the perspiration the day's heat had caused, glad to get rid of the hat hair that I'd struggled with all day.

Dressed, but still toweling off my hair, I sat on the couch in front of the air conditioner. Chester hopped up, landed his bulky gray frame onto my lap, and nosed my chin. I guess it was his way of saying I was his woman. What did I need to mess with Brad for?

I took his furry head in my hands and stroked his ears

just the way he liked. "I am not messing with Brad. Just having dinner with an old friend."

Chester climbed up and rested his head on my shoulder, lying against me like a little baby before letting out a kitty sigh that smelled vaguely of rotting tuna.

"Oh, you're one to judge. You've got it rough, don't you?"

A knock sounded at my door. I rose without disturbing Chester.

Brad stood outside, smiling an iridescent smile, looking dapper in khakis and a stiff-collared polo with the *Fix My Wedding* logo embroidered on it. It looked like it just came out of the package. He held a box of chocolate truffles—the best gift for a florist, by the way. I let him in.

"Audrey, I . . . I thought you'd be ready," he said, probably eyeing my dripping hair.

"Sorry," I said, immediately a little ticked off. I'd forgotten how Brad's obsessive punctuality grated on me at times. And I hated how I always groveled to explain and justify myself, but found myself doing it anyway. "I was working on the bouquet for Monday since Gary upped the taping. I may even have to go back to work on it some more tonight. I was only able to finish one of them. Amber Lee offered to replicate it, but—"

Brad let out a lungful of exasperation. "Sorry. Old habits die hard. Of course you were working. I'll sit and get reacquainted with Chester while you finish getting ready." Brad held his arms out for my cat, but when I tried to hand him over, he jumped out of my arms, leaving a cloud of fur and dander. He hit the floor on all fours with a thud, then scampered off into the kitchen.

"I'll just be a moment." I darted into the bathroom. While using a cool hair dryer, I reasoned with my reflection in the mirror. "Not a date," I said, as I applied a little blush, but skipped the mascara and lip gloss. I added earrings and a scarf, then went back and added the mascara and lip gloss. "You're an idiot. You know that, right?"

My reflection nodded. Glad someone agreed with me.

"Ok, let's roll," I called to Brad as I grabbed my purse and slid my feet into wedges.

"You look great, Audrey." Brad followed me out the door. I turned the lock and pulled the door shut with a bang before Chester could come running and escape. He was never an outdoor cat, but he did like to explore the neighborhood, though usually not getting much farther than my neighbor's truck tires.

"That's not good for the locks, Audrey. You really ought to use the key."

"So my landlord has told me." I raised one eyebrow in challenge.

Brad's smile dimmed slightly, but he grabbed my elbow and led me to his car. Only it wasn't his car. It was a huge black Range Rover.

"Is this . . . ?"

"It belongs to the show," he said. "But I use it quite a bit."

I sank into the seat and watched the town pass outside the windows. A few minutes of uncomfortable silence later, the top of the vehicle scraped the low-hanging branches of a mature apple tree as he pulled into his mother's gravel driveway. Maybe it was a good idea we weren't having dinner alone. So many things had been left unsaid when he left town. Our once-easy conversations were probably as extinct as the dodo bird, phone booths, and rabbit-ear antennas.

Mrs. Simmons greeted us on the porch, her pudgy face flushed, probably from cooking. By the time we'd mounted the steps, she'd enveloped me in a hug, then reached up to pinch my cheeks. "Audrey, so good to see you. You look lovely. So pretty in purple. Come in. The roast is almost ready."

Ceiling fans were spinning rapidly, and the central air whined as it strained to keep up with the heat pouring from her kitchen. Fortunately, several enticing aromas also swirled through the space. Cooking a roast on the hottest day of the year? She must be really happy to see Brad.

At least I hoped it was Brad she was happy to see. Mrs. Simmons had never quite reconciled herself to the breakup, still wanting me to call her "Mom," as she had asked me to do when Brad and I were serious and a proposal on the horizon had seemed a certainty. At least it had to everybody in the world except Brad.

"Dinner's ready," she said as she led us into the small eating area in the kitchen. I was surprised the table didn't buckle under the full bowls and platters of food she placed upon it. A basket of fresh bread, a steaming platter of roast beef. A tureen of gravy. More bowls of hot vegetables. She had enough there to feed at least a dozen lumberjacks.

She coaxed Brad into saying the blessing over the food. Because their tradition was to hold hands while doing it, this sparked one of the first awkward moments of the evening. And as he held my hand under the table, I looked up into his blue eyes and could see only sadness in them.

Why was he sad? Sad to be here with me? Sad that he didn't stay here with me? But the spell was broken when what seemed like three-quarters of a cow crash-landed on my plate.

"Thank you." I avoided addressing her by name for fear of starting the controversy again. By the end of the meal, I was holding my stomach.

"I think it's finally cooling down," Mrs. Simmons said. "Why don't you two go outside while I clean up a little? We'll have coffee and dessert later."

"Let me help you," I offered.

"No, dear. I run a one-woman kitchen, and I'm just pleased to have you back." She shooed me away with her dish towel.

Brad led me out onto the deck. The outside air was indeed growing cooler by the moment, a result of the town's location in a valley near where the Blue Ridge and Appalachia meet. I never truly understood the meteorological hocus-pocus that caused the nights to be cool even on the hottest days, but the sudden change in temperature drew a shiver from me.

"Here." Brad took off his coat and draped it across my shoulders. We sat on the old cushioned aluminum glider that overlooked the wooded backyard.

"This place hasn't changed," I said. "Your mom hasn't changed, either."

He reached out and took my hand. "We do have a lot to talk about."

I yanked it back. I was here to put my negative feelings about Brad behind me, not to rekindle the positive ones. "How are you enjoying your job with *Fix My Wedding*? Are Gary and Gigi much like they are on the show? In real life, I mean."

"You really want to talk about the show?" He used a finger to push back a stray lock of my hair and tuck it behind my ear.

"Yes, I really want to talk about the show." I straightened up and put as much space as I could between Brad and me on the narrow glider.

Brad laughed and folded his hands in front of him before starting the glider in a gentle rocking motion. "Gary and Gigi are . . . entertainers. They're a lot like they are on television, but a little less amplified, if that makes sense. They can be abrupt at times, but they're extremely focused on the show."

"The tabloids say they don't get along."

"The tabloids also say Elvis is an auto mechanic in Buffalo and that Michael Jackson transported down from another planet to study Earth culture." He leaned his head back. "No, I'd say they get along fine. There's an occasional squabble. Those two can fight like husband and wife. But they also have great chemistry, don't they?"

"When I saw my first episode, I wondered if they really were married."

Brad snorted. "I see you still have no gaydar. How have you survived all these years?"

"I don't know. Maybe by trying to treat everyone I meet with the same kindness and respect."

He smiled and took my hand again. "Nice sentiment."

"But I have to admit, it hasn't helped my dating life much." I leaned my head back and watched the birds dart among the branches of the trees. "I did notice that Gary's not as sweet in real life as he appears on the screen."

"No, that part seems to be an affectation," Brad said. "But if I had to describe Gary and Gigi, I think I'd call them professionals first. They have a job to do, and they do what it takes—*become* what it takes—to get the job done."

"If Jackie sticks around, I imagine she might make that harder. Are you worried about her disrupting things?"

He shrugged. "Possibly. Not sure how she found us. We're rather tight-lipped about our shooting schedule. After all, the show is pretty popular in its demographic."

"Was it worth leaving Ramble for?"

Brad turned to me with that same sadness in his eyes. "I told you on the phone that I messed up. I was so focused on the job opportunity. I felt it was my last chance to . . ."

"To what?"

"I don't know. Make something of myself? Run away from home? Keep Ramble from smothering my soul? I can't explain it. It was like I was caught in a giant sinkhole that was swallowing me alive, and if I didn't get out right at that moment, I'd never make it out at all."

"But now you think you messed up."

"Audrey." Our gazes met and the twinkle in his eyes reflected the gathering stars. "I don't regret leaving. Not at all. I regret not taking you with me."

Brad traced my lips with his thumb before leaning in for a kiss—a long, slow, familiar kiss that I hadn't realized how much I'd missed. "Come with me this time," he whispered into my ear, then drew me into another kiss.

I lingered for a moment, feeling nothing but his lips caressing mine. Then an alarm bell sounded in my head. I grabbed his shoulders and pushed him away. "I could never leave Ramble. It's not smothering . . . Well, it's safe, it's cozy, and it's home. I have the shop . . . and Liv." And I had something else, another important reason to stay, but that kiss seemed to have shorted my brain, and I wasn't coming up with it at the moment.

Mrs. Simmons chose that second to walk outside and set a tray on the nearby patio table. "Coffee," she trilled. "And lots of sugar because I remember that's how you like it, Audrey. And sorry I didn't have time to make dessert from scratch. But I got some lovely cupcakes from that Baby Cakes Bakery in town. Well, when I told that nice Nick Maxwell what I wanted them for, he made me promise to say hello to you, Audrey."

Chapter 3

❧

I arrived at the Ashbury at seven a.m. exactly.
A wood police barrier, manned by Ken Lafferty, closed off
the private road leading to the historic inn. Even that early
in the morning, a crowd of curious Ramblers gathered near
the road. They craned their necks from behind the barrier,
binoculars trained on the gazebo where filming was rumored
to take place. Jackie and her bridesmaids sipped coffee while
waving their signs halfheartedly. Then they put them down,
probably when they decided the Rose in Bloom delivery
vehicle didn't contain anyone they needed to impress. As I
approached, the crowd parted peacefully. Then Ken swung
the barrier off to the side to let me pass and waved me
through.

I parked under a shade tree, leaving the flowers in the
CR-V with the air conditioning running on full. Even at this
early hour, it wouldn't take long for the sun to bake the
flowers. The three sample bouquets delicately packed behind
me would look lovely on camera, but I wasn't so sure I was
"bright-eyed and bushy-tailed," as Grandma Mae used to

say. But don't quote me on that. After working into the wee hours, I was too tired to turn around and check for a bushy tail. But I was certain I failed the bright-eyed part. I'd tried to fix that by loading the dark circles with concealer, then applying a perky shadow and mascara, since the packet Brad had sent me disclosed that I'd be responsible for my own makeup.

A table had been placed in the gazebo, and Brad was draping it with a white satin cloth.

"Audrey, white cloth okay?" he said. "It won't wash out any white flowers, will it? I know some people like black for photographing flowers, but Gary likes the white."

"Perfect. The bouquets are carried by brides wearing white, generally."

Was that a tic in his face? Was the bride not wearing white? What other color would a bride who loved bells wear? Silver? Silver bells? Would these bouquets look washed out against a flashy silver background? Maybe we could change the ribbon colors.

"Why don't you get three of the bouquets from the car and the camera crew can take some initial shots and get the lighting right."

I pulled Liv's and my bouquets out first, and Brad carried Shelby's more unusual one. He'd created an elaborate three-foot-long but narrow cascade of curled foliage, into which he'd wired foxglove. I'd never seen anything like it—or the elaborate netted tube of floral foam that formed the back-bone of the bouquet and kept it from drying out. We joked that he was making green sausage. But the finished bouquet, although a bit heavy, looked stunning, and foxglove was certainly a bell-shaped flower. But the meaning niggled at the back of my mind. Then again, Gary had said that the language of flowers would only be part of the Victorian-styled bouquet.

Brad introduced me to the producer, Tristan, a rather ruggedly handsome type with a cleft chin and a gorgeous

British accent. He was kind of James Bond-y, in a young Roger Moore sort of way.

"Glad to have you aboard, Miss Bloom." He winked as he shook my hand.

I watched as the camera crew, all dressed in black, swarmed like ants over the first set of bouquets. Well, most of them swarmed, with the exception of the lone female on the crew, a young woman in short cutoff jeans and a tight black tank. She'd pulled a perky ponytail through the back of a baseball cap that said "Intern." She seemed to major in striking provocative poses and fanning herself with a clipboard. Each crew member stopped to explain his process to her. Assuming he had a process. To me, it looked like they just poked, prodded, folded, spindled, and mutilated the bouquets before taking multiple moving and still shots of the flowers sitting on the table. Now I knew why they needed two sets. Then they took more shots of the bouquets stuffed into a white fabric box.

"It diffuses the light," the cameraman mumbled to me.

Whatever that meant. But he turned to the intern to provide a more thorough explanation. He encouraged her to take the camera while he stood close behind her to point out the controls. But by the time they were done almost an hour later, the bouquets looked like they'd survived an encounter with a Tasmanian Devil—the cartoon version. And I'd seen enough of the intern and the rest of the crew fawning over her to feel as if I'd accidentally stumbled into a porno film when I had intended to see a revival of *Bambi*.

"Are those my bouquets?" A tan, almost orange-skinned young woman rushed up to take a look. She had highlighted hair that ranged from platinum blonde to brunette; almost every strand seemed like it was a different color. She wore a short, scooped-neck fuchsia dress that hugged her ample curves and those strappy sandals that wind halfway up your leg. I think Liv called them gladiator sandals when she'd flattered me into buying a pair. But I doubted any real gladiator ever wore them. He'd be lion food before he figured out how to keep the silly things up. Eventually Chester had found another use for mine.

I also noticed little pink calla lily bell earrings dangling from her earlobes. I found that encouraging since both Liv's bouquet and mine contained calla lilies.

"Now, Suzy." Brad tried to guide her away with a firm hand on her upper arm. "You know you're not supposed to see the bouquets until you're on camera."

But she was having none of that. "Why are they so limp? I'm not going to have limp flowers, am I? Daddykins!" She hollered this last bit, and "Daddykins," a brawny man with thinning hair but a shaggy gray overgrowth of moustache and beard, jogged over. Had he been in camouflage, I might have mistaken him for a regular on *Duck Dynasty*, not *Fix My Wedding*.

"What's wrong, sweetheart?" He put his hand around her shoulder and kissed the top of her head. Indulgent fathers: the first ingredient in raising a bridezilla.

"Look at these flowers." She flicked a finger against a loose campanula, and it came off into her hands.

"They're pretty, aren't they?" he said.

"No, they're all old and limp, and I hate them. And they have nothing to do with bells."

"I warned you about this before you signed up," he said. "If it weren't for this show, you could pick whatever you want. There's still time to back out, you know. We could pay the penalty."

She folded her arms in front of her. I could have sworn the sun dimmed and a breeze picked up, as if a full tantrum were rolling in like a summer storm.

"I am not backing out, and you'll make them fix the flowers."

"But, Suzy, these aren't . . ." Brad whined. "You're not even supposed to see them until the big reveal."

"These have been handled to death," I said. By this time, we were all speaking at once.

"Quiet!" Gary said as he and Gigi forced their way into the circle.

Gigi signaled time-out. "Save the drama for when the cameras are rolling, people."

"Now what seems to be the problem?" Gary stood looking around the recently quieted circle. Feet shuffled and gazes were diverted to the ground, and I felt like I was back in school, the principal asking who it was that plastic-wrapped his Volkswagen.

"Look at these!" Suzy pointed long, spiky nails at the flowers.

Gary put a hand on his hip and sighed, then stared at me through half-closed lids. "Is this the best you could do?"

"No, this is what's left after your crew manhandled them for an hour." I tempered the frustration out of my voice. "I have the fresh duplicates waiting in the SUV."

"They'd better be nicer than these," Suzy said, getting in one last dig. "Let me see them."

"But she's not supposed to—" Brad started.

"Quite right," Gary said. "The flowers are supposed to be a surprise, and they will be, because they should look nothing like these." He pointed to the limp foliage. *"Right?"* The last question was directed at me, punctuated by a commanding glare that made me want to salute.

"No, sir," I said.

"Now, Max." Gary spun on his feet to face Suzy's father, the man formerly known as Daddykins. "Take your . . . daughter inside. The local baker sent in some lovely scones. And we'll call for her when we're ready." He turned to Suzy. "This is part of the show you agreed to. No peeking, and you abide by my decision. There are plenty of other brides who want us to fix their weddings. Our show, our rules. Do you want to be on the show or not?"

Suzy bit her quivering lower lip and took another glance at the flowers, then nodded. "I want to be on the show," she said softly, as if she wasn't used to having anything less than her own way. And by the shocked look on her father's face, that was probably the case.

Max took her by the arm and the two of them walked back down the flagstone path to the Ashbury.

"How did you do that?" Brad asked.

"It's nothing *Daddykins* shouldn't have done years ago." Gary plucked a relatively undamaged foxglove bloom from Shelby's bouquet and attached it to his lapel.

"But it helps that she really wants to be on the show," Gigi said. "Not that we could stop production at this point."

"But Suzy Weber doesn't know that," Gary added. "Over-the-top brides provide more drama. Which is fantastic for the viewers, don't get me wrong. But they can make the whole process a pain in the tush for us."

"Now that this drama is over, I need to head into whatever there is of this little town." Gigi blew kisses at us as she departed. "Ciao, bella."

Gary offered me his arm. "Now, lead me to the other bouquets, and I do truly hope they're better than these."

I felt like Dorothy in Oz. These people couldn't be real.

When the path narrowed, Gary walked behind me back to the CR-V, where the fresh bouquets were enjoying the frigid air being pumped from the AC. I'd make sure gas costs were folded into the show's growing bill.

"You're right. These are much better," he said. "I only wish Suzy hadn't seen the others. But these look so different, we should still get a good facial reaction from her."

I let out a relieved sigh. "So brides like Suzy are typical for you?"

"Often, they're worse. Always sneaking around trying to find out what we're doing. That's where all those secrecy clauses come in. You have to be on your toes to prevent their snooping. And most of them are terrible at faking surprise, so we know right away."

"We haven't shared our plans with anyone, but then Suzy showed up—"

"Don't let Suzy melt you down. Most of our brides get a little witchy, if you know what I mean. But we're here to make their dreams come true, so they get with the program if they don't want their contracts voided. They pay a hefty penalty if that happens and forfeit all the wedding paraphernalia. But you coordinate weddings. That can't be new to you."

"No, I've dealt with my share of bridezillas. Usually I just smile and nod and give them what they want until they go away."

He laughed. "I like you. Audrey, was it? I can see why Brad recommends you so highly. But on this show, if the bride is pleased, it's secondary. We try to please the viewers, and they want a little excitement, a little romance, a little glamour, and most of all, a lot of entertainment. I think you've captured them in these flowers. All strikingly different."

"Thanks." I smiled. "I have a good staff." Maybe this wouldn't be so bad after all. This was the sweet, reassuring Gary I'd seen on television. I only hoped nothing would happen that would push him over that edge again. His temper seemed to rest on a hair trigger. We chatted for a few minutes about the bouquets and flower choices, and then Gary and Tristan huddled, and soon things were under way.

We carried the fresh bouquets to the gazebo, and the crew carefully draped each of them with a white satin sheet so the bride would be surprised. Shelby's took two sheets. Good thing they had extra. I took my position behind the table, reached into my purse to pull out the compact I'd shoved in there at the last minute, and dotted more powder on my nose, already shiny again due to the growing outside heat.

Suzy Weber came out, fanning herself. Her glare spoke volumes, like "You should be worrying about the flowers, not your own face."

I put on my glad-to-serve-you smile and shoved my compact into my apron pocket.

After a few introductory commands and a click of whatever you call that thing they use to mark the start of a film take, Gary began. "Our guest florist today is Audrey Bloom, wedding coordinator from the Rose in Bloom shop in Ramble, Virginia. Audrey, what sets your shop apart and what do you have to show us today?"

Calm. Cool. Yeah, right. "Well, Gary," I heard myself saying, about a half of an octave too high. "What makes us different is our fresh flowers, many from local growers."

I thought I heard Suzy huff, but I wasn't sure the camera or boom microphone hovering over my head picked it up, so I continued as Gary lifted the draping from the first bouquet.

"We have three unique looks for you," I said, "each created by a different member of our staff. The first is a Victorian-inspired bouquet. Many of our brides like traditional elements. I based the design around these lovely campanulas, also called bellflowers because of their bell shape. The Victorians not only chose flowers based on their colors, shapes, and textures, but each flower had an associated meaning. A bellflower meant *constancy*, and the small white ones meant *gratitude*."

Suzy's eyebrows rose as she looked at the flower as if for the first time. It was a lovely variety, almost pure white with just a ring of pink around the outside.

"In keeping with the theme"—I pointed to the green flowers—"I also added some bells of Ireland, to wish the happy couple the best of luck. And calla lilies, which, when inverted, look a little like bells. And which I see in the bride's earrings."

"Oh," Suzy gasped.

Gary leaned over and held her hair back while the camera zoomed in on her earring and then on the flower.

"Calla lilies mean *magnificent beauty*," I added. "Instead of adding more traditional filler, I used lily of the valley, which also resemble small bells. Kate Middleton had them in her bouquet, and they carry a number of meanings. My favorite is *happiness restored*."

"What else can they mean?" All challenge had drained out of Suzy's voice. She was in wonder of her bell-shaped flowers and their meanings.

"*Purity of heart, humility*, and *chastity*."

Suzy snorted. I suspected chastity wasn't high on her list.

"Nice sentiments," Gary said.

"And I've set them in a larger reproduction of an antique silver tussy mussy holder. Very Victorian, and you can see the little wedding bells embossed in the metal." Suzy was enraptured, and I then showed how the bouquet could stand upright on its own or be removed from its stand for that walk down the aisle.

"Now the next bouquet is a little more modern in design?" Gary said.

"Absolutely. My business partner, Olivia Rose, made this one." I pulled the cover from her bouquet. Too late I realized I'd used Liv's maiden name, which she still used in business, so I hoped she'd be okay with that.

"Tell me about this one," Suzy said.

I described the clean design of cascading white calla lilies, with just a little bit of eucalyptus for greenery, hand-tied in a white satin ribbon and secured with little bell-shaped pins.

"Now what does the eucalyptus mean?" Suzy asked. "It smells a little like cough drops."

"It's wishing you health, actually. *Protection* and *healing*."

"And the white calla lilies mean *happiness restored*," Gary said.

"No, actually they mean *magnificent beauty*," I said, "but it's easy to get them confused."

"Cut!" Gary yelled. "Can we take it back?" He cleared his throat and waited until the red lights came on. Smooth as silk, he went on, "And the white calla lilies mean *magnificent beauty*."

"That's right. Good memory." I got it. Don't embarrass the host. I could play along.

"Very clean. Quite modern," he said. "I can't wait to see what else you brought."

I lifted the covering for Shelby's design.

Suzy gasped.

"We were going for something a little out of the box. This was constructed by one of our new young designers, Shelby Frazier. The construction is curled and wired lily grass, which he's used to make an elaborate three-foot cascade. He then embellished that with gorgeous variegated foxglove, so that the flowers start out small at the top, and at the bottom, there's a symphony of bell-shaped blooms. They really look like bells, don't they?" I asked.

"Oh, they do!" This was clearly the bride's pick.

"And a surprise." I picked up the bouquet and shook it gently. The jingle bells Shelby had wired into some of the flowers made their signature chime.

The bride squealed and clapped her hands. "And what do those flowers mean?"

"I'm not sure lily grass has a meaning of its own, but lilies generally mean *beauty* and grass is a symbol of . . . *submission*. You know, the whole love, honor, and obey thing. Right?" I cemented my smile and hoped they'd drop it there. Gary had assured me we'd only talk about the language of flowers for the Victorian bouquet, and yet he'd started carrying that forward into all of them. I hoped and sent up a quick, fervent prayer that they wouldn't ask what the foxglove meant.

As if on cue, Gary and Suzy both said, "So what does the foxglove mean?"

So much for the power of prayer. "Well, of course this flower was chosen primarily for its shape." I paused, hoping that would satisfy them.

They stared, waiting for me to fill in the blanks.

"*Insincerity.*"

Silence reigned on the set for about thirty seconds until the cameraman snorted.

"Cut!" Tristan yelled.

"No, keep it rolling," Gary said.

Suzy became livid. "Why in the world would you put such a flower in a bridal bouquet? Insincerity? What are you trying to imply?"

"I . . . I was under the impression that we were only going to use the language of flowers for the Victorian-inspired bouquet. The others were constructed simply for their beauty and your bell theme." I resisted the urge to say "corny bell theme."

"What made you think we wouldn't ask?" Gary asked in that voice sweet as molasses. Grandma Mae would have said "butter wouldn't melt in his mouth," but butter is oily just the same.

Two could play at that game. I put on my sweet voice. "Well, Gary, had you yourself not informed me that you didn't 'want to get bogged down with that jazz,' as you put it, I would have been happy to make sure all the flowers had positive floriography—"

"So this is your fault?" Suzy turned on Gary. "I spent hours filling in those stupid questionnaires and then more hours with you drilling me about my whole life. You should know what I like by now."

"Trust me, Suzy, it's for your own good." He took her shoulders in an attempt to soothe her.

She jerked away.

"Now look." He turned to me. "I should fire you for what you did . . ."

"What I did? But you did say—"

Gary's scowl stopped me dead in my tracks. This dude was seriously bipolar. Then Liv's voice chimed in my ear: "The customer is always right." Not that she was there, but it was as if she were sitting on my shoulder, like the good angels in the old cartoons. Or like Jiminy Cricket.

"I'm sorry." But the thought of Liv in green makeup and dressed as a cricket made me smile. Fatal mistake.

"You think being fired is funny?" Gary's cheeks turned red, and his bulging eyes made him appear apoplectic. "I'd find another florist right now if we weren't so far behind schedule. I'm going to do you a favor and we'll finish up the interview, nice and pretty. But don't think you're going to be on *Fix My Wedding* again. And no exposés, either. I have enough friends in the wedding industry to ruin you, and don't think I can't. You can expect a more immediate financial hit when we charge you for the taping delay."

"But, Gary." Brad stepped forward. "All she did was—"

"Oh, so the glorified gofer is standing up for her, is he? Are you going to be the big man and protect her? It's because of you that I hired her in the first place. I don't know why I took the word of such a washout. I must have been out of my mind."

And if he wasn't then, he was now. Of course I didn't say it. But I did think it.

Gary advanced on Brad. "She's not the only one who should be in fear of her career. There's going to be some staffing changes around here in the near future. Who knows? Maybe you'll be one of them."

Tristan stepped between them. Brave man. "Hey, how about we break for a few minutes, huh? Get our heads on straight and finish up that last bit. It was going great until that point."

"No, let's finish now, starting at the last bouquet. And you"—Gary pointed at Suzy—"don't ask what the foxglove means."

"Now, wait a minute," Max began, but Gary stared him down.

Suzy nodded, using a finger to sweep upward on her tears so she wouldn't smudge her mascara. We then restaged the reveal of the final bouquet, talking about its shape and flowers without the meanings, and with little enthusiasm.

"How'd it look?" Gary asked.

"A little stiff," Tristan said, "but maybe we can inter-mingle some of the facial expressions from the first go-around."

"Do what you want." Gary turned back to me. "I'll send my *gofer*"—he glared at Brad—"to let you know which, if *any*, of the designs I deem acceptable." Then he stormed off.

I let out the breath I was holding and heard others do the same.

"Is he always like that?" I asked no one in particular.

"It's the weirdest thing," Suzy said. "Sometimes he's sweet as pie. When we were doing the original interviews, he seemed so nice, like he was really interested in me. Well, not in that way, since he's . . . you know. And on camera he's, well, Gary."

As Suzy walked back to the inn in the consoling arms of Daddykins, Brad joined me behind the flowers. "Something seems to be bothering him. And I'm sorry you had to go through that." He put his arm around my shoulder. "If I knew he'd be on edge like that, I never would have recom-mended you for the show. I thought I was doing something nice."

"Oh, you were. It's not your fault Gary's bipolar." Talk about insincerity. "Do you think he really means to fire you?"

Brad offered a half smile in response. "Probably just blowing off steam. I wouldn't worry about it. But at least the taping part of your responsibility is over. And the flow-ers for the reception are okayed by Gigi, so you'll mostly be dealing with her now."

"And here I always thought Gary was the nice one," I said.

"Not this week," Brad added.

"He said that to you?" Liv was livid, pacing the back room after I recounted my story.

Shelby shook his head. "He seems so different on television."

"Oh, Shelby." My heart was broken for my friend and coworker. "I'm sorry so much of the drama centered around your design. It really was spectacular and deserved better than that. He still might choose it. The bride was entranced the moment she saw it. Maybe I should have—"

"It's not your fault," Amber Lee said. "We all were right here when he told you not to mess with the meanings of the flowers for the other bouquets."

"And maybe I should have used something else." Shelby scrubbed his face. "But that foxglove was gorgeous, you have to admit."

"Very," I assured him. "That design could have been featured in any bridal magazine in the country."

"So now we sit and cool our heels until he decides to tell us which design he picked?" Amber Lee leaned against the worktable.

"He's supposed to send Brad," I said, "who's getting the raw end of the deal, too. Gary demoted him from potential associate producer all the way back to gofer in one fell swoop."

"Not quite the dream job he left Ramble for, is it?" Liv said.

As I paused to consider this, I could hear a bell in the distance. "What's that?"

"Don't go changing the subject," Amber Lee said. "Seems to me that you've been seeing a bit of Brad since he got home. And with Nick around, that's bound to be trouble."

"Don't you hear that bell?" I paused a moment to listen. "Something's going on."

"Sounds like the one at old First Baptist," Shelby said.

"Maybe they're filming something for the show," Liv suggested.

"No." I shook my head. "I saw the filming schedule. Everything was over at the Ashbury today."

I walked through the shop and out the front door to the sidewalk. Liv and Amber Lee followed me. Other townspeople had also stopped what they were doing and left the shops and restaurants. Soon, half the population was lining the sidewalk. We stared down the street toward the historic stone church.

A black Range Rover was parked out front. Maybe they were filming after all. Or checking out the bell in the church prior to filming.

But soon sirens joined the pealing of the bell, and a Ramble police car sped down Main Street.

I started running toward the church.

"Audrey, wait!"

I glanced around to see a pregnant Liv trying to keep up. "No, stay at the shop. I'll let you know what I find out."

Without turning again, I sprinted around the rubbernecking citizens and arrived at the church just as the police were going in. I stood hunched over, my hands on my thighs, as I tried to regain my breath, then stared at the building. The Range Rover and a police car with its gum ball lights still flashing were parked out front. The Range Rover was the same car Brad had used to take me to his mother's house. Was it just last night? Did that mean Brad was inside? What was wrong?

I tried to run through the front door, but Ken Lafferty stepped outside and warned me to stay back.

While we stood waiting, more officers arrived and sped inside. What seemed like hours later, one of them led Brad from the building. Thank God he was alive. Even from yards away, he seemed dazed, and his eyes weren't focused on his surroundings.

I ran up to him. "Brad, what's happened? What's wrong?"

He wagged his head.

"Brad!" I grabbed his shoulders and shook him.

He shivered.

I took his hands, which were like ice and beginning to

tremble, despite the warm, sticky air. I turned to the officer. "He's had a shock. Can you help me get him over to the bench?"

"Sure," the officer said. "But don't leave yet. Bixby's going to want to talk to him."

I was so glad for the help that I didn't think about Bixby or why he'd want to talk to Brad until a couple of minutes later when Brad's breathing became more normal and he squeezed my hand in response.

"Brad, are you okay?"

He exhaled. "I think so. Oh, what a thing to have happen."

"What happened?"

"I don't know," he said. "How could he have done that by accident? He must have done it on purpose."

"Who? Done what?"

Brad sniffled and straightened himself.

"Gary. He texted me and asked me to meet him here. Something about the bell."

"The bell was ringing," I said.

He nodded. "The bell started ringing as I pulled up. I figured Gary was testing it out. By the time I got up to the bell tower . . ."

I swallowed hard. This couldn't be good. And Bixby wanted to talk to him?

"What did you see?" I asked.

Brad leaned forward, covering his face with his hands. "Gary was hanging from the bell rope."

"Ringing the bell."

He shook his head. "No. The rope was around his neck. He . . ." Brad shuddered and sobbed behind his hands.

I leaned closer and rubbed Brad's back.

An ambulance pulled up, its lights off and its siren silent. There's nothing worse than a silent ambulance.

It meant Gary was already dead.

Chapter 4

❧

Kane Bixby, Ramble's chief of police, climbed out of his car, looking as happy to see me as I was to see him. Not that he was ornery or incompetent, or even unpleasant to anybody else, it seems, but me. But his severe allergies put him at odds with anyone who was a florist. Of course, then I remembered that he and Brad had never gotten along well, either, probably based on Brad's penchant for getting in trouble as a teenager.

"There's no flowers in there, are there?" he said, as he climbed the steps.

"I don't know. Not any that I put there, but I haven't been inside. Chief?" I tried to make my voice sweet. "Brad has had quite a shock, finding the body and all. I'd like to get him out of this heat. May I take him home?"

"No, Audrey. He's not to leave the premises." Bixby looked impatiently at the church.

"But, Chief!"

"Audrey," he said firmly. "He needs to stay." Bixby lowered his voice. "I have to consider him a suspect until—"

"Brad? Nonsense. And if anything happens to him sitting in this heat . . ."

"Audrey, I'm going to need to get a statement." Bixby raked his hand through his gunmetal-gray hair. "*After* I get a look at the scene. And I'm not going to go traipsing all over the country to—"

"My place then. Just a few blocks. Not even out of your way." I went for a demure smile.

"Audrey, don't baby me. I'm fine." Brad tried to illustrate it by standing up, but swayed so dramatically that I pulled him back down onto the bench.

"Besides," I said, "the reporters will be here soon, and you'll want to talk with Brad before they sink their teeth into him."

Bixby sent me an exasperated glare.

"You can interview him at my place," I pleaded again, "and I guarantee, no flowers at all in the apartment."

"Fine. Your place. Just avoid the press, for now."

"Can you walk?" I asked Brad.

"Don't have to. We can take the Range Rover," he said.

"I'd rather you leave the vehicle here," Bixby said, "until we know if we're dealing with a crime scene and what the extent of it is."

"I can walk." Brad slowly rose from the bench.

I had him lean against me. As we hobbled our way down Main Street, Ramble residents watched us out of the corners of their eyes while pretending not to watch us. Small towns are like that. When we reached the bakery, Nick Maxwell stepped outside.

"What's happened?" Nick's gaze traveled back and forth between Brad and me.

"I'm trying to get Brad back to my place," I said. "He's had a terrible shock and I want to get him out of the heat."

"Come in here for a few minutes, then." He held the door open. I could feel his air conditioner reach out onto the sidewalk, luring us in with its frozen fingers. Or maybe it was the scent of fresh-baked goods that was doing the luring. I'd often thought that heaven must smell like a bakery.

Brad shook off my support as we walked into the shop— maybe some testosterone-controlled male ego thing, not to be seen leaning on a woman. He slipped into a chair at one of the white two-seater bistro tables scattered in the middle of the room. Lining three walls was a glass counter, with all kinds of confectionary wonderment displayed. Nick had started the shop focusing on cupcakes, and those were in good supply, but he had a knack for adding in new items and varieties.

I remembered a couple of months ago, shortly after we started dating, when he told me that he didn't think Ramble could support a cupcake shop. I feared it meant he was considering closing down and moving to a larger community. Instead, he'd expanded into a full-service bakery, adding scones, cookies, and pastries, which he sold in the shop but also supplied to the local coffee house. Later came fresh breads and rolls, which he also sold to the local restaurants. And those gorgeous, scrumptious wedding cakes. He'd hired more employees to help with all the work. Of course, all that baking may have made the room smell amazing, but it really stank when it came to his social life. And my waistline.

Nick slipped three large glasses of lemonade onto the table, then pulled up another chair and straddled it. "I heard the sirens, but wondered what was happening. Nick Maxwell, by the way." He sent a pointed look to Brad, which was his polite way of saying, What in blazes is going on?

"Brad Simmons." Brad held out his hand, and the two men shook. "I've seen you around the set, I think."

"Yes, and we've talked on the phone. I've been supplying coffee and snacks for the show."

"Those were your scones?" Brad asked. "They were amazing."

"If I give you one will you fill me in on what's going on?"

"Gary Davoll is dead," I said. "Brad found him in the church."

"Whoa," Nick turned to Brad. "And you rang the bells to call for help?"

"No." Brad gulped. "Gary did that, I'm afraid."

Nick's brows were not only knit in confusion—it looked like they were purling and casting off as well.

"Gary was hung on the bell rope," Brad said.

"Hanged," Nick and I both said together. Had to give the man a point for good grammar.

"How in the world did that happen?" Nick asked. "Accident?"

"Suicide," Brad said.

But at the same time, I said, "Murder."

"Murder?" Brad pushed up from his chair in protest. "Audrey, what makes you think that?"

"Easy," I said. "Who hangs themselves on a bell rope? Certainly not that egomaniac I met this morning, and not in the middle of filming."

"You can tell that by meeting him once?" Brad sank back into his chair. "I've worked with him for months now, and I don't know him well enough to know that for sure."

"Call it a hunch if you want. Or maybe intuition."

"Or maybe a good schooling on human nature," Nick suggested. "I believe you."

"Thanks." I sent a smile in Nick's direction, then patted his hand, which he turned over to grasp mine.

"Oh," Brad said. "I didn't realize. Of course, I should have known when I left Ramble, I—"

"You know," I said, "I should get Brad back to my place. Bixby said he'd be coming to question him, and if we're not there . . ."

"No problem," Nick said. "Let me get Jenny to watch the front of the house, and we can take Brad in my truck. No sense walking in this heat."

Nick untied his apron and darted into his back room.

"New boyfriend?" Brad said.

"We've dated a little."

"How much is a little?"

"Why? Are you jealous?" I asked.

"Do you want me to be jealous?"

Nick and Jenny emerged from the back room. I'd once considered hiring Jenny to work at the Rose in Bloom, but before I could add her to the payroll, her former fiancé was murdered with one of our shop knives. After that, while we remained friends, she decided to seek employment elsewhere. Nick's expanding bakery seemed like a good fit.

"Audrey, just the person I was thinking of," Jenny said with a broad smile. "Hi, Brad," she added, almost as an afterthought. She turned back to me. "I was wondering how busy things were for Eric. I might have some business to send his way."

Nick must not have told her about Gary. No, probably best not to alert the town before the news could be officially released. "Is it true what I've heard about your mother's restaurant reopening?" While I needed to get Brad back to my place, I could spare a few moments to lobby for the man who married my favorite cousin.

"Maybe." Her eyes sparkled. "It's going to take a while, though. The building needs a major renovation. But the financing just came through, and I know she wants to ask Eric for a quote on the construction."

"I'd tell your mother to get to him quick," I said. "Once the fall hits, people want to start getting ready for winter."

"I'll suggest that to her, then. We're planning to make it a little more family-friendly, this go-around. No wine list because . . . you know."

I nodded. I was happy that Jenny's mom was sober again, but working around wine all day would probably not be the best of ideas.

"Sounds great," Nick said. "Although I never got to see the old place to compare."

"I have," Brad said. "Audrey and I used to go there all the time, didn't we, Audrey?" Brad put his arm around me, while Nick stared.

And somehow my illusions that we could be mature and all get along began to evaporate. Any such thoughts that remained were driven away as I sat between the two men on the bench seat in Nick's truck. Nick sat bolt upright, working his jaw and hammering out a silent rhythm on the steering wheel. Nick was the taller of the two men and had well-developed muscles, which he claimed came from tossing twenty-five-pound bags of flour around all day.

Brad took to throat-clearing and staring out the window. He was fairer in complexion and slighter, with sensitive features and blue eyes that tended to draw you in.

Of course, I didn't need two men in my life. And narrowing my focus to one of them should have been an easy decision. Why is it that easy decisions are always so difficult?

After the truck jerked to a stop, Nick and Brad both rushed to open the doors for me. And instead of dropping us off, Nick remained in my apartment, flopping down on my sofa and riffling through a bridal magazine from one of the stacks I used as end tables.

"I should call Liv and tell her where I am." I cranked up the air conditioner before pulling my cell phone out of my pocket, then slipped into the bedroom, closing the door and leaning against it for support.

"Is everything all right?" Liv asked, the second she picked up.

"Brad found Gary dead at the church." I filled her in on the details at high speed. Only Liv knew me well enough to interpret. I took a deep breath. "And now Brad and Nick are both sitting in my living room while we wait for Bixby to come."

"That man." I assumed she meant Bixby. Ever since the chief had executed a search warrant and absconded with a bunch of our tools, which we eventually got back, and bags full of our stock, which I'm sure rotted in their evidence locker, Bixby hasn't been Liv's favorite person, either. "Maybe Brad should get a lawyer. On TV, the person who finds the body is often the first suspect."

"Don't be ridiculous. Brad didn't kill Gary. He had no motive." And then my mind replayed Gary's threats to Brad's career during the filming. "I'll suggest it to him."

"Good girl. I guess it's too early to tell what's going to happen with the wedding, right?"

"Oh, the wedding." Considering the events of the afternoon, I'd forgotten why they were all in town in the first place. "I don't know. I doubt the rest of the crew has heard about Gary yet. I wonder if they won't cancel it."

"I hope not, kiddo," Liv said. "We've got full coolers and more on the way. Once he recovers, see if Brad knows what they plan on doing."

I could hear the low rumble of conversation from the living room. "I'd better get back."

"Yeah, you won't want to leave those two boys alone for long. We've got the shop covered. Can't really do anything but sit on our hands until we know if and when the wedding is going to take place—and if so, which design to work with."

Before rejoining the "boys," I stripped off my shirt, which was sticking to my back due to the humidity and exertion. Did I really run down Main Street in this heat? Nice to know I could. I ran a cool, damp washcloth over my skin, added fresh deodorant, and slipped on a clean T-shirt.

When I opened the door, I was greeted by two frozen smiles. Three, if you count Chester, who was sitting on Brad's lap.

"I was getting reacquainted with Chest Hair." Brad nuzzled my purring cat under the chin.

A smirk started across Nick's face, but before he could

get out the quip I knew was coming, I blurted, "Liv thinks you should get a lawyer."

"Why would I need—?"

"Think about it, Brad. You found the body, so that puts you at the scene of the crime. You had a fight with Gary this morning—"

"A fight?" Nick said.

"An argument," Brad said. "More of a professional disagreement."

"He threatened to fire you," I said. "And more than that—to end your career."

"That does sound implicating." Nick calmly plucked several gray cat hairs from his baker's whites, a common activity when he wore his work clothes in my apartment.

"But Gary spouted off all the time," Brad said. "And he always cooled down and forgot about it. Besides, he threatened Audrey, too."

"He did?" Nick looked up in concern.

"Yes, but I have an alibi," I said. "I was in the shop with our full staff, waiting to learn what design Gary picked so we could get a jump on the rest of the flowers. *You* were at the scene of the crime. Motive, means, and opportunity."

Brad turned ashen. "You can't think I killed Gary."

"Of course not," I said. "But I can't prove it to the police."

Maybe Brad's grasp of Chester got a little too tight at that point, because the cat hopped from Brad's lap to the sofa, then curled up on Nick's lap. Nick looked a little too proud of being chosen as he stroked Chester behind the ears. At least someone was getting a little love.

"Why don't you tell us what happened," I said, "from the time you got there until I arrived, and maybe we can see how that will sound to the police. Huh? First of all, why did you go to the church?"

Brad closed his eyes and exhaled slowly from pursed lips. He looked like he was meditating. "I got a text from Gary, telling me to meet him at the church. He wanted to check out the bell. Which . . ." Brad's eyes opened in surprise.

"Isn't right," I said.

"The venue has always been Gigi's domain." Nick cocked his head. "Why would he suddenly be interested in the church or the bell?"

"So now you're an expert on the show?" Brad said, a little bit petulantly.

"I have to keep current." Nick held up a bridal magazine. "I'm in the bridal industry, too."

"Which is beside the point," I said. No, Nick and Brad together was not a good idea. I turned to Brad. "Do you still have Gary's text on your phone?"

"Yes. That should help me, right? I can show it to Bixby to prove to him why I was there."

"But it doesn't prove that you didn't arrive and then kill him," Nick said. "Or that the text even came from Gary. Who's to say you didn't kill Gary, text yourself using his phone, set him swinging, and then pretend to find him?"

"Thanks a lot!" Brad said.

"Nick's right," I added. "Nothing in that proves you didn't kill Gary. So let's go on. You got the text and then what?"

"I drove the Range Rover to the church. As soon as I stepped outside, the bells started ringing. I didn't see any of our staff cars, but the door to the church was unlocked. I figured it must be Gary checking it out, so I climbed the stairwell that leads to the belfry and found him . . . dangling from the rope."

"How did you know where the belfry was?" Nick asked.

"I grew up here. I used to ring that bell when I was a kid. It was considered a special honor. I'd leave to ring the bell, and half the time nobody noticed if I didn't make it back to the pew. It was one way of going to church without getting a sermon. Besides, *campanologist* looked good on my college application."

"Campanologist? Like campanula." I smiled. I liked connections I could understand.

"I know campanologist is the study of bell ringing," Brad said, "but what is campanula?"

"The flower she used in the bouquet this morning," Nick said. "If you'd been paying attention. A bellflower."

"You were watching?" I asked.

"They had a live feed set up in the Ashbury," Nick said.

"But you didn't see the argument?" I asked.

"When the cameras are cut, the feed ends," Brad said to Nick, as if trying to display superior knowledge.

"So you found Gary swinging," I said. "Then what?"

"I'm afraid I stared at him for a while. I couldn't believe it. I managed to dial 911, but I think I dropped my phone after giving the location. I didn't want Gary to suffocate. I remembered I had a knife in my pocket. So I grabbed him." Brad blanched again. "You don't suppose that's what killed him, do you? Because when I grabbed him, the rope tried to pull him back up. And that bell must weigh at least a ton."

I bit my lip and thought about what I knew about hanging—which was more than I wanted to know about hanging. "If Gary was dropped suddenly from a sufficient height, like they did in official executions, then his neck would have been broken. Nothing you could have done afterward could have helped or hurt him."

When the two men looked at me, I explained. "Remember, I studied nursing for a while. One time when I was working emergency, we—" I closed my eyes. Interning in emergency at a large urban hospital had seemed so exciting at first, even if I was just supposed to stand in a corner and observe. But I'd felt each trauma as if it were my own, and still had nightmares over some of the things I could do nothing about. "I've seen it."

I looked up to see two sets of caring eyes staring back.

I averted my gaze to Chester, who seemed to be trying to lick his own shoulder. Good luck with that.

"But if the action wasn't sudden enough," I continued, "I suppose he might have suffocated from the pressure of the rope. It could have cut off air flow and possibly even blood flow."

"And when I pulled on him?" Brad asked. "Audrey, I have to know if I made things worse." He seemed to struggle to swallow. And when he spoke again, his voice came out hoarse. "If I could have killed him."

"I'm sure he was already dead." I wish I felt as sure as I tried to sound. Tugging on Gary as the momentum of the bell tried to pull him up could have resulted in the same kind of force as a drop hanging. Brad could have broken Gary's neck while trying to help him. Or closed off an already narrowed trachea. Hopefully the autopsy would reveal something that would clear Brad. "They'll know you tried to help."

"At least that makes me feel a little better," he said.

"It does put your DNA all over the body, though," Nick said.

Brad threw up his hands in exasperation. "Of course it does!"

"Let's keep going. I'd like to hear everything before Bixby gets here," I said. "So you cut him down. Then what?"

"I felt for a pulse. Nothing. So I tried CPR. Moments later the police arrived. I felt a little woozy, so the cop took me outside. And that's when Audrey showed up."

"Was there anything else at the scene? Anything left behind or out of place? Something that would suggest who might have been there?"

Brad shook his head as he focused on an empty corner of the room. "Nothing in the room but Gary. Only . . ."

"What did you notice?" I asked.

"I had told him the belfry wasn't very nice and tended to be a bit dusty. I don't know why he would want to go up there—and why he'd go up there wearing the same clothes he had on from the shoot this morning, including the jacket, even in this heat. He still had the flower in his lapel."

Foxglove. *Insincerity.* I wasn't quite sure why that thought came to mind. And I hoped the one lapel flower wasn't enough to get Bixby all cranky.

"What do you think?" Brad asked. "Do I still need a lawyer?"

"I'd get one," Nick said.

I nodded.

A short time later, Ken Lafferty arrived. At first I was relieved, since I knew Bixby would want to question serious suspects himself. Ken's presence would mean Brad was low on his list. Instead, Ramble's resident rookie was there to ask Brad to come with him to the station for questioning. My relief evaporated.

I watched out the window as Brad was transported in one of Ramble's three police cars.

Nick came up behind me, put his arm around my waist, and leaned his head against mine. "What do you think?"

"Well, he didn't kill Gary, that's for sure."

"That's good enough for me. So where do we start?"

"We?" I spun around in his arms to face him. "Start what?"

"I know you. You're going to jump right in and prove him innocent. Which, I've noticed, you're pretty good at. I'd like to help."

"I can't ask you to do that. You must know that Brad is a former boyfriend."

"So I gathered," he said. "The key word, I hope, being 'former.' But you must have an idea where to start."

"Not really . . . unless. Brad said there were no cars at the church. So how did Gary get from the Ashbury to the church? He could have driven, and the killer took his ride. Or he could have caught a ride with someone else, in which case that person is either the killer or the last to see him alive."

"Or he could have walked," Nick said.

"But not without being noticed by half the town. Maybe somebody saw him with somebody. Maybe somebody followed him."

"How would you find that out?"

"One way." I turned my air conditioner down and headed to the door. "I have to get back to the shop."

Chapter 5

❦

"Whoa, you're going too fast." Amber Lee jotted down questions in a small floral-patterned notebook. We sell them in our gift department, and she gets an employee discount. This one was on the house. "I get the idea. You want us to visit the shops on Main Street, hang around, and then ask if anybody saw Gary Davoll or any of the *Fix My Wedding* people headed toward First Baptist."

"Bixby's not going to be happy when he hears someone's horning in on his investigation." Liv crossed her arms. "Especially after he made you promise last time."

I shot her a look. "Then we make sure he doesn't hear about it. Last time was a fluke, anyway. And Brad needs our help. Besides, everybody in Ramble is going to be talking about the show and the murder, anyway. All we have to do is be everywhere at once to hear it." I looked over my recruited volunteer spies: Nick, Amber Lee, Eric, Shelby, and Darnell. Liv had tried to volunteer, but if I hadn't nixed it, Eric would have. Although there certainly wouldn't be any harm in heading to the coffee shop or drug store, and anything I learned about snooping, I'd learned from spending all those summers and vacations growing up with her. Instead, she would mind the shop.

"Now," I said, "does everyone have their assignments?"

"I head west and stop off at Pete's BBQ for a sandwich and a 'Hey, has anyone heard what happened today?' " Nick said. "And then head back to the Ashbury. I man the catered food tables and nonchalantly try to figure out which of the cast and crew were at the inn at the time of the murder and therefore have an alibi."

"And I head east." Amber Lee checked her notes. "I get a stool at the Underdog Sports Bar and pretend like I'm interested in whatever's on the screen and try to engage someone in conversation. I'm going to have to get a burger, I think. Long time since I had one of their burgers. Then I hit the beauty salon for some gossip time with the girls, casually ask if they saw any of the celebs in town head toward the church. And if there's time, I finish off with ice cream. I love my job, by the way."

"I head back to the office to see if my receptionist has seen or heard anything," Eric said. "Her desk faces Main Street, so it's possible. Then I'll double back to the barber shop and get a trim."

"More than a trim." Liv fingered his hair, which was just beginning to reach his collar. "You're getting a little shaggy."

"Yes, dear," he said with a syrupy sweet sarcasm. "Then I'll head to the hardware store to see if any of the locals saw one of the strangers milling around town. I have a couple of things I need to pick up, anyway. Then to the candy store and the jewelry store—window-shopping for a gift for my wife."

"More than window-shopping, if you're smart," I teased.

"I've got the Brew-Ha-Ha," Shelby said, "and the craft store, and then I'm going to check in with my dad, I think."

"That's not going to be too uncomfortable for you, is it?" I asked. Shelby and his father, who ran an automotive repair garage, were at odds over the young man's choice of vocation.

"Naw, not too bad. We're talking now, at least. And since his shop is kitty-corner to the church, maybe he saw or heard something."

"And I'll hit the deli," said Darnell, "before I double back and hang out at the soccer fields. Should be plenty of people to talk to there."

"And where will you be, Audrey?" Liv asked.

"I want to see if Mrs. June has learned anything." Mrs. June, an old friend and neighbor of our Grandma Mae, worked the front desk at the police department. Very little happened there that she didn't know all about. And while she didn't share it with everybody, a cheery bouquet of flowers for her desk had been known to loosen her lips, just a little. To me, anyway.

"And then," I added, "I'm going to check if that crowd of people is still hanging around outside the Ashbury."

"The protesters and the groupies?" Nick asked.

"I'm sure they had their eyes locked on everything that happened today. Who better to ask?"

"You shouldn't do that alone," he said. "It's one thing asking our friends and neighbors if they saw anything. But those rabid fans and that wacko bride . . . Not all of those people seem completely sane. Give me a call when you get there, and I'll come out and join you."

"My bodyguard?" I couldn't help a smile.

"Worth guarding," he said, not meeting my eyes.

Mrs. June was leaning over to look at something in her desk drawer, her poufy head of "decadent mocha" hair the only thing visible from the window separating her from the lobby. She startled when she looked up to see me there, then flashed me a jowly smile and buzzed me right in.

I set a small vase of colorful gerbera daisies on her desk.

"I still can't believe these aren't dyed." She let her reading glasses fall on the chain around her neck. "I always used to tease your grandma that someone was spray painting her flowers overnight. Child, you have no idea how much I miss her and her garden."

"I think I do."

"Oh." She patted my hand with her pudgy one. "I know you do. I wish someone would move into that cottage and clean up the place."

"Not until I've saved enough pennies. I'd be heartbroken if someone else bought that old place. But I guess there's no danger of that. Eric told me Rawling isn't putting a lot of money into his properties these days."

"I guess I'll have to wait for the right neighbor then. Even if it's someone who primes me with flowers before she pumps me for information."

I flashed her an innocent "Moi?" look before I pulled a couple of Hershey's Kisses from the bowl on her desk and sank into the chair next to her. "Anything interesting?"

"Well, Bixby's still got your boyfriend cooling his heels in the interrogation room."

"Ex-boyfriend. What do you mean, cooling his heels?"

"He left him in there alone. I've seen Bixby do it before. He's trying to freak him out, make Brad more likely to talk. And I'd say it's working. Every time I peek in on him, he's pacing the room, talking to himself. I sure hope he has nothing to hide, because he looks like he's about to spill everything he's ever known. And while I doubt he could have had anything to do with the death of our visiting celebrity, I'll lay odds he was part of the crew that disassembled Mr. Riggleman's old Dodge and put it back together on the roof of the high school. Although I gather the statute of limitations for that little escapade has run out."

"No comment. Did he ask for a lawyer during questioning?"

"That's just it. Bixby hasn't even been to see him yet. He

keeps heading out the door to talk to other possible witnesses. He popped in long enough to interview the grieving widow in his office, and—oh, Audrey, you did *not* hear that from me."

It took a moment to register. "Grieving *widow*?" Although Brad had chided me for my lack of gaydar, even I had enough to pick up on Gary's tendencies. Eventually. "Gary Davoll was married? To a woman?"

Mrs. June shushed me, then pulled her chair closer. "Audrey, you have to keep that on the down low. I'm not even supposed to know it, and I can't believe I let it slip out. But yes, Gary was married. And to a woman. Been married a long time, but it was all hush-hush because of the show and his reputation. Apparently nobody trusts a straight man to choose their wedding fashions. I mean, my husband, God rest his soul, couldn't tell the difference between satin and flannel. I didn't overhear all of the conversation, mind you, but Gary most definitely was married."

"To whom? You saw his wife? Was she someone from the show?"

Mrs. June nodded and then whispered, "Gigi Welch."

Chapter 6

❧

My mind was still spinning when I arrived
at the Ashbury and saw the crowd milling behind the police
barrier where Ken Lafferty sternly stood "guard." Not that
any of the crowd, including Tacky Jackie, couldn't have
taken out the diminutive young rookie with a good kick
to the knees. Perhaps the oppressive heat rising in waves
from the asphalt surfaces was siphoning the fight right out
of them.

Jackie was present with her entourage, mostly her bridesmaids from the wedding. Their protest signs stood propped
into the ground while the women were all draped over the
large boulders that lined the boundary of the Ashbury's
garden, like they had melted in the heat or were part of some
Dali painting.

A few Ramblers mingled among the crowd, waving
cheerfully when they saw a familiar face. And I did spot the
stocky young fan who had taken up a bullhorn in support
for Gary and Gigi at the welcoming ceremonies. Long hours
in this heat had left his blond scalp sunburned, while his

nose, forehead, and the tops of his ears were downright singed. He was sitting in the grass, leaning against the trunk of a tree, as if the tree were the only thing holding him up.

I texted Nick that I was outside, asked him to bring a couple of bottles of water, and made my way over to the groupie under the tree.

"My guess is that you're tired, have a headache, and feel ready to drop."

"It's been a bummer day," he said.

"You're probably also a bit dehydrated with that sunburn." I waved to Nick, who had stepped outside the building looking for me. "I'm Audrey Bloom, by the way, and I've had just enough nursing school to be dangerous. You need fluids."

When Nick jogged up to us, I took one of the water bottles and handed it to the young man. He removed thick glasses and poured a bit of the cold water on his head and face before chugging the rest.

"Thank you. You might be right. I feel better already." He reached out his hand, which I shook. "Dennis Pinkleman. Cleveland, Ohio. If you're on the fan boards, I go by the screen name Gigi's Guy."

"Um, sorry. Fan of the show, but I've never been on the boards. You're a big fan of Gigi, then?"

"Gary and Gigi, both. But yeah, they always seemed so nice on TV. But Gigi . . . it's like she really gets it. There's just this connection. She even answers her e-mails."

I smiled and nodded. I doubted she even knew he existed.

"I came down here because I thought it would be fun to see Gary and Gigi live. The fan boards don't often find out the locations. The network tries to keep it hush-hush. But this one leaked out. And since Ramble was in driving distance, I hopped in my car. Only I never thought . . ." He sank his face into his palms, then screamed and jerked his hands away from his leathery cheeks. That had to hurt.

"Look, Dennis, you would probably feel better if you

were inside with some air conditioning." Although evening was approaching, the air was still warm and sticky. "Do you have a room somewhere?"

"No. I drove overnight and was going to catch a nap in my car before I headed back home. Only now . . . now I can't leave."

"Did someone tell you to stick around?" Maybe Bixby considered this big lug as a possible suspect. The obsessed fan angle?

"How can I leave until I *know*? I'm waiting to see if they make some kind of official announcement about Gary. I keep watching that door. Sooner or later they have to come and tell us something."

"Uh, Dennis, you do know he's dead, right?"

Dennis closed his eyes, resting his head against the tree. Tears snaked down his flushed cheeks. "I keep hoping that it's a bad rumor, like somebody put it on Twitter and people kept retweeting it without checking to see if it was true. Is that too much to ask? That it be just a bad rumor?" He looked up with sad, puppy-dog eyes. "I know it's silly. I can't believe this is happening."

Nick squatted next to Dennis and handed him the second bottle of water. "Audrey's right. Maybe you should go someplace cool."

"But they have to tell something to the fans," Dennis said. "We've been out here all day. They owe us that much. Gigi should come out here. She and Gary seemed so close on the show. She shouldn't be alone at a time like this. We're all mourning. We can be there for her."

And Dennis had no idea how close Gary and Gigi really were. But I doubted seeking comfort from crazed fans was high on her priority list.

"Hey, how come he gets water?" a female voice demanded, just behind me.

I knew that voice. I whipped around to face Tacky Jackie. Her cheeks were flushed, but not with sunburn. I'd say anger, but that was just my guess based on an hour, minus commercials, of watching her fly off the handle while turning that precise shade. I'll have to admit, it was more fun to see on TV than in person.

"Seriously, because he's a fan, he gets water? What about the rest of us dying out here in the hot sun?"

"Will you cut it out, Jackie?" Dennis scrambled to his feet. "A great tragedy happened here today, a fine man was struck down in his prime, and now it's suddenly all about *you*." He took a step toward her. "I take that back. It's not sudden. It's *always* been all about you, hasn't it?"

"Do I deserve that?" she asked, and her bridesmaids pushed themselves off their rock perches to stand behind her. "All I did was ask about water. Water is one of the necessities of life, you know."

I took an unconscious step back.

"Look, ladies, if it's water you want, I can get you some," Nick stammered.

Jackie shook her head. "It's not the water. It's the principle of the thing." She turned back to Dennis. "And here you are, the *faithful fan*." Tacky Jackie, or maybe I should say Wacky Jackie, since she was definitely giving off that vibe, drew close enough to Dennis that when she spoke, her spit hit him in the face. "You think the show is going to give you water, a place to stay, or even some official announcement? They couldn't care less about you, just like they couldn't care less about me. And I was *on* their silly program."

Her face melted into a sneer. "They don't care about weddings. They don't care about fans. And I doubt they even care that much about Gary. You know what they care about? The bottom line, ratings, and advertising dollars. And if I had to guess, I'd say Gigi and that producer are in there right now trying to figure out how his death will affect their pocketbooks and shooting schedule. Well, you know what? I'm glad he's dead."

That last statement was enough to turn Dennis from a sunburned, weepy teddy bear into a ravenous grizzly. "You take that back." He grasped Jackie's shoulders, like he was trying to shake some sense into her, and then her bridesmaids rushed to her aid, beating on him with their signs and purses, trying to scratch him with their manicured nails.

I was glad I'd taken the step back. Nick reached for my hand, and we put a little more distance between us and the fracas.

A whistle blew, and Ken Lafferty's distorted voice came over a bullhorn, demanding they "cease and desist." Why he didn't just tell them to stop, I don't know.

Two bridesmaids pinned Dennis to the ground while Jackie kicked dust at his face with her flip-flopped feet.

And then torrents of water seemed to come from nowhere, from everywhere. A stream blasted the right side of my face and trickled down my arm. Nick found my hand again, and led me even farther from the conflict.

Ken Lafferty was standing on the hood of the police car, a high-pressure fire hose in his hand. I guess he'd figured out a way to handle crowd control after all.

A burst of a siren sounded as another of Ramble's three police cars rolled up. Bixby climbed out of the passenger seat, took off his mirrored sunglasses, and stared at the situation. He gave one gesture to Lafferty, a quick slash at the neck, and soon the water slowed to a trickle.

Bixby grimaced at his rookie. "When you learned crowd control at the academy, tell me something, boy—was your textbook published during the Civil Rights movement?"

The water had left Dennis and the three women sprawled on the ground, arms and legs tangled in a heap like spaghetti. It seemed to take the fight out of them, though.

After a quick, quiet chat with Lafferty, Bixby parted the crowd and demanded that Dennis come with him.

"But that's not fair," I said. "You don't even know what happened."

Bixby didn't answer me. He escorted the man through the crowd and deposited him in the back of the police car. He said a few words to his officer at the wheel. If I can read lips, he said, "Taxi moo gestation." Apparently I can't read lips.

As the car containing Dennis Pinkleman drove off slowly back toward police headquarters, Bixby darted into the Ashbury.

I turned to Nick with a sigh. "That man never listens. At least not to me."

"If it's any consolation, Audrey, at least the police department is cooler than it is out here."

"And watch," Jackie spat, hair matted to her head and water still rolling down her face. "They'll probably even give him dinner." She gaped as the police car rolled down the street, then she reached up to wring out her hair. "Ouch!" She rubbed her arm. "It's police brutality. Did I hear you say you were a nurse?"

"Not really. Former nursing student." Apparently little got by Jackie.

She held her fingers out to me, wincing as she flexed them, my invitation to supply free medical care. Nothing seemed broken. "Maybe some ice would be a good idea. And then have a doctor look at it if it gets worse."

"I'll get you some ice." Nick headed back into the Ashbury.

"How is he getting in that place, anyhow?" she asked. "They won't even let us near there."

"He's catering for the cast and crew."

"He seems nice. Your boyfriend?" Jackie asked.

"Sort of."

"You should do something about that 'sort of.' Never good to let that kind get too far away. And I saw you go in yesterday morning."

"I'm the florist."

"Florist." She rolled her eyes with some disdain. "I hated my flowers. Did you see my flowers?"

"I . . ." I was ready to defend my unknown fellow florist, but I couldn't remember if I had seen her flowers. And here I'd justified watching the show to get ideas for work. I was so distracted by Jackie's other antics, that I never even noticed them. "I can't say I remember them."

"Sunflowers, hypericum berries, and yellow peppers. Vegetables. Can you believe they put vegetables in my bouquet?"

An unusual combination. But the colors sounded harmonious and the meanings were mostly positive. The small sunflowers represented *adoration*. Some say the hypericum berries foretold *protection* and *good health*. But peppers?

You can put almost anything into a bouquet, and I'd had my share of strange requests. Still, I can't say that I'd ever come across the meaning of peppers, even though I'd seen meanings for walnuts, lemons, and watermelon (which not so ironically symbolized *bulkiness*). Although I doubt many bouquets contained watermelon, except maybe those from Edible Arrangements.

"I don't know, Jackie. I've heard of worse bouquets."

"So you do know who I am. You know what they did to me."

I glanced back to the Ashbury. Where was Nick with that ice?

"I'm sure things aren't always what they appear on camera," I said. "And my brief experience with Gary leads me to believe he wasn't always as nice as he seemed."

"Well, you got that right. They messed up everything. I thought I was going to have my dream wedding. I've had it planned ever since I was six, you know. Like some fairy princess story. I was going to wear a sparkly white dress with a huge train. And a glittering tiara. And there'd be music. Violins and cellos. A whole orchestra. And everyone would stand when I walked down that aisle, and say, 'There never was a lovelier bride.' There'd be a horse-drawn carriage waiting when we came out. White horses. With footmen and everything. And large white feathers. On the horses, not the footmen.

"That's what they promised me. A fairy-tale wedding. And instead, they turned me into a laughingstock. Brian won't even talk to me. My divorce just became final. No fairy-tale wedding. No Prince Charming."

"I'm sorry."

"Well, I don't care who hears it," she said. "Gary Davoll ruined my life and my reputation, and I'm glad he's dead. I guess now everyone is going to treat him like he's some kind of hero. I'll bet they even do a tribute program. What do you want to wager that the shot of me trying to deck him with the champagne bottle will be part of it? I'm surprised they haven't hauled me in as a suspect."

Only because Bixby never watched the show.

"Jackie, if you don't mind my asking, why did you come here? What were you hoping to accomplish?"

"Well, I . . . I want . . ." She straightened her posture and tugged at her wet shirt so it wasn't clinging against her skin. "I *need* to get past this. To put the show and everything that happened behind me and begin again. That Jackie you saw on TV wasn't me. I'm really a very private person."

"Jackie, a photo?" a woman called.

Jackie turned to the camera and smiled.

"Great, and now that will be all over the Internet with my hair all wet. Why can't the paparazzi leave me alone?"

I hated to tell her that the person who snapped her picture wasn't from the media. Mrs. DeYoung teaches second grade at the elementary school and probably wanted the photo for her scrapbook. And it also seemed to me that someone who wanted to be left alone would have been home, trying to mend her marriage and not traveling the country carrying signs. But maybe that's just me.

I glanced back toward the Ashbury to Nick, who was lugging out a big insulated beverage cooler. After a quick confab with Lafferty, Nick lowered the cooler onto the trunk of the police cruiser. "Lemonade," he announced to the crowd. "Courtesy of *Fix My Wedding*."

Soon people queued up to fill the little paper cups from the side of the dispenser.

Nick then trotted over with an ice bag he'd balanced on top of the cooler. "Sorry it took so long. I thought the lemonade might help the spirits of the crowd out here."

Jackie took the ice pack and applied it to her hand. "So it's not really from the show after all."

"Well, sort of. They paid for it. They just didn't finish drinking it," Nick said with a wink.

"Good man." Jackie tapped my arm. "Remember what I said."

Those nearby who had been sitting on the grass started to rise.

"Someone's coming," Jackie said.

A gleaming black limo rolled down Main Street and approached the inn. The front window descended. The driver spoke briefly with Ken Lafferty, then Ken moved the barrier out of the way and let the vehicle pass. But at the same time, the tinted back window lowered and a dapper gray-haired man leaned out and waved royally to the crowd—the whole Princess Di wave that's no more than a swivel of an upraised hand, the kind they train royals to do.

Jackie tried to jump to see above the heads of the people in front of her. "Who is it?" she cried, almost frantically. "Can you see who it is?"

Nick and I and half of the crowd said the name almost simultaneously: "Henry Easton."

"That rat." Jackie crossed her arms in front of her. "He messed up my dress. I hope he dies, too."

Chapter 7

❧

"Audrey, I didn't see you on the shooting schedule for this afternoon." Ken Lafferty stood, arms crossed in front of him, feet spread. Probably trying to look imposing. But seeing Henry Easton drive up in the limousine had immediately overwhelmed my curiosity and set my feet in the direction of the Ashbury.

Everyone who's anyone in the bridal industry knows Henry Easton. His chain of posh bridal salons dots the major cities from coast to coast, and he carries only the top designers, some exclusively. His dapper image, wearing an immaculate tuxedo, is in every ad his salon places in the major bridal magazines, and he'd made guest appearances on more than one episode of *Fix My Wedding*.

"Ken," I said, "I need to find out if there will even be a shooting schedule. If they're going on with filming, I need to know the revised schedule and which of the floral designs they're going for. And if they're not filming, I need to know that, too, so I can figure out what to do with the thousands of dollars of expensive foliage sitting in our cooler."

"Well, I guess it'll be okay. You are a designated supplier."

I barely waited for Ken to get out his last words before I took off running toward the historic inn, Nick trailing behind me. I climbed the steps to the stone portico and flung open the restored wood door.

It took a few moments for my eyes to adjust to the much dimmer light in the lobby. A dark wood staircase stood in front of me. To my left, at the restored hotel registration desk, owner Kathleen Randolph was the only person in sight. Her head jerked up from the book she was reading, before she nodded and returned to it.

To my right was the original historic restaurant—not the larger modern addition often used for community dinners and wedding receptions. Here, at least according to Kathleen, was where Washington chowed down on hoecakes for breakfast and cracked walnuts in his teeth. The space, normally booming during mealtimes, was closed for filming. Loud greetings, not meant for Nick or me, I was sure, sounded from the room. I peeked inside.

Most of the tables had been stripped of their cloths and stacked against one wall of the restaurant space. A couple of tables retained their coverings and were laden with coffee, lemonade, and baked goods kept fresh under gleaming glass domes. Nick's catered tables.

Technical equipment, cameras, and screens were bunched in the other side of the room in a makeshift studio. There, crew members shook hands and mingled with Henry Easton, greeting him as if he were a hero recently returned from combat.

I overheard one of the cameramen saying that he'd go get Gigi. Another yelled to get the whole cast.

Nick went to stand behind his table. He looked innocuous, and I decided that might not be a bad observation point for me, either.

For the next few minutes, I helped pour and restock, as

cast and crew assembled and grabbed coffee. They greeted Henry Easton and whispered among themselves.

When Gigi came in she looked a little worse for wear: red-eyed, fragile—which was a word I'd never associated with Gigi before. She was escorted by Bixby, who whispered something into her ear. Gigi nodded, then Bixby asked everyone to lend him their attention.

He waited while various crew members and some of the cast pulled up old wood chairs and sat. Suzy and Daddykins, his beard and mustache now neatly trimmed, slipped into seats next to a young man I hadn't met—possibly the groom. Bixby caught my eye before he began, but my presence didn't seem to bother him enough to ask me to leave.

"I'm Kane Bixby," he said. "Chief of police of the town of Ramble. I've spoken to some of you already, and I expect to speak to all of you over the course of the next few days as we actively seek to discover who might have killed your friend and coworker. If you have any information or witnessed anything that you think might be relevant to our investigation, please stop me at any time."

A hand shot up. The sound man, I thought, if I recognized the back of his head. Bixby nodded to him.

"Are you the only ones working on this? Aren't you calling in somebody? The state police or FBI?"

"I assure you," Bixby said, "we are not a backwater little town. I am a trained and experienced homicide investigator."

I swallowed hard. Trained, probably. Experienced, sort of, if you could call it that. But we'd only had one homicide in Ramble before Gary's demise, at least that I could recall. And although the murderer was eventually caught and prosecuted, I wasn't sure that Bixby had all that much to do with it. Modesty forbids me from retelling the story.

Still, I wouldn't call Bixby incompetent, either. Our crime rate is low, and the town remains a safe place, so he must be doing something right.

"And," he went on, "we have a good working relationship

with the state police, who have placed their resources at our disposal at any time we need them."

"So it's true then?" Tristan asked. "Gary was murdered, and didn't commit suicide?"

Bixby nodded. "Even if we felt his death was self-inflicted—"

Gigi shook her head.

"—we treat all suspicious deaths as homicides unless the evidence proves otherwise. What we saw at the crime scene leads us to believe this was no suicide. Nor was it an accident. It would have been nearly impossible for Gary to have hanged himself, based on the height of the—"

Gigi clutched at his arm. Whether to stop him from saying more or to keep herself from going down is anyone's guess. But she accomplished both.

"The next week will be difficult for all of us." Her voice was soft, but the room grew quieter to hear her. "We've decided to go ahead with the wedding."

The crowd erupted in noise, talking among themselves and shouting out questions.

I turned to Nick. "Who decides that? The network? The producer?"

"From watching them, I'd say Gary and Gigi literally ran the show. Now I'd say it was probably Gigi."

Bixby signaled them to quiet down. Someone from the crowd echoed my question, "Who decided that the wedding is to go on?"

"I did," Gigi said, "after much consideration about what is best for the show and what Gary would have wanted us to do. And after talking with Chief Bixby, of course, to make sure that it was all right for us to continue. But we do have a contractual obligation to fulfill."

Suzy stood. "Contractual obligations? To me? Does that mean my wedding will turn into some morbid remembrance? Or are you just going to march us before the justice of the peace so you can cross us off your to-do list?"

Gigi shook her head. "No, plans go on for the wedding, and it will be as fabulous as you could dream it. That's why we've invited Henry Easton. He'll be taking Gary's place, overseeing the fashion and makeup and flowers, just as Gary would have."

"For this episode?" Tristan asked.

"For this episode," Gigi said. "And any more that we might film."

"Might? Does that mean we're canceling the show?" A murmur went up, probably as the crew were determining if they'd have to dust off their résumés.

Henry Easton hopped up and joined Gigi and Bixby. "Gigi's lawyer and my agent are in negotiations to make me a permanent part of *Fix My Wedding*," he said. "I believe they will come to terms, and we can go from here." He paused until the crowd quieted again.

"I understand the grief of your hearts. I made plane reservations to join you from Philadelphia the minute I heard what had happened, even before my agent called. And I understand that no one could ever replace Gary. He was a great man and a good personal friend. His death is an unfathomable loss to the show, the bridal industry, and the world. But I am grateful for the opportunity to follow in his shadow and make my humble attempt to walk, however falteringly, in his shoes."

I wondered how long he'd practiced that speech.

"And I can assure you," he went on, "the show and the wedding will be done to the best of all of our abilities, to Gary's memory. Accordingly, it should be the best work we've ever done."

This seemed to placate Suzy, and she resumed her seat. Her father reached out to hold her hand and whispered something into her ear. She shook her head.

"Now some practical issues," Gigi said. "We're not sure about using any of Gary's footage. The network is going to run it by a test audience. Fans might want to see Gary again, or they might be weirded out by it. But since we're early in the film schedule, we're going to re-film all segments using Henry. That would be what? The opening interviews, trashing the original wedding plan, and what else?"

"The flower samples," Tristan suggested.

"And then the voice-overs," Gigi said. "We re-film everything with Henry, and then we can decide in postproduction which version to use in the final show."

And as they huddled to discuss the practical aspects of filming, Bixby sauntered back toward the catering table. I hoped he was coming for coffee.

He poured a cup of black coffee from the insulated carafe into a stoneware mug, bypassing cream and sugar and all the delectable baked goods. He thanked Nick, then squinted at me.

"Moonlighting?" he asked.

"Just helping a friend."

"I'd have thought you'd have all that froufrou flower stuff to do, what with the wedding still going on."

I decided to ignore the implied insult. "That's part of why I'm here. I needed to know if the wedding was still going on. And Gary never told me which design to go with. I've been working mostly with Brad, and I'd ask him what I'm supposed to do, but it seems that he's being detained."

Bixby cleared his throat. "Who said anything about detaining him? He's not been arrested and no charges have been filed against him. He's free to go at any time."

"Did you bother to tell *him* that?"

Bixby didn't answer my question, but screwed up his face. "Naturally, after we learned of his altercation with the deceased, we simply invited him in to ask him some questions."

I couldn't help notice Bixby's use of the plural *we*. Apparently he was insecure enough in his accusations that he was hiding behind a group. If he were taking credit for a job well done, I'd imagine he would be crowing in the singular *I*. I wasn't about to let him off the hook, either. "I had an altercation with Gary, too. And I suspect I'm not the only one in this room who did. Why zero in on Brad?"

"You make it sound like I'm a sniper with my sights on him. Like I said, we're keeping our options open and will be looking at any altercations Gary might have had with anyone inside—or outside—this room."

"While they're putting on a wedding, and knowing that there's a killer probably walking around town, you're just going to sit back and watch them? What if Gary isn't the only one on the killer's hit list? I can't believe you're putting them—*us*—all in danger by letting this wedding take place."

A smirk tickled the corner of his lips.

"What?" I demanded, maybe a little too loud.

Bixby took my arm and led me into the hallway. "Okay, Audrey, I shouldn't be telling you this, but I know you've seen some of the more unseemly parts of life. And you're quick-witted. I think you can understand this. If we told them they could no longer film here, everybody connected with the show would be free to leave. And the chances would be pretty good that we'd never solve this thing."

"But can't you tell them not to leave town or something?"

"Only in the movies. Unless I arrested all of them, I have no power to keep them anywhere near Ramble. And if they left now, carrying any evidence with them, then the killer most likely gets away. He cools down, rationalizes to the point where he might not even think he killed someone. The whole town of Ramble gets a black eye. But, if we go on with the filming while my men and I pursue the investigation . . ."

"The heat stays on. You can watch them. Watch their reactions. The killer might make a mistake that gives himself away. And the town preserves its reputation." And Bixby would preserve his.

He might not like it, but I'd be watching, too.

"See, I knew you were smart. Look, Audrey, I don't want to put anyone in Ramble in danger. But I have a duty to find whoever killed that man in our town, even if it's one of our own who did it."

I found myself in a blinking match with the chief, as we stood there assessing each other.

He lost. "So, tell me about this altercation you had with Gary Davoll."

Bixby seemed less than excited about my confrontation with Gary, especially when he learned I had an alibi. Which, good news for me, probably kept me off the suspect list. As he walked away and I turned to face the cast and crew, I couldn't hold back a shiver. Unless the killer were a local, which I doubted, then he or she might be milling around this room. Or standing outside behind the barrier. And while I understood the chief's reasoning and agreed that Gary's killer needed to be caught, I wasn't sure I wanted a murderer hanging around longer in our little town.

But I did have a flower job to do. And doing that job meant that I'd have to talk and work with these people. And keeping my eyes open meant I'd have to start associating some names with the faces of the crew instead of treating them like some homogenous machine.

Gigi finished up a conversation with Tristan, who winked and waved at me before he jogged away. Tristan was the one I could remember, with his James Bond looks and British accent. Normally, I might be attracted. I've been a sucker for a man with an accent ever since my first Cary Grant movie. But I already had one man too many. Besides, I had a firm rule to not flirt with murder suspects.

I caught Gigi's eye and was surprised when she made her way across the room toward me. Maybe it was my frantic waving at her that did it.

"Audrey, was it?" She held out her hand.

As I shook it, I fumbled with words. "I'm sorry about your loss . . . of your co-host." I reminded myself I wasn't supposed to know about her secret marriage.

She was made up like I was used to seeing her on television, but the rims around her eyes were red, and puffy circles were barely hidden under thick under-eye concealer. How hard it must be to hide a marriage, much less the loss of a spouse.

She didn't answer, just stared at our hands, which I had inadvertently held for too long a time to be polite.

"Sorry," I said.

"Thank you." Whether she was grateful for my sympathy or my letting go of her hand, I couldn't tell. "How are the flowers coming?"

"Stalled, for the moment."

She tilted her head and stared. On the show, that expression meant a snarky tirade was coming.

I decided to head her off. "Gary never picked a design before . . ."

She sucked air between her teeth, then nodded. Her face was a mask. I couldn't tell if it was the result of good acting, pancake makeup, or Botox. I tried to read something from her eyes, and I thought I saw a hollowness, a depth of grief chained deep inside, forbidden to bubble to the surface. Or maybe that's what I wanted to see.

Or maybe I read that in a novel somewhere.

At that moment, a cell phone rang—the theme song for the show—and Gigi pulled a smartphone from her pocket. In a flash, I saw the caller name: a major life insurance company. "Just a moment." She walked away to an empty corner of the room.

Of course, even if their relationship were a secret to the rest of the world, she would have life insurance on her husband. This would probably mean that she, more than anybody, had something to gain from his death. Aren't they always saying on those TV shows that it's usually the spouse? Probably why cop shows are not my favorite. I'm rather fond of happily-ever-afters that involve two people walking off hand in hand, not one being led off in handcuffs while the other decomposes in a casket.

I didn't want to believe that these two people who made wedding dreams come true for so many others could have had such a train wreck of a marriage that one of them resorted to murder to end it. But could Gigi have killed Gary—or had him killed—for his financial holdings and insurance money? As I watched her talk on the phone, she turned away, letting me know that I'd been staring. Maybe she was worried I could read lips. Unless her phone conversation was about a "white rhinoceros," her privacy was safe from me. I made a mental note to look online for lipreading courses.

I wandered away and absentmindedly picked up a scone.

Nick handed me a lemonade. "She sure holds it together well, doesn't she?" He nodded off in Gigi's direction. "Cold as ice, that one."

"I don't know. I think she's more upset than she's letting on."

"They had such great chemistry on television, but maybe they weren't all that close."

"No." I shook my head. "They were closer than people even knew."

Nick raised an eyebrow, and I longed to tell him what I'd learned about their secret marriage. But in a small town, rumors were hard to stuff back into the bottle, and I wouldn't hurt Mrs. June for anything.

"Have you met the rest of the crew?" I leaned in closer. "And any idea who was present and accounted for at the Ashbury at the time of Gary's death?"

"I may have learned a few things. But please don't go getting into trouble."

"I figure I'll have less trouble if I know who I'm dealing with. Any impressions?"

"A few. That producer is a bit full of himself. Not sure how that ego would have gotten along with Gary. And no one at the inn recalls seeing him earlier this afternoon."

"Tristan? He seems nice."

"Appearances can be deceiving. He's nice to the people who do stuff for him and ignores the rest. He's really nice to Gwyneth, if you get my drift." He gestured discreetly toward the buxom young intern I'd seen the first day of filming. "And no one can account for her whereabouts earlier, either."

"Got it. The cameraman's sweet on her, too, by the way."

Nick huffed. "Wouldn't doubt it. Marco seems like the type."

"Aren't all men the type?"

Nick drew a hand to his chest and feigned innocence with a flutter of his eyelashes. "Not all men are the type to take advantage of a young girl like that."

I chuckled. "I'm not sure she's not the one taking advantage of them. A lot of interns end up filing, retrieving coffee, or doing the jobs everyone wants to get rid of. But with her, the rest of the crew is tripping over each other trying to teach her the business."

"You may have a point," Nick said. "And yeah, the only coffee she gets is her own. Here she comes."

"Gwyneth?"

"No. Gigi. And you've got . . ." He pointed to my chest.

I brushed off the scone crumbs and whirled around.

"Sorry about that," Gigi said. "More loose ends. Where were we?"

"I was saying that the flowers were stalled until I know which design to go with."

"Hey, Marco!" she called across the room to the cameraman. "You got the footage with the flowers handy?"

"I can pull it up," he said.

"Do it."

She gripped the back of Marco's chair while he punched

buttons on a console. Soon the preview screen displayed footage of Gary, Suzy, me, and the bouquets. Gigi leaned forward and squinted. "They all look fine to me. Not sure I should be the one picking them. We're going to have to re-film that scene with Henry, anyway."

"But if I could get a hint of which one, I could get started on the designs for the rest of the flowers. We're well behind schedule until we know."

"Henry?" Gigi waved the man over. I was intimidated enough by Gigi, but Henry Easton? His bridal designs had graced anorexic models on catwalks the world over, and he was heading our way, looking me over from head to toe and grimacing.

He was still looking dapper and exquisitely preened, the little bit of a purple pocket square artfully displayed in his pocket suddenly making me think of larkspur, standing tall and proud in the field. Generally, larkspur can mean *brightness* or *levity*, but the purple signified *haughtiness*.

"Please tell me this is not a bridesmaid," he said. "I didn't bring any plus-sized gowns."

My jaw dropped. "I'm not . . . I'm a twelve. You can check the labels." And I was sure of that because I only shop in stores where size twelve fits me.

"Sixteen. Maybe a fourteen if you do a body cleanse and lay off the scones. I have a trained eye, my dear. Don't try to deny it." He turned to Gigi. "Maybe we should get that on camera. That would add some tension, don't you think? Perhaps a close-up of bursting seams?"

"Possibly, but she's not a bridesmaid. She's the florist."

Henry breathed out a relieved sigh. "That's the first thing that has gone right all day." He placed a hand on my arm. "What can I do for you?"

Frankly, as far as I was concerned he could go jump into the creek. And I'd have told him that, but it seemed petty and probably wouldn't have been good for our business reputation. "I need to know about the flowers."

"What flowers?"

"Exactly," I said. "Gary never picked which bridal bouquet to base the rest of the flowers on, so now I guess that's up to you."

"Quite right, quite right. At least for this episode, but I have hopes." He smiled at Gigi. "Not that I could replace Gary, of course."

Gigi cast him a frozen smile. "You're in good hands," she said to me. "Ta-ta!" And she walked out of the room.

"That poor woman," I said.

"Naw," Henry said. "She's a trouper. She'll bounce right back. Just watch."

I bit my lower lip.

"So are we done here? That was a bumpy flight from Boston, and the security lines were terrible."

"Boston? I thought you were coming in from Philly."

"After a while, they all look the same. Jetlagged, you know, so if you don't mind . . ." He started to walk away.

"No, wait. Could you at least take a look at these? It would help us get caught up."

Henry leaned toward the screen and then pulled out a pair of reading glasses. "Ahh . . . huh. Umm . . . I can't really . . ." He pulled his glasses to the tip of his nose and smiled at me. "I was right."

"What?"

"See that?" He pointed to the preview screen, where Gary and I stood behind the foxglove bouquet. "I happen to know that Gary wore a woman's size sixteen, and don't ask me *how* I know that. But look! You could be his body double in that shot. Sixteen."

Twelve. "But what about the flowers?"

"What do I know about flowers?" he said. "That's what they're paying you for, right? You choose."

"I couldn't do that." No way was I going to pick between Liv's, Shelby's, and my designs.

He balled a fist on the table. "No rest for the weary." He

was leaning closer to the screen when Tristan came up behind him.

"Henry, Audrey. Just the people I was looking for," he said. "We're re-taping the flower segment tomorrow at eleven."

"Good," Henry said. "I can't tell from that tiny picture, anyway. Tell you what. I'll decide tomorrow after a good night's sleep."

"Sure, sleep well." I managed a smile. Meanwhile I was plotting how I could sneak a jar of bedbugs into his room. Jetlagged from a trip south—that was a new one. And three more bouquets. And still no answer on the design. At least we'd sleep tonight, too. I wasn't sure about the rest of the week.

Chapter 8

❧

I was marching my size-twelve frame down Main Street, shoulders held high, swinging my arms in a brisk walk, when something felt wrong. No, not some spooky premonition. I just didn't normally walk that way. I must have left my purse—that torture device with the same ergonomics as a cannonball—at the Ashbury. Sure, my favorite over-packed bag gave me the posture of Quasimodo, but it fit all my stuff, so I habitually swung it over my shoulder anyway.

As I turned, I spotted Suzy Weber standing in front of the Ramble Historical Society building looking at the display stand of pamphlets. I would have never picked her for a history buff. Then again, one didn't need to be a history buff to appreciate the significance of the building, a monstrosity of a reworked and over-renovated home. The society had long dedicated themselves to restoring the eyesore to its original glory. The problem was none of them could agree as to what it once looked like. So it sat untouched, a perpetual embarrassment to the society whose name was placarded on the building.

But since Suzy's wedding seemed to be at the center of whatever was going on, I decided it might make sense to spare a few minutes and keep an eye on her—to see if she did anything suspicious while she was milling around town. So I turned to the nearest building, which happened to be the bank. I pretended to study the latest interest rate information while I watched her out of the corner of my eye. What I discovered was alarming—not that Suzy did anything. But interest rates, while not through the roof, were slowly climbing. I decided I should probably put in an offer on Grandma Mae's cottage sooner rather than later.

When Suzy put the pamphlet back and headed in my direction, I moved along, too. I figured it would look less like I was following her if I could keep ahead of her. So I inched down to the next building, which happened to be Olé, the town's Mexican restaurant. Rather than stare at the patrons noshing on their empanadas and enchiladas by the front windows, I kept strolling casually until I was in front of the cheese shop. I was fond of cheese, but never really bothered with anything but cheddar, American, and mozzarella. One of these days, I'd have to rectify that. Some of the cheeses in the display window looked yummy, except maybe for one marked Sofia. I wondered if the owners of the shop knew it was moldy.

While ogling the cheese, I looked for Suzy in the periphery. She'd stopped in front of the Tractor Supply store and seemed to be engrossed by the price tag on a wheelbarrow. She flashed a glance in my direction, then went back to studying the tag. Who was following whom?

I recalled what Gary had said about some brides going to elaborate lengths to snoop. Was that what she was up to? Or did she have something more sinister in mind? I walked to the next building, which happened to belong to the local Realtor. Overpriced homes glared at me from the full-color, glossy listings taped to the windows. Suzy advanced to the bank and stopped.

That was all the proof I needed. I whirled around and quickly made up the distance between the two of us.

"Why are you following me?"

"Oh, hello, Audrey. Following you?"

"Or do you need a bank loan to pay for that wheelbarrow you were pricing a few minutes ago?"

Suzy opened her mouth, as if to argue, then blew out a breath. "Fine. You got me. What's the big deal?"

"Have you ever thought that following someone right after a murder might be just a little creepy?"

"Wait, no. It's nothing like that. I saw you talking with Henry Easton. I wanted to know what bouquet he picked." Suzy wrung her arms. "He didn't pick the insincere ones, did he?"

"Don't you want to be surprised?" I asked.

"Hey, lady, don't you think we've had enough surprises today?"

Suzy's father, Max, jogged down the sidewalk and joined us. "What's going on?" He was red-faced, but not out of breath from his exertion.

"Just trying to find out more about the flowers, Daddykins," Suzy said sweetly.

"Only there's not much I can tell you," I said. "Henry didn't pick any of them."

"He wants new flowers?" Suzy asked.

I couldn't tell if the question was hopeful or nervous. "No, he didn't want to choose from a picture. He said he'll decide tomorrow after the reshoot."

"Did he really not pick? Or do you just not want to tell me?"

I chewed on my tongue for a moment while I considered how to answer. Of all the things that had happened in less than twenty-four hours—Gary's death, Brad's detention, Henry's unexpected arrival, and the announcement that the show must go on—and here her biggest worry was that she'd end up with foxglove in her bouquet.

"Suzy, all I can say is that your wedding flowers will be lovely. What they will be, I don't know. And if I did know . . . I couldn't tell you. I'm under contract."

"Couldn't or *won't*?" With that, Suzy spun on her heels and walked back toward the Ashbury.

Max shook his head and watched her go, looking like he'd aged about ten years. "Sorry about that. Audrey, right? I don't know what's gotten into her."

"It happens." I shrugged. "The stress of weddings. A lot of young women become . . ."

"You can say it. She's a bridezilla. But I can't help thinking this is my fault. After Suzy's mother passed away, I'm afraid I became a bit overindulgent. I was so stressed out over managing a growing business while worrying about doing the whole single-parent thing wrong that I just wanted her to be happy. I could never tell her no. Especially in the summer when I'm gone so much. I'm in landscaping, you see.

"And I did want to tell you I thought you did a great job with the flowers. A nice blend of colors. If you ever want a career change, look me up. I'm always looking for people who know flowers." He handed me his business card, which boasted landscaping services in seven different metropolitan areas in the Northeast.

"Oh, wow," I said, looking at the card. "That's quite an empire."

He sighed. "But at what price? Now I suppose Suzy thinks her happiness should be the main goal of everybody's life, and she'll pursue it at all costs."

That perked up my ears. What if she felt Gary stood between her and the perfect wedding—and therefore between her and happiness? I could see the headlines: "The Bridezilla Murder" and "Homicide and the Guilty Bride."

"I heard you try to talk her out of this," I said.

"Not the wedding. I have no problem with the groom. It

takes a special kind of a guy for Suzy. As soon as she brought him home the first time, I knew he was the one. I just wish she hadn't signed up for this show."

"I can see the appeal. Gary and Gigi have put on some lovely weddings."

"And some major disasters."

I nodded. I wasn't sure I totally agreed. Even the disappointed brides had elaborate weddings, probably much nicer than what they would have planned on their own. With the exception of Jackie.

I started strolling back toward the Ashbury.

Max walked beside me. "I offered to pay for one of those special destination weddings, anywhere she wanted to go. After all, it's not like I can't afford it. I sent away for all kinds of brochures. A tropical seashore. A Greek temple. An Irish castle. She could have been a blooming princess. I'd still do it, if she'd agree. Under the circumstances, it would make sense for us to pay the penalty and to let the crew out of the contract. Compassionate, even. They have to be reeling. But no, Suzy's still set on her bell wedding and being on TV."

"An Irish castle sounds great to me. She must really love bells."

Max shrugged. "Always loved them for some reason. Bells all over the place when she was a kid. Hand bells, wind chimes, you name it. Other kids wanted to go to Disney World. She wanted to see the Liberty Bell. I thought she'd grow out of it, but it's really a part of her now. I think her fiancé is taking her on a tour of European bells for their honeymoon, but she doesn't know it yet. Big Ben and all that." He rolled his eyes.

"I take it you don't share her enthusiasm."

"There are worse hobbies, I guess. And although I'll miss having her around, I will enjoy being able to sit on the deck at home when there's a nice breeze without having to wear earplugs because of all those wind chimes."

By this time, we had arrived back at the inn. Max gave my elbow a kindly squeeze in lieu of a good-bye. I headed toward Nick's table deep in thought.

In a few days, Suzy and her groom (Marvin? Mark?) would be headed overseas. The crew would pack up and leave for their next destination. Even Tacky Jackie and Dennis Pinkleman would go back to their normal lives, if you could call them that. And if the killer wasn't ferreted out by then, he might get away with murder.

I did what anyone else might do when confronted with the stress of that realization. I grabbed another scone. Then put it down.

"You touch it, you buy it," Nick said with a grin.

"Sorry. I didn't mean to pick it up. I'm not really hungry."

"Dopamine and serotonin. Probably the stress."

"What?"

"Two very potent chemicals released when one eats carbohydrates. Mood enhancers."

"You, my friend, are a drug dealer."

"The legal kind. And I'm a drug dealer who's about to quit for the night, anyway. Would you like these scones to go? I'm assuming you'll be working into the wee hours again."

"I can share them with the crew. I don't think we can do much more tonight—just three more bouquets so Henry can choose tomorrow."

Nick nodded. "You know, I'm almost glad I didn't get the contract for the wedding cake."

"For the show? I didn't know you were even in the running."

"I was. I pitched the idea to Brad when he called to arrange the catering. Came real close to making it happen. Gigi claimed she liked my designs, but in the end, I guess she decided to go with a nationally known baker." Nick didn't meet my eyes, but used a sheet of waxed paper to transfer the remaining scones into a white bakery box.

"That would have been some nice publicity for you. I'm sorry."

"Not sure how much the publicity would have done for us. You can't ship a wedding cake, so we're not likely to expand our territory much. No, I think expanding our product line was the best decision." He shrugged, but I could see sadness pull at the corners of his eyes. The chance to take one's work to the national arena—that's the opportunity the show had given to Liv and me, and the opportunity that Nick missed out on. A lot of people would kill for a chance like that. Thankfully, Nick wasn't one of them.

But I couldn't help thinking that it was a good thing for him that it was Gary and not Gigi found hanging in the belfry, otherwise Nick might have made Chief Bixby's suspect list.

"Before I head back to the shop," I said, "I wanted to ask if you've been able to figure out more of the whereabouts of the crew during the murder."

"A few." Nick gestured to a table where three middle-aged women were sipping tea and playing cards. "For a start, you can eliminate those three."

"That's good. Who are they?"

"Two of them are Gigi's wedding planners. From what I gather, they do most of the real work. The other is Gary's makeup and hair person. She does up the brides and bridesmaids. And according to rumor, sometimes Gary. But they were apparently here in that same spot at the time of the murder."

"They look dangerous," I quipped. "Glad we won't have to tangle with them. Anybody else?"

"Jordan the sound guy and Nathan—I'm not sure what he does. They were in here, too, arguing about something. Kathleen had to tell them to take it outside."

"And did they? And what were they arguing about?"

Nick shook his head. "Something to do with the filming. But no, they never left, just settled down and worked things out. So they have an alibi as well. But I'm afraid those are the only folks accounted for at the Ashbury. Everyone else was either in their rooms or about town."

"Thanks. At least we can eliminate a few people. And the dangerous dames at the corner table."

He smiled, but it was a weak smile that didn't quite reach his eyes. "Audrey, we don't seem to be able to find much time to spend together. Do you have a moment to talk?"

"Sure. What's up?"

"Not here." He glanced at the milling crew members. "Let's walk." Then he grabbed my hand and led me through the French doors out onto the patio. A narrow fieldstone path led toward the gazebo and a decorative pond.

Large koi clustered near the surface as we leaned on the wood railing of the bridge that spanned a narrow section of the pond. Water bubbled from a fountain. The sky shone bright blue and small birds and bees jumped from flower to flower. It was an almost idyllic setting. And I hoped Nick didn't bring me out here to break up. With the busy shooting schedule, we'd never talked about my dinner at Brad's house. Not that I had anything to hide. But then why was I avoiding the subject? And call me a pessimist if you must, but the Ashbury didn't hold many happy moments for me in the romance department.

"Look at that guy." Nick pointed to a large orange and white speckled fish that was eyeing us hungrily.

"I think that's Curly," I said. "Kathleen started out with three fish."

"Let me guess. The other two are Larry and Moe?"

I nodded. "And when she added more fish, she kept on with the theme. She added Chico, Harpo, Groucho, and Zeppo."

"There's a fifth Marx brother," he said. "Gummo. He was in the vaudeville act, but never appeared in any of their films. And . . . Shoot, Audrey. I didn't bring you out to talk about the Marx brothers. I think I'm stalling because this is so difficult for me."

Here it comes. "Look, if it's about the other night . . . "

He shook his head. "You know how many hours I've put into the bakery."

"It takes a lot to get a small business going. Trust me, I know."

"Yes, but I don't know that it's fair to you." He pulled me to face him, and then lifted my chin so that I was looking into his eyes. "What I'm saying is that I do understand if you want to date other people."

"You're breaking up with me."

"I didn't say that. Call me old-fashioned, but when it comes to relationships, I can't think of advancing to the next level unless I had . . . Look, I live in a barely habitable studio apartment above the bakery. In the winter it's toasty, and in the summer, it's a sauna. The business just started turning a profit, but not what I'd call a living wage, and certainly not enough to consider . . . well, to consider getting married and having a family. Audrey, if you waited for me, you could be waiting a long time."

I swallowed hard. Turning toward the pond, I leaned my arms against the aged wood railing and stared down into the water.

Curly hit the surface, sending ripples in all directions. A moment later Harpo did the same, and the ripples met, added to one another, creating an elaborate pattern in their interaction.

But the ripples didn't touch me.

I could feel the bubble forming around me, that protective isolation shutting me off from the rest of the world. The illusion that I was healed—whole again—evaporated, and the feelings of abandonment returned. Even the blood that ran through my veins seemed to respond. I once learned that in hypothermia, the blood leaves the extremities to protect the organs. But even in the summer heat, there didn't seem to be enough warmth there to prevent crystals forming, freezing my heart itself.

Nick stood silently next to me, waiting for a response. Even the stupid fish in the pond swam together, mated. But I couldn't interact anymore. I concentrated on breathing, on keeping a calm expression on my face, but I wasn't sure that this time I could pretend everything was all right.

"Dating me can't be a lot of fun for you," he said. "Unless you enjoy long evenings of Scrabble and cupcakes."

I happened to adore long evenings of Scrabble and cupcakes. "So you *are* breaking up with me."

"No! I'm saying that I understand if you wanted to break up with me. Especially since Brad is back in town and seems to be interested in you. I'm not saying that I would like it, but I'd understand it."

"So you're not breaking up with me. You're just giving me your blessing to break up with you."

"If that's what you want."

I stared down at the water, not really seeing it. "Brad and I dated for a long time. Maybe too long. I won't lie to you. Before he left Ramble, I had entertained thoughts of marriage—of spending my life with him. And I spent quite a few weeks after he left dreaming that he would come back and fall on his knees, admit he was wrong to leave, and beg me back."

Nick's water reflection nodded ruefully. I neglected to tell him that Brad had done pretty much that shortly after arriving back in town.

"But," I said, "a relationship with him now . . . I'd be constantly wondering whether he was going to leave me again. So while I suppose part of me still cares for him, I'm not sure I could trust my heart and life to him."

"You're not sure you could, but you're not sure you couldn't."

I bit my lower lip, then shook my head. I also wasn't sure if I could trust my heart and life to someone who'd just suggested I date other people.

"Maybe you should explore that."

"Are you trying to push me away?"

"No." Instead, Nick put his arms around my waist and drew me closer. He gazed into my eyes and removed an errant strand of hair from my cheek before leaning in to kiss me, a long, slow, tender kiss that instantly took most of the tension from my body. I leaned into his embrace and clung to him, part out of affection and part because his kiss left me weak in the knees and I needed the support. Maybe an ice crystal or two melted, just a little bit.

"Does that feel like I'm pushing you away?"

"Nuh-uh," I murmured into his chest. One of the advantages of dating a baker is that he always smells of cinnamon and vanilla and anise. I breathed deeply of his scent.

"But I want you to be happy, even if it means it's with someone else."

I leaned back to speak, but he put his finger over my lips. "That's all I wanted to say. Now I suspect it's back to the grindstone for both of us."

I walked into the shop with a box of scones and a heart so heavy, I was sure it had sunk to somewhere near my belly button.

Liv, Amber Lee, and Shelby must have sensed my mood, because, after I informed them that we needed to make three more bouquets, they kept up a cheerful banter between themselves without requiring me to say much. But Liv shot me more than a few concerned glances, which I avoided. Until she cornered me in the cooler.

"Are you going to tell me what's got you so down in the mouth?"

"Well, let me think about that for a minute," I said. "A nationally known wedding planner has been murdered. A killer is free, roaming the streets. My ex is back in town and being questioned by the police. We have a major job to do, but can't get the go-ahead on any of the designs. And I think Nick wants to break up with me."

"Last thing first. Nick wants to break up with you?" Leave it to Liv to narrow in on the one thing that was throwing me the most.

"I think. He said he wants to give me the freedom to be happy, but—"

"Has he given you reason to doubt that?"

"Not him, personally, but all the other men in my life seem to . . ."

Liv set down her flowers and drew me into a hug—a little farther apart than usual because of her growing baby bump. "Oh, kiddo. I know you haven't had the best of luck with the men in your life. And I'm no expert on the species myself. But one thing I've learned is that you can't blame one for the mistakes of all the others."

"I'm not. I'm blaming him for his own." Before she could defend Nick further, I brushed past her and back into the shop.

"So," I said, faking a smile as I stripped the foliage from a stem a little bit too forcefully and ended up splitting it down the middle, "did anyone learn anything today?"

"I did," Amber Lee crooned. "But I got a whopper and I kinda want to go last."

"Darnell will be back from a delivery in a few minutes." Liv peeked at the clock. "And Eric should be here, too."

The door swung open. "Eric is here," he said, bringing in several pizza boxes. "And brought dinner." He kissed Liv on the cheek.

She pulled back, ran her hand along his newly trimmed beard, then leaned back to inspect the hair behind his ears.

"Do I pass?" he said.

"You'll do." She reached up to return his kiss.

Eric looked around. "Is Nick here?"

"No," I said. "He's working at the bakery tonight."

Eric opened his mouth as if to add something, but Liv elbowed him in the ribs. Eric and Nick had become buddies. If Nick and I broke up, Eric would miss his camaraderie.

Darnell arrived as we carried the food to the fieldstone

table in the consulting nook, and soon everyone had divvied up their favorite slices dripping with gooey mozzarella.

"So, what did everybody learn today?" Eric said.

Shelby licked a blob of sauce from his thumb. "I got nothing at the Brew-Ha-Ha, just chatter. And my dad was out on a job, so I haven't had a chance to talk with him yet. But I think I might have gotten a hint as to the wedding design in the craft store. They're having a great sale on ribbon, by the way. But I started chatting up Miss Laurie. Next thing I know, she pulls out her cell phone, and there's a picture of Gigi in her store. Holding *silver ribbon*. So I bought some just like it. I thought maybe we could sneak some into the bouquets."

"Make sure I get the receipt so I can reimburse you," Liv said.

"Do you know when the picture was taken?" I asked.

"I was getting to that," Shelby said. "Miss Laurie told me she'd just finished her lunch."

"And Miss Laurie likes to eat her lunch early," Amber Lee said, "because people stop in for yarn and such during their own lunch breaks. So that picture was probably taken sometime after eleven, but probably before noon."

"Which puts Gigi only a couple blocks from the church with plenty of time to get there if she wanted to off Gary," Eric said.

"To *off* Gary?" Liv stared at him. "That's it. I'm getting rid of the TV."

"But why would she want to kill her co-host?" Shelby said. "Their chemistry made that show."

I took a bite of my pizza and chewed. I hated withholding information from my coworkers, but Mrs. June's job was more important. I struggled to swallow and sipped my soda, forcing a glob of congealing cheese down my esophagus. "There could be any number of reasons. We only know their television personas. They could be much different in real life."

Amber Lee turned to me, her wide eyes flashing.

"Did you want to go next?" I asked.

"Nope. I still want to go last, but you are very perceptive."

"Well, I didn't get anything from my secretary," Eric said. "Said she had her head buried in our monthly reports all day, trying to fix a discrepancy of twelve cents."

"Slave driver," Liv teased.

Eric sent a smile in her direction. "But I did learn a thing or two at the barber shop. Not sure if it's all that relevant."

"What is it?" I asked.

"Lou told me two strangers came in. An older gentleman and his daughter. He thought they might be part of the show."

"An older man. Did he have a straggly beard?"

"I guess he did when he came in," Eric said.

"He left clean shaven?" Amber Lee asked.

"He would have if the daughter had her way. Lou said they argued something fierce over it." Eric blushed. Liv had insisted he show up for their wedding clean-shaven, and he had complied. But that was before Liv realized that his baby face would make him look like a twelve-year-old groom. They've since hidden their wedding pictures and Eric went back to the bristly look. "I heard he got a decent trim. Should look fine on camera. Although Lou also told me that she made an appointment for him the day of the wedding. They're making bets down at the barber shop on how much facial hair he'll be allowed to keep."

"So that puts the bride and Daddykins also a few blocks from the church," I said.

"Audrey," Liv said, "this is Ramble we're talking about. Everything is a few blocks from the church. So what did you learn today?"

While they ate, I told them about Bixby making Brad cool his heels and my visit to the Ashbury.

"So that adds a couple more suspects," Liv said.

My jaw dropped. "Now, wait—"

"Not Brad." Liv rolled her eyes. "He may be a jerk at

times, but I don't think he could kill anyone. I meant Dennis Pinkleman and Jackie. Any thoughts about either?"

"Well, Bixby took poor Dennis into custody without even asking who started that altercation outside the Ashbury. I kind of feel sorry for the guy."

"So he drove all the way from Cleveland just to get a glimpse of Gary and Gigi?" Eric asked.

"I guess he's a rabid fan," I said.

"Fan as in he likes watching the show?" Amber Lee said. "Or fan as in having a roomful of grainy images pasted on all his walls? That makes a difference."

"He must be a bit obsessive to travel that far. And then there's Jackie," I added. "Jackie and Dennis acted like they'd both been outside the Ashbury all day, but that area was kind of chaotic. They must have left to find food and to use a bathroom somewhere."

"Not at the Ashbury?" Darnell asked.

I shook my head. "The Ashbury is closed except to cast and crew. Ken Lafferty is guarding it, so to speak."

"Then he should know who was coming and going," Liv said.

"Not sure. He was there this morning when I arrived for shooting the flower segment, and when I arrived later this afternoon, but . . ."

"That sounds like an interesting 'but,' " Amber Lee said.

"He was at the church when I got there." I tried to play the scene over in my head. "First one at the scene. He was there before Bixby, even."

"That's because he was at the deli when that bell started ringing," Darnell said. "Officer Lafferty, that is. I heard he got a call and charged out of there, leaving his lunch unpaid for and sitting on the table. His waitress was not happy."

"They know where to find him," Amber Lee said.

"Then someone must have replaced him guarding the Ashbury," Liv said. "You know, I bet Mrs. June might know. Wait—didn't the show have its own security guards?"

"Yeah, the first day," I said. "The guys with the black clothes and the mirrored glasses. Fat lot of good they did. Come to think of it, I haven't even seen them since. I'll keep an eye out for them when I head back to the Ashbury tomorrow."

I turned back to Darnell. "Learn anything at the soccer fields?"

Darnell stroked the stubble on his chin. "Just rumors. One guy said he saw Gary walking down Main Street. Asked for an autograph for his daughter, but Gary passed him like he didn't hear."

"Was Gary alone?"

"The guy didn't mention anybody with Gary. And I think he would have told me. Some of the guys in town seem to think his murder had something to do with Gary's orientation."

"Hogwash," Amber Lee said. "Is it my turn now? Because I can't wait any longer."

"Spill it," Liv said.

Amber Lee's face broke out into a huge grin. "Well, speculation at the Underdog was the same as at the soccer field, only they were all buzzing about how they met one of the crew. Said he ordered the All-American number four with onion rings and a Diet Coke."

"They didn't get a name?" I asked.

Amber Lee shook her head.

"Did he have an accent?"

"They didn't mention one."

"Probably Marco, the cameraman." I figured if he had an accent, they would have mentioned it, since they got his lunch order down to the minutest detail. "This puts him in town near the church. Did they have anything else to say about him?"

"Not really. Said he kept to himself—although my burger was excellent."

She waited, obviously enjoying the rapt attention of her audience before she dropped her bombshell.

"But then I went to the beauty parlor. Or salon, or whatever they're calling it these days. I had no sooner sat in the chair, before it all came out. It seems that Gary's orientation was all a big act for the camera. He was straight, and . . . wait for it . . . he was secretly married. To Gigi Welch."

Oh, Mrs. June. The secret's out. But they didn't hear it from me.

Chapter 9

❧

A small nosegay bouquet wasn't going to make it all better, so I went for a large vase full of gorgeous purple Dendrobium orchids (*love, nobility, beauty*). Not that orchids would make it all better if Mrs. June lost her job over the revelation of Gary and Gigi's secret marriage. And not that I had anything to do with the word getting out. Unless someone overheard my conversation with Mrs. June and repeated it.

So first thing in the morning, I was marching the flowers up the sidewalk toward the municipal building that housed police headquarters, as well as most other government doings in Ramble, and almost literally ran into Rita Watkins, the mayor's wife. She burst out the door, letting it close behind her. When we met midway on the sidewalk, we did one of those little dances where you try to get out of the way, but whichever direction you step, the other person steps the same way. After four or five of these side-to-side steps, she brushed past me without a word of greeting or help for the florist struggling with the large arrangement.

I was about to set the vase on the stoop when the door flew open again. This time the mayor rushed out and chased after his wife. He didn't verbalize a greeting, only a gruff nod, but at least I was able to get an elbow in the door before it closed. Now, why were they in such an all-fired hurry?

Mrs. June buzzed me in and oohed and aahed over the flowers while one of the officers seemed to take forever to gather his equipment from a nearby desk. When he headed out, she leaned closer to me. "Orchids, Audrey? What did I do to merit orchids?" She raised an eyebrow. "Or what did you want me to do? Because there's not much I wouldn't do for orchids. Legal, that is."

"Mrs. June." My words stuck in my throat. The police department was her whole life. She'd been working there ever since her father was the chief, and I knew she had no plans to retire until they carried her kicking and screaming from the building. I swallowed and tried again. "I don't know how it happened, because I didn't tell anybody. But I wanted to give you a heads-up that"—I lowered my voice to a whisper—"word of Gary and Gigi's marriage is getting around town."

I studied her face for any look of worry or concern. It was a quick study. She threw her head back and laughed.

"And here I was fretting that it could mean your job!"

"It might have, but the leak has already been discovered and traced. Seems Bixby was so proud of his revelation that he told the mayor."

"The mayor?"

"Who told his wife. Who mentioned it to half a dozen people. I mean, what good is it to be the mayor's wife when you can't deliver dirt every now and then?"

"Is that why Rita and the mayor were running out of here just now?" I asked.

"Oh yeah. Big blowup. I guess someone from the hair salon sold the information to a group of reporters that just arrived—staying at the bed-and-breakfast. A whole 'undisclosed source close to the investigation' thing. Now Bixby has egg on his face, and the mayor is doing damage control. I think he's taking his wife over to the Ashbury to apologize personally to Gigi."

"That has to be galling."

A sly smile crept across Mrs. June's face. "Yes, terrible, isn't it? Wish I could be a fly on that wall."

I couldn't resist a giggle and a dip into her candy jar.

She shook her head. "But I think what's got the chief so worked up is getting to the crime scene last. He's the most experienced investigator we have. He's spitting fire that he wasn't there earlier."

"But Lafferty was there first, I guess."

She shook her head. "Because the chief was guarding the Ashbury so Lafferty could break for lunch. When the call came in, Lafferty rushed straight to the scene of the crime. He contaminated who knows how much evidence in the church bell tower, but the chief was stuck at the Ashbury until he could find someone to replace him. What a mess. He was not a happy camper. He's been playing catch-up since."

"So when did Bixby get around to questioning Brad?"

Mrs. June looked at her watch. "About twelve minutes ago."

"No!"

"Yep. He came in this morning to find Brad sleeping on top of the conference table. Frankly, I think Bixby plumb forgot he was here. He messed up, trying to play like the big boy cops, and he knows it. I think it will end up working in Brad's favor. His mama and her people are voters, too. You don't do that to a native son. Not that the chief gets elected directly, understand. He's appointed by the mayor. And I'll bet he's going to get an earful."

The door to the conference room banged open, and Bixby's over-friendly voice filled the corridor. "Again, I am so sorry. Not quite sure what happened there, but thanks for voluntarily coming in to give your statement."

Mrs. June whispered to me. "I bet he threw me under the bus. Like I was supposed to keep reminding him."

"I'll set Brad straight. Don't worry." I winked.

"Just to be sure, I reminded him twice this morning that he has that Pinkleman kid still at the detention center. But I think they're letting him go right after breakfast."

"At least he had a meal and a place to sleep."

Soon Brad rounded the corner, carrying a coffee with a doughnut balanced on the lid of the thermal mug. His clothes were rumpled, his hair mussed, and he had a double dose of a five o'clock shadow. He looked bedraggled and sleepy-eyed and sweet. Like the Brad I used to know, the struggling videographer living with his mother in a town where not much happened worth taping, not the ambitious young man who dumped me for a career in reality television.

"Audrey, I . . ." He stroked the stubbly growth under his nose as if rubbing it would make it go away. The movement jostled his coffee, sending several drips to the floor.

"Don't worry about it," Bixby said. "Our receptionist can clean that up." He nodded to me. "Miss Bloom." Then he backed into his office and closed the door.

Mrs. June rolled her eyes.

"I can't believe you spent the night in the conference room." I picked up a small stack of napkins from the table housing the department's coffee, tossed them on the few drips from Brad's cup, and wiped up the mess with my shoe. "Didn't he tell you that you were free to go?"

"Apparently he missed that part." Brad set down his coffee and rubbed the sleep from his eyes. "I need a shower and a shave."

"Would you like me to run you home?" It was only a couple of blocks from the shop to the municipal building, but I'd taken the CR-V to transport the flower arrangement I'd made for Mrs. June.

"Actually, I'm staying at the Ashbury with the crew, but if it's not too far out of your way, I'd love a ride."

Soon we were buckled in. I glanced at the clock and decided to make a pit stop back at the shop to pick up the new bouquets for our shoot. I also grabbed my change of clothes and makeup case.

Brad craned his neck when I put the flowers in the back. "I thought you already finished that segment."

"Not with Henry Easton."

"Easton's here? Is he taking over for Gary?"

"Yes, he arrived last night—"

"I'll bet Gigi and Tristan have been trying to get in touch with me." He scrubbed his face with his hands. "Bixby kept my phone."

"Probably because it had Gary's text on it."

Brad drained the rest of his mug. "I hope they have coffee out. And something better than this doughnut." He banged it on the dash. "That's one thing your boyfriend does well."

"He does a lot of things well," I started, then held my tongue.

"Sorry." He drew in a breath. "I mean it." He rolled down the window and tossed the doughnut outside.

"Brad—" I started.

"What? It's biodegradable. Maybe the birds can digest it better than I can." He smoothed a wrinkle out of his pants. "So what have I missed?" His tone was artificially cheerful. "If Easton's here, I guess the show's still on."

"They made that announcement while you were locked up."

"I wasn't locked up."

"Detained, then," I said.

"As Bixby explained it, I wasn't even detained. I was asked to come in for questioning. And stayed there voluntarily."

"You like sleeping on conference tables, then?"

Brad wagged his eyebrows in a teasing gesture. "Wouldn't you like to know."

I gripped the steering wheel just a little bit tighter as Lafferty waved me through. We rolled into the Ashbury parking lot past the group of gawkers, which at the moment contained a couple of news crews. I left the CR-V running to keep the flowers cool and fresh, but locked it. And then checked my purse for my extra key, which was thankfully there. I walked with Brad into the inn, with my change of clothes dangling over my arm.

Nick was pouring coffee behind the table and looked up with a smile. Then the smile drooped and he averted his gaze.

I guess my arrival with Brad in such a state didn't look good. Take that, Mr. Free-to-date-other-people. But that attitude lasted only a split second. I didn't want Nick thinking Brad and I were back together, so I said good-bye to Brad, who was then surrounded by other members of the crew. I headed over to the table and joined Nick behind it.

"Good morning." I poured myself a cup of coffee.

"Audrey . . . I." He sighed. "I guess when I suggested that it would be okay for you to date other people, I didn't know you'd be so quick about it."

"Look, I'm not dating . . . Brad spent the night at the police station, sleeping on the conference table."

"He did?" Nick seemed to enjoy that information a little too much.

I looked around the room. "Has the mayor or his wife made an appearance yet?"

"A few minutes ago," Nick said. "They found Gigi, then headed to one of the conference rooms and shut the door."

I nodded.

"What's that about?" he asked. "Something to do with the murder?"

"Well, I can tell you today, because it's probably going to be on the news soon. Gigi and Gary were secretly married."

"Married?"

His outburst turned the heads of several members of the crew, including Brad.

I hushed Nick. "I don't think the crew knows yet."

"But that would mean . . ."

"What?"

"It's just that . . . that Easton fellow did everything but outright say that he and Gary were . . . close. Was that a put-on?"

I shrugged and grabbed a scone.

I was still chewing when the mayor and his wife strode down the hall and directly out the door. Rita was red-faced, but otherwise unreadable. Soon Gigi rounded the corner. When the din in the room didn't subside, she put two fingers to her mouth and whistled. All eyes turned to her, including a sleepy-looking Easton, who had entered the room and was halfway to the coffee bar.

"I hoped we were done with surprise announcements for a while," Gigi said, as the group gathered around her.

At the mention of surprise announcements, almost every set of shoulders in the room tensed. The crew had clearly reached their quota of surprises.

"Oh, hey, Brad," Gigi said. "Nice of you to join us today."

The group laughed—one of those laughs where nothing may be funny, but a tension-relief valve opens.

"Well, I don't know how to say it but to say it. Gary and I had a secret, one we kept quiet for the good of the show. He and I were married. Happily so . . ."

The crew shared glances. I wondered if any of them had suspected. As I scanned their faces, I saw one smile flicker, ever so slightly. I studied the young man's face. Strong, clean-shaven. Blond. His rapt attention was on Gigi.

"But because of the investigation," Gigi went on, "that fact has become public knowledge. News outlets are going to start reporting on it. But I wanted to be the one to tell you. Gary and I . . ." She stopped to wipe a tear. "Now you understand that I didn't just lose a co-host and a friend. I've lost my soul mate." She swallowed.

I kept my gaze on the man. His jaw tightened ever so slightly at the words "soul mate," and the rest of his face turned into a mask. The muscle-bound blond Adonis was obviously part of the crew, but I hadn't seen him before.

"Please understand," Gigi continued, "that our little subterfuge was only to forward the business. We love you all and trust you. Only we knew that once the secret got out, it would spread like wildfire, which is what is happening now. I . . ."

For once she didn't seem to have a closing remark. The last word. She didn't need to. The crew surged forward and enveloped her in a series of embraces. All except the blond man.

Nick whispered in my ear, "You called that one."

While Gigi was still surrounded by the crew, Henry Easton walked over to the coffee table, shaking his head. I stuffed the remains of my scone in my pocket.

"Wish I'd seen that coming," Easton said.

And somehow, his inference that he'd seen Gary in women's clothing came to mind. Size sixteen.

"The fashion industry must be terribly difficult for a straight man to maneuver." I chose a conversational tone.

Easton's gaze caught mine as his shoulders went rigid. He added a lethal dose of artificial sweetener to his coffee before answering. "I suppose. Women who come into my shops, for example. They don't want a man in the fitting room with them, ogling them, stuffing them into strapless dresses. If the man is gay, however, they don't seem to care. And then there's the stigma that straight men don't know fashion. Perhaps it was convenient for Gary and his career to playact the stereotype."

And I wondered if Gary wasn't the only one playacting. Foxglove. *Insincerity.*

And with insincerity comes secrets. I wondered what other secrets Gary could have been hiding, secrets that could have motivated someone in this room to kill him.

A moment later, Gigi freed herself from her staff and headed to the coffee table.

"What's the strongest you got?" she asked Nick. "It's going to be a rough one."

"Just regular coffee," Nick said. "Nobody requested espresso. Although I could run and get one if you wanted."

She waved off the offer. "Make it a double. Black."

"Gigi, again may I offer my condolences," I said. "Not just on the loss of your co-host, but of your husband."

"Oh, Audrey. Thanks. In a way, it's a relief for the information to be out there. Now I can grieve publically, without people questioning why I'm so upset."

"Who would . . . ?"

She rolled her eyes. "Twitter and the tabloids were already spitting out their theories. I killed Gary because of professional differences. I killed Gary to make myself more valuable and better my contract terms. I suppose they'll say I killed Gary for his life insurance. Oh, now they'll be even surer. Isn't it always the spouse?" She reached out and nabbed herself a scone. Good move. I swear Nick's scones are better than Prozac.

"Sometimes. The police must have asked your whereabouts yesterday."

She chewed and swallowed. "Mmmm, that's good. Yeah, they did ask. Unfortunately, I was all over this little town yesterday, including the church. Scouting the venue, picking up some materials. This town is just as quaint as it can be, but not the easiest place to shop."

"Did you hear the church bell ring?"

Gigi closed her eyes and inhaled. Then shook her head, while breathing out a disgusted sigh. "By that time, I was headed out of Dodge. Someone, I think it was Brad, clued me in to the strip mall in the next town over. Felt like I was driving through the Amazon to get there, though. All these little roads, twisting around these hills. And the GPS lost signal twice. I was half cursing Gary for bringing us out here, at the same time he . . ." She swept her long, manicured fingers under her eyes to remove the beginning of tears.

"It was Gary's idea to fix this wedding, then?" I said.

She nodded. "Frankly . . ." She looked around before leaning toward me and whispering, "I never understood his fascination with this one. I told him that bell theme was lame-o. But he wouldn't listen to anybody. He had more fascination with this particular wedding—I would have said with this particular *bride*—than he ever had before."

Kathleen Randolph stole up to the table. "Excuse me, Miss Welch. I found this envelope on the desk, addressed to you."

Gigi took the envelope that sported only her name and pulled out a single sheet of paper. She scanned it, then tossed it on the table as if it were radioactive.

I could read the large block letters, even upside down.

"GIGI, LEAVE NOW WHILE YOU STILL CAN. OR YOU'LL GET WORSE THAN GARY GOT."

Chapter 10

Bixby was there in a flash, taking possession of the letter and questioning Kathleen Randolph. Apparently I wasn't in the way, because he let Nick and me remain, standing behind the coffee table.

"No, it was on the desk when I came back," Kathleen said. "I have no idea who might have put it there."

"The envelope and the notepaper are distinctive," Bixby noted.

"And, yes," Kathleen said, "they have the name of the inn embossed on them. I provide them for guests in every room. A personalized touch, a reminder of their stay. And I keep more at the desk for anyone who asks."

Nick leaned in closer to me. "You know, it has to be someone in the cast and crew, then. Because nobody else could have gotten into the inn."

"I don't know," I whispered back. "Security isn't all that tight. Someone could have sneaked past Lafferty pretty easily. Have you seen any of the show's security around?"

"What do they look like?"

"When they rode into town, they wore dark glasses and had the word 'Security' in big letters on their T-shirts."

"Come to think of it, I haven't seen anybody like that at all at the inn."

When I looked up again, Bixby had moved away from Kathleen Randolph and had Brad pinned against the wall. Well, not literally pinned, but Brad seemed shocked and appeared to cower before him.

When Bixby was done speaking, Brad's shoulders sank in relief as he made his way over to us.

"Bixby looked like he had a lot to say," I ventured.

Brad poured himself a cup of coffee and stared into the brown liquid. "He wanted to ask me about the latest threat." He looked up. "Audrey, what is happening? This is a nightmare. He has a point that the person who wrote the note has to be one of the cast or crew. Who else could get in? But why would any of us want to stop the show?" His eyes panned the room until he stopped to look at Nick.

Nick raised an eyebrow and stared back at him.

Brad set down his cup. "You have motive to stop the show."

"Why would I—?" Nick started.

"Brad, don't be silly," I said

"No, I mean it." Brad set his focus straight on Nick. "You were turned down to be on camera. That could have done your career some good. But then I come back to town. Maybe you thought I was a threat to your relationship, is that it?" Brad had raised his voice. Several cast members—and Bixby—were looking in our direction.

"Brad," I said, purposely calming my voice and trying to drag him into a quiet corner. "You can't possibly think Nick had anything to do with this?"

But Brad held his ground, even if he did lower his voice a little. "You've had access to the Ashbury. You could have written the note and slipped it on the desk as easily as I could have. More so, since nobody is watching *your* coming and going." He said that last part extra loud and focused his attention on Bixby, who wasn't even trying to hide the fact that he was listening intently to this conversation.

"But I didn't," Nick said. "And I was in the shop baking, with another employee present, during the time of Gary's death."

And I hoped that Jenny would not be pulled into this. She'd had enough of Bixby earlier this year.

Brad's eyes became no more than slits as he scrutinized Nick. "Well, if they're watching me, I'll be watching you."

"Why do you have such an intense interest in turning suspicion in my direction?" Nick said. "I think you're grasping at straws to save your own neck. If anyone needs watching, I say it's you."

"Fine, watch each other," I said, crossing my arms, not trying to disguise the pique in my voice.

Two heads swiveled in my direction.

I propped up what was probably a scary-looking fake smile. "And while you're busy watching each other, Gigi and the rest of the crew—and the whole town of Ramble—will be in danger, because there's a killer still out there, maybe plotting another murder, while you have your jealous little staring contest."

"Sorry," Nick said, almost instantly, with just the right amount of penitence in his brown eyes.

Brad worked his jaw for what must have been a full minute, then turned to Nick. "Look, I don't know you very well, but I do trust Audrey to be a pretty good judge of character. I have no reason or right to accuse you like that. Sorry." And he held out a hand.

Nick whipped off his food service glove and shook.

Bixby walked away, and other heads turned back to their work. Show over.

"Listen, Brad," I said. "I was wondering if you could help us with something."

Despite the hand-shaking gesture, Brad looked leery. "What is it?"

"We were trying to figure out what happened with security."

"What do you mean?"

"The security guards who were with the crew the first day. I haven't seen hide nor hair of them since."

One corner of Brad's lip curled up. "There is no security—well, except for the local LEOs. That's 'law enforcement officers.'"

"I know what it means. I watch *NCIS*," I said. "But who were those guys in the shirts and dark glasses?"

"Audrey, look at the crew."

I turned to look at the crew members milling about. Then shrugged my shoulders at Brad.

"You weren't looking at their faces that day, were you? Most people don't. They see security guards and decide they're too much trouble to mess with."

"I still don't . . ."

Brad shook his head. "The crew *were* the security guards. We put on those black shirts and dark glasses when we roll into town, and then cross our arms and try to look imposing. People think we're secure, so they don't try to horn in on filming and shout and wave to their grandmothers. Up until now, it's been all the security we've needed."

"You were there, at the welcome rally?"

"'Fraid so. I saw you on the stage with your tuba."

"You did?"

Brad smiled and nodded. "And that cute little hat."

Nick cleared his throat. "That still leaves the rest of the crew. And the cast."

"How many are there?" I asked. "Have I seen the whole crew? There are still too many nameless faces." I was especially curious about the blond I'd met earlier.

"Then let's fix that right now." Brad took my arm and tucked it around his, sent Nick a curt nod, and then began escorting me around the room.

"You met Gary and Gigi, of course. Beyond them and their

staff, we operate a basic six-man crew. I know I introduced you to Tristan, the producer. Marco, he's the camera operator."

"I've met him, too," I said.

"He's been in the industry a long time and been with *Fix My Wedding* from the beginning. Really knows his stuff. Nathan is his assistant. This is his first gig." Brad pointed to a young man weighed down with shoulder bags and backpacks. Looked like he functioned more as a pack mule.

"Hey, Jordan!" Brad shouted and waved to a man wearing headphones. He was the same one who'd been holding that dreaded boom mic over my head. He waved halfheartedly and went back to his work. "Jordan is our sound mixer."

Brad then pointed to Gwyneth. The young woman wore a low scoop-necked top and short shorts. "And that's Gwyneth, our production coordinator. She's interning with us for the summer." Gwyneth smiled a flirty smile at Brad.

"That's basically the production crew."

"So six people from the production crew could be considered suspects, but Nathan and Jordan were here at the Ashbury when the murder took place, so that leaves four viable suspects without an alibi."

"If you want to include me in that list, yes."

"Sorry," I said. "Three suspects from the production crew. Marco was seen in town at the sports bar, and nobody saw Tristan or Gwyneth all afternoon."

"And then there's Gary and Gigi's staff. They're the ones that make the weddings work. Gigi has a couple of event planners who do almost everything—or hire locals when we need more help. Sven, our lighting guy, is here." Brad pointed to the muscle-bound blond I'd seen earlier, who could have been Sweden's contestant for Mr. Universe.

"For the filming?"

"No, he does the up-lighting for the reception. Travels to all the weddings. Gigi wouldn't have anybody else."

I'm sure she wouldn't.

"Gary also traveled with a seamstress and stylist."

"The stylist and the wedding planners were here playing cards at the time, so they're out. I guess that leaves Gigi, Sven the lighting guy, and the seamstress without alibis. I think I'm getting a headache."

Brad chuckled. He leaned in and gestured his head toward a striking young brunette sewing beads on a filmy veil that she'd stretched across a table. "I'll introduce you to the seamstress, but I warn you, she's Bulgarian and knows very little English. Not sure how long she's going to be with us. Spends half her time talking to the State Department and Immigration Services."

"*Zdrasti,* Nevena," Brad called with a wave. She looked up and smiled.

"Nevena, meet Audrey," he said, and she reached over and shook my hand.

"Nevena—that's a very pretty name," I said.

She paused for a moment, then nodded. "You the flower lady. Nevena mean marigold," she said, as if establishing some long-lost connection. "When I young, I have the yellow hair."

In the language of flowers, marigold had come to mean *grief* and *pain.* Maybe I let the language of flowers seep into my impression of this woman, because her blue-gray eyes seemed older than her twenty-some years—and infused with pain. Was she that upset to lose her boss? Or could he have been more than a boss?

Brad led me toward an empty table and we sat down. "That's pretty much everybody it takes to put on one of these weddings. Of course, the national baker won't be arriving until later today, and Henry Easton didn't arrive in town until after the murder."

"Easton might have had more motive than anybody. Any chance he could have sneaked in earlier?" After that bursting-seams crack, I hate to admit it, but I would have loved to see him handcuffed and put into the back of a Ramble police car.

"I don't know, Audrey. He'd be pretty recognizable."

I nodded. I recalled how the crowd instantly called out his name and made such a fuss when he rolled down the window of his limo. Certainly someone would have seen him around town.

"And then there's the cast," Brad added. "The bride, her father. The groom. His parents. They won't arrive until tomorrow, so you haven't met them yet."

"I've barely met the groom." I tried to recall his name. Martin? Matthew?

"I suspect Suzy is a little more . . . predominant," he said. "You think the future in-laws might have wanted to stop the wedding?"

I shrugged my shoulders. "It seems like an extreme move, don't you think? Even if for some reason they hated Suzy, there have to be simpler ways to stop a wedding."

I rubbed my forehead, trying to process all this new information. "That's a lot of people with means. Maybe we should concentrate on motive. Any chance that Dennis or Jackie could have gotten in?"

"With Ramble's finest parked out front?" Brad rolled his eyes. "But, Audrey . . ." He leaned forward and reached for my hand. "I'm not sure I like you poking around into a murder. Maybe you should let the local police handle it. I'm sure they're processing evidence and following leads. They might have a suspect under surveillance at this very moment."

I glanced up at Bixby, who was still staring at Brad.

Brad followed my gaze, then slumped into his chair. "Or maybe not."

It was déjà vu all over again as Suzy and I—this time with Henry Easton and not Gary—stood in the gazebo looking over the flower bouquets.

"Come stand by me, Daddykins?" Suzy asked her father. But Max shook his head and took a place on the other side of the camera, standing beside Nathan, the camera assistant. With, I might add, a good view of Gwyneth in her short shorts. She was probably the only one of us not wilting in the heat.

By this point, Suzy had time enough to practice making her pick. She oohed and aahed and her eyes lit up during the reveal of my Victorian-inspired bouquet.

"I love the bell-shaped flowers and all the meanings. And the little silver holder is just to die for."

At this point, Tristan cut the filming, and had her go back.

"I love the bell-shaped flowers and all the meanings. And the little silver holder is just *super cute*."

"Very lovely." Henry barely glanced at the flowers. "But tell me, why bells?"

"I don't understand." Suzy scrunched up her face.

"What is it about bells that you love so much?" It was a good question. I didn't get her fascination, either. Apparently Gary was the only one who had.

"I don't know. I just do." Riveting answer.

"Think about it," Tristan coaxed. "Take your time."

Suzy thought. And thought. By this point, sweat was pouring down my back from standing outside in the increasingly warm and humid weather.

Finally, she cocked her head to one side and started talking softly. The boom mic dropped even lower over her head.

"I think I love them most when . . . I miss my mother. There's something comforting about them when the wind catches them. The sound doesn't stop right away. It echoes, and I can almost hear her voice in the echo. Like she didn't just end right away when she died, either. Echoes of her live on . . ."

Where did that come from? The crew must have been thinking the same thing. Tristan had a huge smile on his face. Max wiped away a tear.

To my right, Henry Easton leaned over and gave Suzy a big hug, his voice cracking with emotion as he murmured assurances in her ear. The boom microphone continued to hover overhead.

And I found myself trying to wipe away an unexpected tear without streaking my face with mascara.

After Tristan yelled, "Cut," he turned to Brad. "Seriously, 'Echoes of a Mother' would make a good episode name. What do you think?"

As the rest of the crew started packing up, Henry began to walk toward the Ashbury.

I chased after him. I was not leaving without a decision on the flowers.

He startled as I touched his arm.

"Look," he said, "I must get out of this heat. I'm simply melting away like the witch in *The Wizard of Oz*."

"Fine," I said, half jogging to keep up with his pace, and agreeing wholeheartedly with his analogy. "All I need from you is a decision on which bouquet."

"The first one, obviously. That Victorian fussy mussy one. The bride was nuts over it. That last one was interesting. Very dramatic. But it would take away from the dress, I think. The dress should be the center of attention."

"You mean the bride."

"Um, yeah."

With just three days before the most elaborate wedding we'd ever done, we were on full staff and late nights. A couple of Shelby's fellow students from nearby Nathaniel Bacon University—good old Bacon U—took time from their summer break and joined our crew. They'd helped us in the past when we've been swamped, and seemed to enjoy the experience. Melanie was a peaches-and-cream young lady who displayed an affection for ponytails, pastel floral shirts, and denim skirts. Opie, short for Opal, was our resident goth. Whatever wasn't covered in black leather was tattooed with flowers. Shelby had made some great recommendations, I thought. Both girls were hard workers, had good attitudes, and could barely hide their excitement about working on flowers that might be seen on a reality TV show. And despite their differences, they seemed to work pleasantly together.

We'd put Darnell to work, greening up some of our more elaborate arrangements. He tried to pretend he was too macho to work on flowers, despite a clear natural gift. But since the greenery didn't have petals, it wasn't the same, right? At least we'd been able to convince him of that distinction. Both Liv and I were longing to see what he could accomplish with flowers, with a little instruction. Anyway, he did a fantastic job with the greenery.

"My dad wasn't too happy about me coming." Opie set her cell phone on the corner of her workstation. "'Cause of the murder. He's saying Ramble is becoming a dangerous place. But I told him I wouldn't miss this for anything. Still, I have to text him every two hours." She rolled her eyes.

"Oh, pshaw." Liv repeated one of our Grandma Mae's favorite phrases. "This latest . . . unpleasantness . . . has nothing to do with Ramble. It has to be one of those outsiders with the show."

"Maybe," Amber Lee said. "Or one of our locals with the show."

I bit my upper lip. No, best to face this one head-on. "Meaning Brad. That's what people are saying."

"Not everybody, mind you." Amber Lee sliced her knife through a fresh block of floral foam. "Lots of people say Gigi. But then folks can't help notice Bixby paying close attention to Brad."

"Chief Bixby doesn't always get it right," Shelby said.

"And Audrey is too good of a judge of character to have dated a murderer." Liv patted my shoulder on the way to the cooler. "And no one else from town had motive, really."

"So, could Gigi have done it?" Darnell asked.

"It's usually the spouse," Opie added.

There was that rule again. "I don't know. Gigi got a threatening note today, warning her to stop the show. She seemed genuinely shaken up by it."

"Gigi also spends a lot of time on TV," Amber Lee said. "She should be able to fake being shaken up by now."

"True." I thought about Gigi's call from her insurance company. "And it looks like Gary's death will help her financially."

"Not if they connect her with the murder," Opie said.

"You know," I added. "Henry Easton also had a financial motive to kill Gary, since he wanted to take over as co-host. But that note muddies things up a bit. He wouldn't want to stop the show."

"So you're thinking Gary was killed to stop the show," Liv said. "And when Gigi decided to continue filming, the killer resorted to the threat to scare her and the rest of the crew off."

"Then the question to ask is who would want to stop the show?" Amber Lee asked.

"Someone less than satisfied with the work environment," I suggested. "Brad doesn't really seem all that happy in his dream job. Gary had hinted at advancement, but then referred to him as a gofer. That had to be a tremendous letdown. Perhaps that's why Bixby suspects him."

"Your friend should call my dad." Opie's father was a high-powered lawyer who lived in the next town over. "Maybe he wouldn't mind my coming out if I sent a little business his way."

"I'll mention it to him," I said. "But Brad wasn't the only crew member with motive. I happen to know from personal experience that Gary wasn't the easiest person to work with, and it didn't take much to put him over the edge."

"Prima donna?" Liv asked.

"Oh, yes, and he threatened not only firing, but blackballing. I think he liked the crew to be cowering in the corner, afraid to cross him."

"Well, that makes for lovely morale," Amber Lee said. "Have I mentioned lately how much I love my job?"

"And I don't think we can totally eliminate the idea that the killer was someone on the outside angry with the show." I took a moment to stretch my back.

"Like Tacky Jackie," Shelby said.

"Or maybe it's not the show. Maybe someone wants to stop the wedding," I said. "I'd like to poke around there a little more."

Liv set down her tools, then tented her fingers under her chin. "There's one thing I don't understand. Why kill Gary and *then* send a threatening letter? Why not start with the threat? Seems out of order."

"Unless . . ." Darnell said.

"Go on," I urged.

"What if the threat's a fake out? Like in football, when you fake to the left but run to the right. Maybe the killer just wants us to *think* Gary's death had something to do with the show."

I studied the centerpiece I was constructing, then gave a calla lily a little push to make it symmetrical. I liked symmetry and order. This murder lacked that sense of order. "I suppose Gigi could have murdered her husband for any number of reasons and then sent the threat to divert attention from herself. Make herself look more like the victim." I explained about Sven, the stud muffin of a light guy, and the pretty Bulgarian seamstress who seemed a little too sad.

"So Gary and Gigi's secret marriage wasn't necessarily a happy one," Melanie said. "How sad. I mean, a secret marriage is so romantic. Like Romeo and Juliet."

Liv let out a snort. "If I remember my English lit, that didn't work out so well. As I recall, both of them died."

"I think we can rule out double suicide," I said.

"But if Gary and/or Gigi were both carrying on . . . extra-curricular activities," Amber Lee started, "then those they were carrying on with each also have a motive."

"Gigi's lover, if she had one, might want to eliminate Gary as a rival," Liv said. "So Sven stays on the list."

"And if Gary had a lover, things might not have been rosy there, either," Amber Lee said.

"I'd like to eliminate Nevena. I don't know that she'd have the strength to string Gary up like that. Wouldn't he have fought back?" I made a mental note to check with Mrs. June to see if Bixby had gotten any of the autopsy results in. "I also don't think Nevena's English is good enough to write the threatening note."

"That's *if* the killer wrote the note," Liv said. "It's always possible that they're not related. That someone who wanted to stop the show is using the murder to make their case stronger."

I leaned my elbows on the table and rubbed my temples. If Bixby's line of deduction was going anything like ours, then someone might have just gotten away with murder.

Chapter 11

"I can't wait. Can you point out the suspects?"
Liv scanned the restaurant of the Ashbury, which had been
transformed into the staging area for *Fix My Wedding*.

"I will do no such thing." I turned to face Liv. "You
promised Eric, right to his scruffy face, that you were going
to stay out of the murder investigation and work on the
flowers."

Liv put her hands into the air. "It's not like I'm going to
interrogate anyone." She smirked. "At least not obviously.
But while I'm here, if someone should respond to an innocent question . . . Besides, people trust pregnant women.
They tell me all kinds of things they never used to. Of
course, they mainly tell me their labor and delivery horror
stories." She shuddered.

"Just don't get into any trouble. Eric would kill me."

"Oh look, there's Nick. And he has scones." What can I
say? It must be a family trait. She pulled me over to the
catering table and soon had a scone and a decaf in her hands.

And I had half of a scone and a regular.

"I was telling Audrey," Liv said, "that as soon as this wedding is over and the cast and crew leave, we all ought to have a nice picnic at Ramble Falls—Eric and me, and you and Audrey."

"It's up to Nick," I said at the same time as he said, "It's up to Audrey."

"Great!" Liv was undeterred by the ambiguity. "It's a double date."

I should have known Liv had more than snooping on her mind when she'd begged to come with me. She was probably right. Surely the feelings that had resurfaced for Brad were no more than concern over him becoming a suspect in the murder investigation. Soon he and the rest of the crew would be climbing into those black Range Rovers and heading out of town. And Nick and I would still be in Ramble. Was there a future in either relationship?

Not if Nick had no qualms with me dating other people.

But that would only matter *if* Brad rode out of town with the rest of the crew. If he ended up locked in the county holding center awaiting trial, things would get messier from there.

That was my cue to leave the tattered remnants of my love life behind and do my job, which today was meeting with Gigi to show her our sample flowers for the reception. This time there'd be no three samples to choose from. We simply needed to show her what we had constructed so far to see if she required any tweaks.

At least that was the plan.

I extricated myself from the catering table as Liv nabbed another scone to the tune of "I guess what they say about eating for two is true."

Gigi was nowhere to be seen, so I headed over to the desk where Kathleen Randolph stood. "Good morning," I said.

She raised her eyebrows. "Is it? I hadn't noticed." She closed her eyes and exhaled. "Sorry, Audrey. I shouldn't take it out on you. When I agreed to let *Fix My Wedding* take over the inn for the week, I thought it would be great exposure. But between catering to the cast and crew, meeting Gigi's demands for the reception space, and the police crawling around the place asking questions . . ."

"It's a lot of stress, I'm sure."

"It would have been better for my Chi had I closed up the place and taken a cruise. Although maybe not as good for my pocketbook. It depends on what happens with bookings when this whole fiasco is over. I'm not sure if folks will associate my place with Gary's murder. Or if that's a good or a bad thing, business-wise. At least it didn't happen here. Not that I'd want it to happen anywhere . . . Oh, that sounded rather heartless, didn't it?"

"I understand. You've thrown your whole life into this place. And it shows. You have a perfect right to be concerned."

"But the hotel did already survive one murder."

"Another murder?"

"Back in 1876. Our nation's centennial."

I settled in for the duration. Once you got Kathleen started on an historical account, that was pretty much what you had to do.

"The inn was run by a middle-aged couple, the Buckmans. Never had kids. From what I gather, he'd run the stables, and she would do just about everything else, from making the beds to doing the bookkeeping, to cooking in the restaurant, with only one servant to help. Then Mr. Buckman got sick."

"Let me guess. Poisoned? Another entry in the category that it's usually the spouse."

"Take it from someone who's had three, there are easier ways to get rid of them." She smiled. "I guess there was some initial suspicion of Mrs. Buckman. But then others started getting sick, including the woman herself. Then she died."

"Mrs. Buckman?" I asked.

Kathleen nodded. "So they arrested her husband."

"Even though he got sick first?"

She kept on nodding. "I guess the working theory was that he'd tried the poison on himself first, either to try out the potency of the poison or to get her arrested. Then, when that didn't work, he used it on her."

"Huh. At least they got him."

"But it wasn't him," she said with a hint of a smirk.

"How did they figure that out?"

"He died in jail of the same symptoms."

"How did—?"

"Back then, they'd get the food for the prisoners from the hotel. Turns out, the man's brother, the elder Mr. Buckman, came to town to take it over, and the servant girl did all the cooking."

"So was it the brother or the servant girl? Or were they in, as they used to say, cahoots?"

"Neither." Kathleen stopped there, her broad smile coaxing me to ask. "Well, they might have been cahooting for all I know . . ." She winked. "But they were cleared of the murders."

"Okay, who did it?"

"Best they were ever able to figure, it was Mrs. Buckman, after all. Only she hid her poison in the flour, and apparently it leached out. A lot of other guests, the brother, and the servant girl all got sick, but since the intended victim got a double dose, it killed him. True story. The elder Mr. Buckman married the servant girl, and the hotel flourished after that—after they'd thrown out all the flour."

I shook my head. "Amazing."

Her broad smile dimmed. "I shouldn't be so excited about that story."

"But the hotel survived that mess. You should find encouragement in that."

"I shouldn't be so obsessed with this place, the history of it. After all, a man died."

"Gary was someone you barely knew, so no one is going

to blame you for not falling to pieces over it. But I don't think you need to worry about business. I suspect the TV exposure will probably do you some good."

"As long as people perceive the place to be safe. And that's only going to happen if the murderer is caught. Bixby's been asking me a lot of questions about Brad. Did I see when he left the inn? Was he anywhere near the desk before I found the note? Did he have notepaper in his room?"

"What did you tell him?"

"The truth. I was running like crazy, trying to get light-bulbs that would suit that Gigi woman and her boy toy. Is that really her name?"

"I think Gigi is her real name. But this boy toy. Blond fellow?"

"Yes. Sven something. I could check the records."

"No, I've seen him."

"Well, I have, too. With Gigi. Not very discreet for an affair."

"You're sure they were having an affair?"

"Audrey, I run what is basically the only hotel in Ramble. I could tell you stories about a lot of your upstanding neighbors, only it wouldn't be good for business. I know what an affair looks like. Trust me on this. But all Bixby wanted to know is where Brad was and if he had access to notepaper."

"What did you tell him?"

"I had no idea where anybody was. And the notepaper is in all the rooms. Audrey, I sure hope you're poking around in this."

"Me?"

"Oh, don't start playing all humble. The whole town knows how you caught Derek's killer."

"And it almost killed me."

"Would it help if I offered to pay you?"

"What?"

"For investigating. Maybe a reward. If you can find the killer, that would help my business."

"Look, maybe you should call in a professional. A real private eye."

"Whom no one would trust, and who wouldn't have the same access to the cast and crew that you do. Look, maybe you don't have the training or the experience."

"Or a license or a gun."

Kathleen waved off my concerns. She pointed to her forehead. "But you've got instincts."

"I couldn't agree to that. Look, if I'm poking around, it's more to help Brad."

Kathleen nodded. "Fine by me. But my money is still on you."

I started to walk away, shaking my head. Audrey Bloom, PI? Ridiculous. Although I might look good in a fedora, if I could find a cute one large enough for my head. Then I remembered why I had come to talk to Kathleen in the first place.

"Kathleen, could you tell me which room Gigi is in? Or buzz her? Liv and I were supposed to go over the centerpieces with her, but I haven't seen her."

Kathleen bit her lip, then waved me closer. "That's a bit of information you might need to know. Gary had a room here—not that it was slept in, mind you. He showered in it, but the housekeeper told me the sheets weren't even touched. Gigi, on the other hand, was staying in the RV parked out back. One of my staff said they saw Gary headed back there. At the time, I thought maybe they were having a meeting or something, because that's when everybody thought . . . before they knew Gary and Gigi were married."

"So Gigi's staying back there now?"

She nodded.

Liv and I, each holding a large arrangement of flowers, stood at the door to the jacked-up RV. I don't mean jacked up as in "put the jack underneath to change a tire." I mean sleek and shiny, with pop-out compartments in every direction. Only, since they'd had the RV wrapped with huge pictures of Gary and Gigi, those images jutted out like severed body parts as the pop-outs were extended. An ear here. A nose over there. A ghoulish smile just over the tires. Picasso would have been inspired.

It had everything but a doorbell, so I knocked.

This part of the Ashbury was private and shaded, just a small patch between the back door of the kitchen and a wooded area that abutted the hillside. Probably why the RV was parked here. I heard no response to the knock, except the birds calling to each other in the trees and a rabbit that tore across the grass and darted into the bushes.

"No answer," I said.

Liv banged on the door. The echo came back off the hillside.

"Show-off," I said.

Almost a full minute ticked by with no sounds except the buzz of a bee that dove in a little closer to check out the flowers we were carrying.

"I wonder where she is," I said. "She told me three o'clock."

"Conference with her lighting guy?" Liv quipped.

"No sense standing out here. Might as well wait in the Ashbury."

"Or . . ." Liv reached forward and tried the doorknob. It turned in her hand. "We could check out Gary and Gigi's little love nest."

"Wait, you can't do that. It's trespassing."

"How can it be trespassing if Kathleen owns the property? I think police can search hotel rooms with the permission of the owner. That's what they do on *CSI*."

"But this isn't a hotel room. And we're not the police."

"True," she said. "So I don't even think all those evidence-gathering rules apply to us."

"I have no idea. But we could still get arrested for breaking and entering."

"The door's unlocked. No breaking. Just entering. And if the police come, we're just two local yokels wanting a peek at the luxury RV. I doubt they'd do any more than slap our wrists."

"I still don't think it's a good idea."

"Neither do I." The voice came from behind us, and I spun around to see Gigi, her arms crossed and her signature smirk on her face. "I'd apologize for being late, but I'm more curious why my florist wants to snoop around in my RV."

Gigi pulled open the door and gestured for both of us to enter.

It took little time for my eyes to adjust to the darkness. I wished my apartment kitchen were as big as the one we stepped into. Sleek cherry cabinets were interrupted by gleaming stainless appliances, with a flat-screen television over the gas fireplace in the corner. We set the flower arrangements on the stone island. Yeah, Bixby would have believed the yokels-wanting-to-see-the-RV defense. This was worth seeing.

"The flowers look great, by the way. Perfect." Gigi circled the island, studying them from every direction. "I wouldn't change a thing." She placed a hand on her hip. "And now that you've seen the place, can you tell me why you were so anxious to look around?"

I glanced at Liv, who was practically bent over backward trying to peek into the bedroom down the hall. I hit her on the arm and Gigi chuckled.

"Seriously, you can't hide much in an RV." Gigi kicked off her heels by the door and slid into a bench seat by the table and gestured for us to do the same. It took Liv a few moments to maneuver her growing belly in the space. "So what was the draw? *Rabid* fan? *Morbid* curiosity? And I can't think of anything else that has an 'id' in it. Except *lurid*, and you two don't look the type."

"Gary," I said.

"Oh. Morbid."

"Not really. See, Brad and I used to be . . . well, close. And the police seem to think he might be involved. And I really don't see it that way."

"So you're doing your best Nancy Drew impression, trying to clear the old lover."

"She has had some experience," Liv said. "Not as an old lover. I mean . . ."

"Works for me. I don't think Brad could have had anything to do with it. And I seem to be their only other suspect, so I can't say I'm all that impressed with the investigation so far. Have at it."

"Excuse me?" I said.

"Look around. I have nothing to hide, but if it helps find out who killed my husband, I'm in. I'll help you look."

Searching the RV with Gigi seemed even more awkward than it might have been searching without her. Liv riffled through the desk adjacent to the bedroom, while I rummaged around in the closet, checking all the pockets of his jackets and trousers.

"What's this?" Liv fanned through a stack of paper.

Gigi looked over her shoulder. "Oh, that's his contract for next season."

Liv flipped through to the back. "Is this a copy? It's unsigned."

Gigi sighed. "A bone of contention between us. I guess that looks bad. Truth was, Gary was considering a change in career. Again."

"Again?" I asked, plucking a packet of artificial sweetener out of the pocket of a pair of skinny jeans.

"Well, yeah," she said. "Here . . ." She crossed the room to the closet, reached over my head, and retrieved a cardboard box from the shelf. She set it on the bed and opened it up. "I don't know why Gary insisted on traveling with this." She unloaded almost a dozen videotapes and a single DVD before pulling out a small photo album. "We don't even have a VCR on the RV. All that's left of his dream career." She bit her lip. "All that's left of the real Gary." She sank down on the bed next to the box.

I rummaged through the tapes, which were labeled with dates, all going back to the early nineties.

Liv picked up the album. "Gary was a reporter?" She showed me the photo of a very young, serious-faced Gary, microphone in hand, in front of a burning building.

"Apparently all he ever dreamed of doing," Gigi said. "He used to sit for hours sometimes, watching those old tapes. I don't think he ever got over being fired."

"Why'd they fire him?" Liv asked.

"That was before I met him, and he seemed really sensitive about it, so I never pressed him." Gigi shrugged. "I remember him saying he couldn't get a job in serious news. He ended up writing men's fashion for a string of newspapers. And then party planning, under a pseudonym. And then wedding planning. And then women's fashion. At one point, I think he was regularly appearing in print as six different people. That's when we met at a party. I was plugging my show *The Bridesmaid Chronicles*."

"I don't know if I ever heard of that one," I said.

"Neither has anyone else. Maybe that was a good thing. But Gary interviewed me for the paper. He was the first straight man I had met in months. We fell in love. We were already talking picket fences when we came up with the idea for *Fix My Wedding*."

"But why the secret marriage?" I asked.

"When we were pitching the show, Gary had a little too much to drink at one of the schmoozing parties. Ended up sitting behind the piano and doing his Liberace impersonation. I thought he blew the deal for us, but the network people loved it. They didn't tell us we had to, but they strongly implied that the show would have a better chance if people thought he was gay. So we put aside the picket fences for later and got married by a tight-lipped justice of the peace. It took us two years to get a signed and sealed contract with the network. Things were starting to go well, ratings were up, and all of a sudden Gary talks about quitting."

"Why?" I asked.

"Claimed he figured out a way to break back into the serious news game. Said he was tired of parading around on camera. I was still hoping he'd change his mind."

"Where would that leave you, if Gary hadn't renewed?" Liv asked.

"Probably pretty much where I am now, so don't go thinking I had anything to do with his death. Gary wasn't a fool, either. He wasn't going to turn down the contract without a sure thing to fall back on."

Chapter 12

❧

"Do you know how hard it is to track down a working VCR?" Eric said, as he hefted the black box onto the counter.

"My hero!" Liv threw her arms around her husband. He claimed a quick kiss.

"It was nice of Gigi to let you borrow the videotapes," Amber Lee said. "I'm kind of curious about what Gary was like before all that *Fix My Wedding* stuff."

Eric hooked up the VCR to the small portable television he'd carted in earlier. I was curious, too, although since we were working full steam on the flowers for the reception, we'd probably be listening more than watching.

But I paused long enough to see the static stop and, after a brief introduction by the Boston news anchor who mispronounced Gary's last name, serious journalist Gary Davoll made his first appearance. He stood tall and proud and oh-so-young in a starched white shirt and new tie as he grimly faced the camera. The first story we watched—and I mean *watched*. Our hands halted, flowers forgotten, as we stared transfixed at the screen. Gary provided voice-over for footage of people coming and going from a house that looked to be in an ordinary suburban neighborhood. He explained how they shot the secret footage using a night-vision camera. The footage showed late-night arrivals to the house, leaving with small packages or bulging pockets. Another clip showed two men looking over their shoulders as they hauled in propane tanks.

And then Gary approached the house, dressed down in a stained hoodie and old jeans, knocking and asking if he could score some meth. The camera caught his outline as the guys inside hemmed and hawed, before taking Gary's generous offer of cash. Before the door closed, you could make out the diapered figure of a toddler, the child's face blurred out for television anonymity.

Gary then replayed his taped call to the police, followed by an interview with local law enforcement as Gary showed them the footage. Finally, they showed the raid, as drug enforcement agents approached—most wearing Tyvek suits over bulletproof vests because of the toxic chemicals involved in meth manufacture, Gary explained. The final clip showed men being escorted away in handcuffs, avoiding the harsh glare of the camera lights, and the child, bundled up in blankets, as it was rushed away by social services.

Liv pressed pause.

"Wow, what a start!" Opie said. "He must have made some enemies."

Liv and I looked at each other. Then Liv face-palmed. "He was an investigative reporter. We have about twenty hours' worth of suspects to watch."

I sighed and stared at the stack of videotapes. Was the answer there? "Even if Gary's murder was inspired by one of his old investigations, why now? Those tapes are all more than twenty years old."

Liv shrugged. "It's worth a try. Look them over to see if we recognize anybody? If someone Gary investigated showed up in Ramble, that would be highly suspicious, right?"

"Probably a long shot," I said.

Poor Liv. I knew her curiosity must be raging, but no way was Eric going to let her hit the pavement as part of our little amateur investigation, especially in her condition. Watching these videos might be the best solution to keeping her and her probing mind actively involved, but out of danger.

"Wouldn't Gary have recognized him?" I said. And then my words sank in. "And when Gary recognized him, the killer struck." I could almost see the scene played out in silent-movie pantomime in my mind. A look of surprise on Gary's face, a finger pointing, and the surprise turning to fear as the camera faded to black.

"Only it doesn't explain how he ended up in the old bell tower," I added. "Or why they'd want to stop the show. But definitely worth a look."

I felt hungover the next morning. If I were a drinker, I could have told you for sure. But if being hungover means that you're blurry-eyed, bleary-minded, disoriented, achy, and fatigued, and you wander around your apartment forgetting what you're supposed to be doing, then, yes, I felt hungover.

We'd made good progress on the flowers and plowed through about eight hours of Gary's early reporting days. The images of drug dealers, prostitutes, and politicians played and replayed in my dreams in those few precious hours I'd managed to sleep.

And, oh yes, I'd been looking for my cell phone.

The buzz of my silenced cell started up again, and I still had no idea where it was. Chester glared up at me from the sofa, his ears pinned back.

"I'll feed you as soon as I find my phone," I said.

He stood up, stretched, and pranced out to the kitchen, revealing my cell on the sofa where I had placed it—and where he had been lounging on it.

"Stinker."

My phone showed a text message from Nick, so I clicked on it and started reading as I walked to the kitchen. Then I stopped in my tracks.

"Something's happening at the Ashbury," it said. "Can you get here ASAP?"

That was followed by two other texts, minutes apart, talking about the arrival of the police.

I pulled a can of cat food out of the cupboard, ripped off the top, and slid the can across the floor. "Whole can today, bud. Enjoy. I gotta run." I grabbed my purse and was out the door.

I was halfway to the Ashbury when I began to wonder if I'd brushed my teeth. They didn't feel fuzzy, but I flipped my mirror down to check when I was stopped at the traffic light. (Ramble has only one.) I had pretty much decided that I had brushed when the blast of a horn set me moving again.

Outside the Ashbury, there was no sign of Tacky Jackie and her bridal party/protest group. Perhaps they were sleeping in or, knowing what I did of Jackie, sleeping it off. Good thing, too, since there was also no sign of Ken Lafferty. The three police cars, Ramble's full fleet, parked askew on the front lawn would have probably served as a deterrent, however.

When I burst in the door, Nevena was shouting at Lafferty in Bulgarian, several more of Ramble's finest were milling around, and a tear-streaked Henry Easton was sitting on a gurney being attended to by a paramedic, who had pumped a blood pressure cuff so tight that I think Henry's eyes were about to pop out of his head.

Nick waved me over.

"What in the world?" I asked.

"He's had a shock. Screamed like a little girl. They just quieted him down."

"What happened?"

"It was hard to understand what he was saying. But I overheard the cops talking. Someone broke into one of the production trailers last night and vandalized the wedding dresses."

"Vandalized? All this is for a vandalism?" I gestured at the full room.

"Well, it was how they were vandalized. Apparently, they were spattered with blood."

"Was someone else killed?"

Nick shrugged. "No idea. But they've been going through all the hotel rooms, doing a head-check, not that anyone could have slept through that screaming. The cast and crew are present and accounted for."

"Why would somebody . . . ?"

"There's more. There was a note pinned to one of the dresses. Written in blood."

"That's kind of gory."

Nick nodded.

"I don't suppose they shared with you what it said."

Nick smiled. "Not exactly. But since I was on-site and couldn't leave anyway, I thought it might be the friendly and neighborly thing to do to start serving coffee to the cops."

I smiled. "You're almost as devious as Liv."

"You want to stand around complimenting me, or would you rather know what it said?"

"What did it say?"

" 'Go home.' "

"For Henry to go home? Or the whole crew?"

"No idea. Whoever wrote it wasn't big on nouns of direct address. That's all it said. 'Go home.' "

"So somebody still wants to stop the show."

"Or the wedding," he said

"Or the wedding. Or make it look like he wants to stop the wedding. But the more I think about it, the less I think the killer is carrying out these warnings as a smoke screen—

if this one *is* just a warning. We still don't know where the blood came from."

I had a moment of panic. What if Liv had come back snooping around? I tried her cell phone and got her instantly.

"What's up?" she said.

"Just wanted to make sure you were okay," I answered. "See you in a bit."

"Audrey, wait. You can't do—" But I ended the call.

Someone had handed Easton a damp towel. He wiped the mucus streaming from his nose and sat up a little straighter.

"Would you like a coffee, Mr. Easton?" Nick called across the room.

Easton nodded.

"Better make it decaf," the attendant said, putting away his stethoscope.

Nick poured a cup, added a little cream and sweetener, and walked it over to Easton. He grabbed it with shaking hands. "Thank you."

I looked around. Bixby was nowhere in sight, so I pulled a chair next to the gurney. "You must have had a terrible shock."

"Oh." He shuddered. "I don't know what was worse, the thousands of dollars in dresses absolutely ruined, or the blood. Blood everywhere."

"But no sign of where it came from?"

Easton shook his head. "Not a clue."

But then the sounds of high-pitched screaming entered through the open windows.

Chapter 13

✿

"She's gone! Someone took her!" Kathleen Randolph spat out the words, then scanned the faces of the people milling around the Ashbury restaurant as if she were reading everyone's minds and narrowing in on a suspect.

Bixby was across the room in a shot, Lafferty trailing behind him.

"Who's gone?" Bixby said. "Who's missing?"

"Beth. Beth is gone!"

"Who in the world is Beth?" Bixby asked. "And you're sure she's missing."

"Yes, just . . . here. Come see for yourself." Kathleen turned and ran back out the door.

"Wait!" Bixby pulled his gun from his holster and checked his clip before following her outside. A buzz went up around the room, people asking if anyone knew who Beth was.

I had an idea, but I needed to confirm it with Kathleen. I rushed to the door to follow them, but Lafferty stopped me. I craned my neck to see a number of loose white feathers in the grass, and I suspected I was right. I waited for a few minutes until they returned, Bixby a little red-faced.

"Kathleen, I'm so sorry." I placed what I hoped was a comforting hand on her upper arm. "Isn't Beth the name of one of your chickens?"

"Only my prize laying hen!" she said. The fish in the ponds might have been named after famous classic comedians, but the chickens—well, the first four were Meg, Jo, Amy, and Beth. Kathleen called them her "Little Women" and had been known to feed them leftover bagels and cream cheese from the dining room. Some say that's why the eggs at the Ashbury were so creamy.

I pulled her into a hug. I might not understand it, but Kathleen was attached to the bird.

Bixby wasn't as sympathetic. He placed his gun back in its holster. "Seriously? A chicken?" As peeved as he looked, I wondered if he was allergic to feathers, too.

Lafferty rocked on his heels, a smile teasing the corner of his lips.

Don't say it, I thought. Please don't say it.

"I guess it's a case of *fowl* play," he said.

Apparently Lafferty never got my telepathic warning.

"Some joke." Kathleen turned on her heels, stormed back to the registration desk, and started slamming things.

Bixby shot Lafferty a disgusted look. "Can I trust you to go out back and collect the evidence?"

"You mean the *chicken feathers*?" Lafferty cast him an incredulous look, as if he was being sent to the local KFC.

"Yeah, the feathers. And look around the area to see if you can find anything else relevant. Footprints. Dropped articles. Any idea of which direction the . . . uh . . . assailant came from. Take pictures before you move anything."

"Of the *feathers* . . . ?"

"Yes, of the feathers. And while you're out there, poke around in the woods a little. See if you can find that bird. Look, I don't know if this has squat to do with the murder, but it's possibly theft." He lowered his voice. "And maybe cruelty to animals, if someone used the chicken's blood in the vandalism. It's an active crime scene. Now, go."

Lafferty hightailed it out the door. Bixby paused for a few moments, then strode over to the registration desk. I followed.

"Miss Bloom, I'd like to talk to Mrs. Randolph, if you don't mind."

"She stays," Kathleen said. "Anything you want to say to me you can say in front of Audrey."

"Fine." Only Bixby's inflection indicated he considered it anything but fine. "Any chance that the chicken could have simply escaped and wandered off? Or maybe a wild animal . . . ?"

"Beth's never gotten out before. If it were Amy—well, Amy's a little slippery. I could see her doing that. But not Beth."

"Could one of your kitchen staff have killed the chicken?"

"My kitchen staff knows the difference between a laying hen and a table bird." Kathleen was wringing her hands. "None of them would have killed that bird. You think that might be her blood on the dresses?"

Bixby didn't answer. "And when was the last time you saw your chicken?"

"Last night. I went out to feed them a few leftovers. Beth was there then. And are you humoring me, or are you going to find out who did this?"

"I'm going to try," Bixby said.

"Only because it might have something to do with the murder." Kathleen huffed. "I should have never booked that show here. Been nothing but trouble since they arrived. Can't you just make them go away?"

Bixby shook his head. "I can't do that. I can't even prove that this incident had anything to do with the murder."

I rolled my eyes.

"You have something to add, Miss Bloom?"

"Someone takes Kathleen's hen, then possibly douses the

wedding dresses with its blood, and you don't think they're connected?"

"I didn't say that I didn't *think* the . . . act . . . had something to do with the murder. I said I couldn't *prove* it. First we need to find out if it's really blood on the dresses and on the note. If it is, I suppose we'll have to send the dresses and the feathers to confirm that the blood on the dresses came from that chicken. We can send the chicken if Lafferty finds it . . . Oh, the state lab is going to love me."

I could almost have pity on the man. Police work seemed to involve so much more tedium than ferreting out the murderer. No assumptions were allowed, at least on his part. I, on the other hand, was pretty sure the blood came from the chicken. And the only question was, who could have done it?

Who wanted the show stopped badly enough to kill Gary and send such an elaborate—but effective—threat?

At that point, I noticed Bixby squinting at the area behind me. I turned around to see Brad coming down the stairs.

I whisked him away before Bixby could.

"Have you heard?" I asked.

"About the dresses? Yes."

"Not just about the dresses. About the chicken." I clued him in on Kathleen's missing hen.

"At least it wasn't a person."

"But it's clearly someone wanting to stop the show. Tell me, who in the cast and crew would want that? Who was unhappy? Might someone have wanted out of their contract?"

"Audrey, that's . . . I don't have time to talk about this. Apparently it's now my job to help Easton recover and try to salvage the filming schedule."

"Who, Brad? Who would benefit most from getting out from under the terms of their contract?"

Brad looked up to the ceiling beams before gesturing toward an unoccupied table. We sat and he picked at a scratch in the wood with his fingernail.

"Brad, if you're in such a hurry, why are you stalling?"

"Well, that's just it. People in this business spend half their time trying to get a contract, and the other half trying to get out of it. When you're not working, it seems like it's almost impossible to break in. But once people know you . . . opportunities arise, and . . ."

"Who, Brad?"

"Frankly, me." He looked up at me through those long lashes of his, probably trying to gauge my reaction before he went on. "See, before I got the job on *Fix My Wedding*, I'd submitted a proposal to the network."

"I didn't know that."

"It was a long shot, so I didn't mention it to anybody. And like I thought, squat, zippo, bubkes. Not even so much as a 'Go away, kid. You bother me.'"

"And then?"

"And then I'm working on *Fix My Wedding* not more than a couple of months and all of a sudden, they answer me. Could I produce the pilot? So I dig out my contract, and there's this lovely non-compete clause."

"What was the show about?"

"See, that's the thing. It's not exactly in direct competition with *Fix My Wedding*. You know that medieval encampment they have every year out in the hills?"

"I've heard of it."

"Well they're growing. Not only that, but there's a bit of a conflict between the serious recreationists and the Renaissance fairs all over the country. And conflict is good."

"In reality television," I said. "Personally, I could use a little less conflict."

"I know." He patted my hand. "Trust me. I know. But anyway, the idea was to focus on the crazy world of medieval re-creations. I was going to call it *Mid-Evil*. Get it?"

I groaned.

"Well, it was only a working title. But it didn't matter. I

was informed that I have an airtight contract. I'm afraid that means I probably had more motive than anybody."

"Did you tell this to Bixby?" I asked.

He nodded.

"Brad—"

"A few others on the crew knew about it, too. I thought it would be better if he heard it from me."

So Bixby had yet another reason to be suspicious of Brad.

I looked up as a uniformed officer walked in the front door carrying a plastic bag. I wondered if he'd been recruited for the great chicken hunt, but then I noticed that the patch on his shirt said he was from two towns over. Had Bixby called in reinforcements?

He looked around at the bedlam the restaurant had become. Cast and crew assembled, some still in their pajamas. The three older ladies had resumed their card game. Kathleen was sobbing. Nevena, the seamstress, sat at her corner table, arms crossed, sending an angry glare in Easton's direction. Easton was off the gurney and glued to his phone. The paramedic who had attended him was eating a scone.

"Is there a Chief Bixby around?" the officer asked.

Bixby walked over and shook the man's hand. "Thanks, you're saving my life, man. Well, possibly my job. Over here." And the officer followed him into the next room.

Yes, I'm not ashamed to admit it. I got up and followed. I watched from the doorway as Bixby led the visiting officer over to the bar where one of the wedding dresses was draped on top, covered with bright red spots.

Even from my distant vantage point, something didn't seem right. Blood oxidizes. Considering how much time had passed, those spots should have been brown.

"Are you sure that's even blood?" I asked.

"That's what we're about to find out," the officer said.

I watched from the doorway as he pulled on latex gloves and drew a couple of small tubes from the plastic bag, shook them up, then dabbed a bit of the liquid inside onto a spot on the dress. He shook his head. Then ran a similar test on the note. "Not blood."

Bixby blew out a relieved sigh, and I let out the breath I was holding. "Can I see the spots?" I asked.

"Don't touch," Bixby said, as he let me get nearer to the dress and the note.

He turned to talk to the officer. "Thanks for bringing the test kits. I would have felt like a fool asking for a DNA test on something that's not even blood."

I leaned down over the note and sniffed.

"Audrey!" Bixby whirled and grabbed my arm. Hard, I might add.

"I didn't touch it!"

"Well, don't go sniffing it. We don't know what that is. It could be toxic."

"No." I shook my head. "I think what you're going to be looking for is an empty ketchup bottle. Kathleen cans her own. Lots of cinnamon. I'm pretty sure this is hers."

A commotion in the other room drew our attention. Lafferty had Dennis Pinkleman's arm twisted behind him. The rookie officer pushed the obsessed fan into the restaurant, pressed his head down until the young man was bent over a table—which I'm happy to report, did not collapse—and then handcuffed him.

"But I didn't do anything." Dennis's eyes were panicked and sweat rushed down his red face.

Lafferty beamed with pride. "Found him camping in the woods out back."

"There's no law against camping," he said.

Lafferty pulled a plastic bag out of his pocket. "And these were nearby."

The bag contained two broken eggshells. Not supermarket eggs, but the brown and speckled kind that Kathleen's hens produced.

"It's just a couple of eggs. I was hungry. What's the big deal?"

"Killer!" Kathleen lunged at Pinkleman. Bixby grabbed at her waist and swung her back.

"No," Lafferty said. "The chicken's out there, too. Alive. Partway up the slope." He held up his hands, which were bleeding. "I would have brought her back in, too, but she pecked me half to death."

Anger drained from Kathleen's face, then relief flooded in its place. She ran out the side door calling to her beloved Beth.

"That guy doesn't know how to stay out of trouble," I told Nick, as I happened to score the last scone on the plate. After looking to make sure Henry Easton wasn't around to comment on my size.

"You don't think Pinkleman could be the killer?" Nick whisked out a full box of scones. He started stacking them on the empty plate using gloved hands.

I poured myself a cup of coffee to go with the scone. "What would his motive be?"

"Obsession," he said. "Makes people do crazy things. I looked him up on the *Fix My Wedding* message board."

"And?"

"Some crazy stuff there."

"From Pinkleman?"

Nick rolled his eyes. "From all of them. But Pinkleman is involved in all of it. Every thread, every inane topic, every controversy, he's there expressing his opinion. Posts from all hours of the day and night. Some in all caps with multiple exclamation points."

"So, we know he's an excitable guy. Nothing illegal in that."

"It does suggest a certain lack of balance."

"What does Pinkleman have to say about Gary?"

"There were a few times he was perturbed with Gary for snarky remarks he made to Gigi."

"But that doesn't make sense. Gigi was the queen of snark. He barely said a word back. At least on the show."

"That's what the other fans said. They really took Pinkleman to task for it. He stood his ground. Said a perfect gentleman would never contradict a lady publicly like that."

"What do you think?"

"If I disagreed with a lady, I probably would have chosen a less public venue than an Internet message board."

"No." I chuckled. "Although that's good to know. But I was curious about what you thought of Pinkleman's state of mind. What does your gut tell you?"

"Well, the response online got pretty heated. A flame war, I think they call it. At one point, the other fan left the board, saying Pinkleman was a sad, lonely human being—that all he had in his life was the message board."

"That can't have gone over well."

"I believe Pinkleman's words were, 'I hope someone peels you like a potato, crinkle cuts your sorry hide, and dips you in hot oil.' "

"Unbalanced," I said.

"And when someone's that far gone, you can never tell what they're capable of."

Back at the Rose in Bloom, stems and leaves were flying. I walked in as Opie and Melanie were in the middle of an animated discussion.

"Something small," Opie said. "And it doesn't need to be where anyone can see it."

"If nobody sees it, what's the point?" Melanie picked up her completed arrangement and carried it back to the cooler.

"What are we talking about?" I asked.

"Tattoos," Opie said. "Melanie's thinking about getting one."

"I was thinking about a small rose," Melanie said. "But not sure it's worth it if I put it somewhere nobody is going to see anyway."

"But you know it's there," Opie said. "A little secret you can hide from the rest of the world. It's strangely liberating."

"It looks strangely painful." Melanie cleared the stem cuttings from her work space. "And what if ten years from now I decide I don't want one?"

I left them to their debate and joined Liv and Amber Lee.

"The prodigal has returned," Liv said.

"Sorry I'm a little late. Nick called me this morning and asked me to rush over to the Ashbury."

"Did it have to do with the wedding, the flowers, your love life, or the murder investigation?"

"The wedding and possibly the murder investigation. Someone destroyed the wedding dresses. Doused them with what looked like blood."

Amber Lee swung her head from concentrating on the flowers she was working on. "That's a little Stephen King, isn't it?"

"More than a little," I said. "With a dash of *The Godfather*. Henry Easton sure took it hard. They had to call in paramedics. Until we figured out it was only ketchup."

"Are they going to cancel the show?" Liv asked.

"No. No sign of that."

We worked in relative silence for a few minutes, the only sounds the satisfying clipping noises of pruning shears and the *scritch*ing of Darnell's broom as he swept up the growing mounds of foliage on the floor.

"Are we ready for another tape?" Amber Lee asked.

"We're almost rounding the final stretch." Liv pulled out another videotape and popped it into the VCR.

Soon the melodramatic news theme was playing and Gary appeared on the screen. This time he was exposing a clerk who had bilked thousands of dollars from a local volunteer fire department.

"He's playing with her," Shelby said, as the interview began.

Liv paused the tape.

"Playing with her?" I asked.

Shelby nodded. "We saw it on a few other interviews. Gary will ask a few innocuous questions, put the interviewee at ease, and then *pow!* he goes in for the kill. You should have seen him with the Balkan baby mill."

"What on earth is a baby mill?" I asked.

"Great story," Shelby said.

Liv shuddered. "Terrible story."

"But great how he exposed it," Shelby added.

"Some sleazeball nonprofit group," Amber Lee said. "They were luring young, unwed, pregnant Balkan women to the U.S. with promises of good-paying jobs and help raising their babies."

Liv huffed. "Unwed, undereducated, and desperate."

"I take it the jobs weren't here when they got here," I said.

Amber Lee shook her head. "They helped the girls apply for *visitor* visas. The girls then delivered their babies in the U.S., making the children automatic U.S. citizens. 'Fourteenth amendment babies,' Gary called them."

"Section One"—Opie cleared her throat—"and I quote, 'All persons born or naturalized in the United States, and subject to the jurisdiction thereof, are citizens of the United States and of the State wherein they reside.'"

"So the kids were citizens," I said.

"But the mothers weren't," Darnell added.

"Everything seemed on the up-and-up for the girls," Amber Lee said, "until the visitor visas expired and the girls were facing deportation. The nonprofit then pressured the young women to give up their babies for adoption. 'Why take them back to the Balkans? Don't you want your child to grow up as a U.S. citizen?'"

"Most surrendered their rights," Liv said. "Records were

spotty and had a habit of disappearing, and the nonprofits closed and reopened in different places under different names. Could be dozens of children. Might be hundreds."

"And Gary stopped this?" My admiration for the man was growing.

"With the help of an unnamed whistle-blower," Liv said. "One of the mothers. He showed only her silhouette on the screen and used a translator, but it must have been scary for her. Gary kept going after the organization. Took down more than one corrupt official who was taking bribes to speed along the paperwork."

"Ruthless," Amber Lee said. "Definitely not the same sweet, flamboyant dude on *Fix My Wedding*."

Liv pressed play again.

Chapter 14

❧

Before heading into the shop Thursday morning, I stopped at the municipal building that housed the police headquarters.

Mrs. June shook her head. "They took that Pinkleman kid right back to the county detention center. He must like it there."

"Any idea what they are holding him on?"

She shuffled some papers around on her desk, then glanced around the empty room, her tell that this was information she wasn't necessarily supposed to share. Not that she wouldn't—at least to me. "Right now, only a destruction of property charge, but that doesn't mean there's not more coming."

"Like the murder?"

Mrs. June scrunched her face. "That, I can't say. There's not much to tie Pinkleman to Gary's murder. Not evidence, at least. A couple of chicken eggshells at his campsite. And the bird. And the chief's fit to be tied thinking about how he's going to take that to the DA."

"What do you mean?"

"He'd at least have to provide evidence that the eggs came from the Ashbury's chicken, and that's a lot of lab time to prosecute a hungry camper for stealing a couple of eggs—which is all Pinkleman admits to."

"He was camping in the woods?"

"Apparently. Although nothing more elaborate than a sleeping bag and a small campfire. There's a burn restriction in the whole county because of the drought, so he's lucky the entire hillside didn't go up. I guess Bixby could charge him on that, but I'm not sure I want to remind him."

I tilted my head. I didn't really have to ask. Once Mrs. June gets started, she doesn't stop until she's said all she's going to say.

"Pinkleman just seems like such a sad, lonely person. He's a young guy. He should be out having fun, learning how to make his way in the world. From the way he talks, the show was his whole life, and now it seems like that's being taken away from him. I figure a few nights in jail might do the kid some good. Shake him back to reality a little."

I bit my lip, thinking of the threat that he, as Gigi's Guy, made to the last person who said something similar. "He seems to be carried away with Gigi in particular. Maybe even romantically."

"And you think that could give him motive to kill Gary? That he really thought he might have a chance with her? She's old enough to be his mother. Not that she's not a knockout in her forties. But is he that delusional, to think that he could eliminate mean old Gary and she'd rush into his arms?"

"It doesn't take much motive for an unbalanced person. Maybe it's simpler. What if he thought Gary was mistreating, or even outshining, Gigi?"

Mrs. June's eyes grew larger. "Or if he somehow found out about the secret marriage . . . But that was before word got out."

"Yes, but if he was camping in the woods behind the Ashbury, he might have seen Gary and Gigi go into their RV the night before Gary was killed. I know Pinkleman said he slept in his car that night, but we only have his word on that."

I leaned against a stool in the back room of the Rose in Bloom and looked at the checklist Liv had created to keep track of the arrangements. "Oh, wow. We're almost done with the reception flowers."

Normally we would not have made them this far ahead, but with the size of the order, it was a necessity. Since we were working with unopened and barely opened flowers, we might have to make some last-minute adjustments—maybe swap out a bloom or two that was too far along, or manually open some that were not far enough—but it was better than waiting until the last minute.

"Maybe I'll start the pew-end arrangements," I said.

"Just make one or two," Liv said, "and I can get the girls to start working on them."

"Is there something I should be doing instead?"

Liv and Amber Lee shared a glance.

"You've obviously discussed this," I said.

Liv set down her knife and came to stand beside me, putting her arm around my shoulder. "We've talked about this, and we think we have a handle on the flowers."

"What do you mean, you have a handle on them? You don't need me?"

Liv shook her head.

"What am I supposed to do? Go home and take a nap? Did I do something wrong?" Could Liv have been upset over my lateness?

"No, no, honey." Amber Lee rushed over. "We thought you might be more helpful over at the Ashbury."

"How? We have this huge wedding—"

"Which won't take place if someone out there has his way."

"And I'm supposed to stop him?"

"Yes. Well, no," Amber Lee said. "Bixby should stop him and throw his sorry butt in jail. But you could be there to help him. It's practically your civic responsibility."

"I doubt Bixby is going to think so," I said.

"What's he going to do about it?" Amber Lee said. "You have every right to be at the inn, since you're working with the flowers."

"And didn't Grandma Mae always teach us we needed to fulfill our civic responsibilities?" Liv said.

"I think she was talking about voting and not littering in public parks." I reached for my apron. "I might be just as curious as the next person, but—"

"But nothing." Amber Lee tugged my apron from my hands and hung it back on the peg. "You'll be no good to us here if all you're doing is wondering about what's going on at the inn."

"And I know I'd feel safer if you were there keeping an eye on things," Liv said, rubbing her rounded belly. "It's not like we want you to go in guns blazing. Just watch, listen, and then tell Bixby if you figure something out."

"Like Bixby's going to listen to me."

"Bixby might not be tickled that you're involved," Liv said. "But I think he knows you well enough by now to pay attention to anything you have to say."

"I don't think he's happy about it, but I'd say he's learning to respect you," Amber Lee said.

I replayed my earlier confrontation with him at the Ashbury. Maybe there was some merit to the claim. "But I don't want to leave you in the lurch here."

"No," Liv said. "Right now, we're on schedule, and we'll need you tonight. But if you want to take a few hours and poke around some more, it would help us all more in the long run."

"Help us?"

"Eric was looking over that contract. If the wedding doesn't take place, we don't get our final payment. When we signed the contract, it made sense. But that was before we ordered all these flowers. If that wedding is canceled, we're going to have to eat the cost of all that added stock."

"And even if we had a sale," Amber Lee said, "there's not near enough folk in town to buy all these flowers."

So, with everyone else busy at the flower shop working on our largest order ever, I was back at the Ashbury, drinking coffee and trying to make sense of Tacky Jackie's latest protest slogan, which streamed in whenever someone opened a door. Eventually I decided it was "Tell the truth. Stop the lies. *Fix My Wedding*, I despise." I was also fighting off the temptation to indulge in another scone.

Jenny was manning the table, setting out cups and artfully stacking pastries—not that Nick's baked goods needed much staging to look appealing. Nick was nowhere to be seen. I suspected that when Jenny and her mother reopened the old restaurant, she'd be sorely missed.

And I was also watching Henry Easton as he sat at a table, his eyes reflecting the colors from his laptop while he barked orders into his cell phone. "Five is too late. I need it by two, even if you have to drive it here yourself." He poked the off button with his finger, then gripped his phone as if he wanted to throw it.

I swallowed my last sip of coffee and brushed a few scone crumbs from my shirt. (I never said I won the battle against temptation.)

"The bad thing about technology," I said as I made my way to his table, "is that it's taken away the pure joy of slamming down a telephone."

"You got that right," he said. "It's a bad habit to lose my

temper like that, but it's highly effective at times. I should be able to get the dresses in plenty of time for alterations."

"So no delays in the filming?"

"Just some shuffling around a bit. One of the dresses Gary was going to use is unavailable, but I found an alternate."

He turned the laptop in my direction and pointed at a lacy high-necked monstrosity with Morticia Addams sleeves that practically touched the ground. "What do you think of *that*?"

I raised an eyebrow. "That's . . . ?"

"Vintage," he said, with a note of pride. "From the seventies. Bell sleeves. Get it?"

I smiled and nodded. If Suzy flipped over foxglove, I could imagine what she'd think of sleeves she could trip over.

"But it will need some alterations to make it current, and I still need Nevena to sew the bells on the other dress. You don't happen to speak Bulgarian, do you?"

"Sorry."

"No matter. I was always good at charades. And I have a few people in mind if she doesn't work out. But I suppose I should give her a chance. She seems to do beautiful work."

"She appears rather upset at Gary's death, don't you think?"

"I noticed that. I tried to tell her to take a few hours off. Clear her head. But that was when her work was almost done. Now . . ." He sighed. "Now we have to do it all over again."

"The experience of finding those dresses must have been very traumatic."

"Oh, honey, that took two years off my life. The first thought that popped into my head was that they were going to cancel the show for sure. The next was that something happened to Gigi."

Nice to know he had his priorities in order. "Gigi?"

"Well, she did get that first threatening note. And now I've been targeted."

"You think this latest threat was directed at you personally? That someone might have wanted you to pull out of the show?"

"Honey, if they killed me, I'd come back as a zombie to do this gig. Of course, they'd have to film me in soft focus." He chuckled.

"So it's actually advantageous for you that Gary is dead."

"Yes, I suppose it . . . No. Now, wait a minute. You're not suggesting that I had motive to kill Gary."

"You did just step into a job that you seem pretty excited to get."

"Well, I am excited. I'm sure you would be, too, if they had reality shows about flower arranging, or whatever else you do, and you got high billing. But, sweetheart, I didn't have to kill Gary to get this job."

"No?"

"No. He called me weeks ago to let me know he was thinking about not renewing his contract. He told me he didn't want to let Gigi down, and would I consider stepping in and taking his place on the show? Said he'd back me to the network. Would I? I almost wet myself."

"Did Gary say why he wasn't going to renew?"

"I asked him. Why step down when you're on the top? He said he had a sure way back into professional journalism. Claimed it was the chance of a lifetime. Then he talked as if what he did on the show . . . as if fashion wasn't important. I guess that should have been my first clue."

"That someone was going to kill him?"

"No. That he was straight."

When Henry rushed off to work on the dresses, or rather dump his work on Nevena, I scanned the room. Gwyneth the intern was leaning over a table looking at a screen the sound guy was showing her, exposing her considerable assets in a way that would have been blurred out on daytime TV. Maybe even cable. One thing's for sure: she never got Grandma Mae's lecture on the proper wearing and fitting of foundation garments.

She was another of the crew that I couldn't account for during the time Gary was killed. So when she headed toward the door, I rushed up to her.

"Gwyneth, I believe?" I said, then introduced myself. "I've been wanting to talk with you."

"Well, I've wanted to talk to you, too, and explain."

"Explain?"

"I feel terrible about everything, and now that I know, I wish I hadn't done it."

Was she confessing? "Done what, exactly?"

"Somebody told me that you and Brad . . . Well, I suppose you must have heard me flirting with him and somehow gotten the wrong idea. Trust me, Brad's a very nice guy, but it was all innocent. I'm no threat to you."

"Well, thank you, Gwyneth. I didn't think you were." I scribbled a mental note to ask Brad about this "harmless flirting." Then crossed it off my mental to-do list. If Brad and I were over, it was really none of my business.

"Besides," I said, "Brad and I broke up quite a while ago."

She clapped a hand to her considerable chest, which started a mound of mammary tissue jiggling in a complex wave pattern. "I'm so relieved."

"But you're not really interested in Brad, are you?"

She looked around the room, then gestured me to a far table. She kicked off her impractical heels as she sat, and I took a chair next to her so we wouldn't have to shout across the eight-foot diameter.

"You see, it's like this," she said. "This is my second internship—my second and last chance to get some real hands-on experience in the film business before I graduate. I thought I'd lucked out on a primo assignment last year.

Sounded like a great opportunity. Man, that was a wasted summer."

I tilted my head and waited. In my experience, people always shared their stories of wasted summers.

"We were supposed to film the surfers who braved the shark-infested waters off certain Hawaiian beaches. How cool is that?"

"Sounds like a fantastic experience."

"And it might have been. Except I listened to my mother. 'It's time to grow up and act like a professional,'" she mocked in a snooty voice. "Worst mistake of my life."

"It doesn't sound like such bad advice."

She snorted. "She took me to her favorite store and bought me a whole wardrobe of professional business casual clothing. When I met the crew, they looked me up and down. Do you know what I did that summer in Hawaii? I fetched coffee and made photocopies, and then they had me alpha-betizing their take-out menus. I was shut up in some office building nearly all day. And the only marketable skill I left with was how to make a decent pot of joe."

"So you changed your image."

"My image, and my whole approach." She tugged up her tank top. "It's the only way any of these men will teach me anything. Think about it. Why should they spend time with an intern? What's in it for them? They don't earn any more money for showing me how to do stuff. And if I end up being good at what they teach me, I'm just more competition in an already competitive job market. And I'll never break into the business without good contacts. I need solid recom-mendations and people in the business who remember me and want to work with me again."

"But will they respect you?"

"I think so. It may not look it, but I do have certain lines I don't cross. And I make sure to take an interest in the job and stroke the guys' egos by telling them what great teach-ers they are. And I am learning."

"How did that work with Gary and Gigi?"

"I didn't need it to," she said. "I mean, I'm not into chicks, and I didn't think Gary was, either. Besides, they're the on-camera people. I'm more interested in the camera and sound work and the behind-the-scenes stuff to start. Maybe be a producer someday."

"It's a pity," I said. "The camera would love you."

"Thanks for saying that, but I don't want to get into a job where you peak in your twenties and then it goes downhill. Besides, Tristan is a producer, and he's quite the attractive man."

"So Eric is going to do those renovations for us," Jenny said, sliding into the chair across from me. "Said he can start next week."

The cast and crew had deserted the Ashbury. Maybe they had to get some work done. Or maybe it was time for afternoon naps. Or maybe they got tired of watching Bixby and me watch them.

"I'm glad. He does nice work. I hope to hire him myself someday, if I ever save enough to buy back Grandma Mae's cottage . . ."

"Are you still pining after that place? Audrey, I drove past it the other day, and it looks like it's going to fall down any minute."

"Pining hardly seems the right word. But, yeah. I'd like to fix it up. Live there."

"Your childhood escape?"

"I'm not sure I'd call it an escape."

"Are you going to talk to me or argue about my choice of words? It was precisely an escape. Every summer you and Liv would go and poke around in that garden, like the whole rest of the world didn't exist. I know things weren't great between you and your dad—"

"Things seemed fine between me and my dad, thank you

very much. Right up until the time he just wasn't there any-more." I had raised my voice. I looked around the still-empty room, and then lowered it. "As far as I'm concerned, he ceased to exist the day he walked out on us."

"Walked out on your mother," she said.

"No, walked out on *us*. Don't you go picking at my choice of words, either. Did he call me? Send birthday or Christmas gifts? Take me out for caramel corn the day I got my braces off? No, not a word since that day. The only way we even knew he wasn't in an accident or kidnapped or something was because his suitcase and half his clothes were gone. I don't know when he packed those up."

"And coming to Ramble helped you forget, but . . ."

"Coming to Ramble was my salvation. Grandma Mae . . ." My eyes started to tear. But I forced my words through the crack in my voice. "That little cottage was a haven. No shouting or swearing. Quiet. Peace. I never felt unloved when Grandma Mae was alive."

Jenny clasped her hands so tightly that her knuckles turned white. "I didn't mean to bring up . . . It's just that it's such a rickety old place, and the things you treasured aren't there . . ."

"But I could fix it up. Make it the same pleasant place I remember."

"It won't be the same, all alone in that house. You would be living there all alone, right?"

She sat up straight, as if she'd just remembered the year the Magna Carta was signed for a history test. And no, I have no idea when it was signed, or even why it was such a big deal. History was never my subject. But if I could have remembered I'd have had the same excited glint in my eyes.

"You're *not* planning on living there alone, are you?" she said slyly.

"Let's not go there."

She pulled closer to me. "It's Nick, right? You and he seemed like you were getting serious."

"Nick and I had a long talk the other night."

"And?"

"And he told me I was free to date other people."

Jenny's jaw dropped. She was speechless for a good fifteen seconds. "Someone needs to hit that man upside the head. Why would he say something like that?"

"Maybe he's not all that interested."

"He's crazy about you," she said. "There has to be another reason."

"He mentioned something about not wanting to commit when he can't make a go of the bakery, but I don't know . . ."

"Well, that makes more sense. He is responsible to a fault."

"But then there's Brad."

"Brad? Brad's back in the picture?"

I nodded. "Possibly. Unless Bixby arrests him for murder."

"So that's why you're hanging around here and not doing flower arrangements back at the shop."

"Liv practically booted me out the door."

"To help Brad?"

"That, and with the added motivation that if someone succeeds in their attempt to cancel the wedding, we don't get paid." And paying suppliers out of our own pocket would set my down-payment fund back months—if not years.

I caught movement out of the corner of my eye and spotted Nick standing in the doorway. He went to the catering table.

Jenny rose to get up, but he waved her back.

"Nobody here, anyway. Might as well get a break in." He poured himself a lemonade and joined us. "I thought you'd be slaving away over flowers."

"Audrey's hot on the trail of the killer," Jenny said.

I rolled my eyes. "I wouldn't say *hot*."

"Nick has been investigating, too," Jenny said.

"Oh?" I said. I could have sworn Nick blushed.

"Seems you guys have a lot in common." Jenny stood and poked me in the arm. "Well, I'll let you two intrepid investigators conference for a minute. I want to make more lemonade before the crew comes back out of the heat."

"What were you investigating?" I asked.

Nick took a sip of his lemonade and set the glass down on a cocktail napkin. "I was looking over all that message-board material on that Pinkleman character, and then it hit me that I could go talk to the man. So I drove over to the regional jail this morning and visited for a bit."

"Learn anything?"

"I asked him why he didn't leave town when he had the chance. He told me he'd considered it, but that someone had to stay to protect Gigi."

"Protect her?"

"That's what he said. He said he figured that if someone was after Gary, Gigi might be next. Said he'd lay down his life for her. A little melodramatic, but kind of gallant, in a way."

"Dennis didn't have access to the Ashbury, at least not officially," I said. "But he heard about the threat against Gigi? Or did he know about it because he's the one who sent it?"

"He didn't mention the threat directly, so I'm not sure he even knows about it. I didn't tell him about it because—if he gets out of jail—I think Bixby would rather Pinkleman clear out of town completely. Maybe have Mrs. June bake him a cake with a file in it just to get rid of the guy."

I tapped my nails against the table.

"What's brewing in that pretty little head of yours?" he asked.

"I think Bixby would rather Dennis Pinkleman stay close by. Pinkleman has some kind of obsessive attraction to Gigi. So he would have motive to get rid of Gary. And he'd also have a twisted reason for writing the threat to Gigi . . ."

"How's that?"

"It allows him to stay and be her protector, her white knight."

Nick leaned forward, resting his elbows on the table. "That actually makes sense. Although . . ."

I quirked an eyebrow at him.

"Pinkleman is obsessive, I grant you that," he said. "And that preoccupation could lead him just about anywhere. But his posts are frank and straightforward, even if they're a little off. I don't see him as cunning or twisted enough to concoct that whole plot."

"No, not unless he's putting on an act. It also doesn't explain the damage to the dresses."

"Pinkleman did have access to the chickens."

"But he could have simply been hungry," I said. "He didn't hurt the chicken. He just ate her eggs. There'd be no connection at all if people hadn't assumed those dresses were spattered with blood." I winced as I realized I'd left myself out of the group that had made that assumption. I'd been as quick to jump to conclusions. "Why would Pinkleman want to sabotage the wedding fashions?"

"To frighten Gigi more?" he suggested.

I bit my bottom lip, which was becoming chapped from the sun. And probably from biting it so much. "Possibly, but why the dresses? That's not an area that Gigi handled. As an avid fan, Dennis would know that was Gary's department."

Nick nodded. "I wouldn't cross him off the suspect list just yet."

"That's the problem," I said. "Can't really cross anyone off the list. The answer has to lie in the motives to cancel the show."

"Easton?"

"Would have had a motive to kill Gary to get the job, but he certainly doesn't seem like he wants the show canceled. If anything, he's frantically trying to keep his new job."

"Gigi?" he said.

"Would have had a financial reason to kill Gary, and more could have been wrong in their marriage than that. And she admitted that she was angry that Gary wanted to walk away from the show. But why would she want to stop it now?"

"She wouldn't," he said. "But threatening herself would divert suspicion away from her. And it could also explain why the dresses—and not any of her materials for the reception—were sabotaged."

"I didn't think of that."

"Who else would have motive?" he asked.

"Well, Brad sure does seem to come up a lot."

"That's another guy with a habit of getting himself into trouble."

I shrugged.

"Sorry, I know it's a touchy subject. Why would he want to stop the show? I thought that's why he left."

Nick didn't say, "I thought that's why he left *you*," but I could hear it in his voice.

"He has an opportunity to film a pilot for a show of his own, but can't do it while under contract."

Nick nodded thoughtfully.

"But he didn't do it," I quickly added.

"Too bad," Nick said.

"What!"

"Sorry." He patted my arm. "I really didn't mean it that way. I was thinking . . ."

"That you'd like Brad to be guilty?"

"Audrey, I happened to think that if Brad were behind the threats, that you were safe. I don't think he'd hurt you. Whether or not the killer is the same person who's sending the threats, someone wants the wedding stopped badly enough that they sabotaged the dresses. Who's to say the flowers aren't next? It's not safe for anybody involved."

Chapter 15

❧

"Do I need to genuflect or something?" Gigi asked, spinning in the aisle while taking in the stained glass of the historic First Baptist. "This really is a spectacular old church. I guess if Gary had to pick . . . what a place to go." She wiped the corner of her eye.

"Not nearly enough natural light," Marco said. "Those colors in the stained glass are going to mess up the skin tone of the bridal party—not to mention how they can dull a white dress."

Aha, so the bride's dress was white after all. I texted Liv.

"Good thing I travel with my own lighting guy," Gigi said. "I'll have him take a look at the church, too. So, Audrey, tell me what you have in mind for the church flowers."

I put my phone back into my pocket. "Do I have to talk into the camera?"

"Not unless you have something earth-shattering to say. Marco is mainly here to check out the lighting."

I walked her through our plans for the church flowers:
altar flowers, nice arrangements on the window ledges,
swags from the rafters, and the calla lily and silver bell
markers on the ends of every pew.

"Perfect," she said.

"Perfect?" Even most of our brides were pickier than that.

She shook her head. "I'm having a hard time getting into
it. But it sounds like you did your homework, so I'm not
going to mess with anything. I'm leaning on you to make
me look good."

"Thanks for the vote of confidence."

"How is your friend liking those old videotapes?" she
asked. "Pretty boring stuff, I imagine."

"Liv? She's poring through them."

"While working on flowers, I hope."

"While working on flowers. We also called in some more
part-time help."

She nodded. "I need to get out of here. Audrey, where is
Jans?"

"Jans? You mean the funeral home?"

She nodded.

"I didn't realize they were doing the arrangements."

"They're not, really. Just the embalming and hair and
makeup, I guess." She wrapped her arms tightly across her
chest. "We'll have the funeral back home where his family
can attend. But the coroner released the body today, and I
had to figure out someplace to take him. I wonder if I should
get our makeup woman to touch him up, if she's not too
freaked out about it. Unless Jans is any good."

"The only ones in town. But yes, they're pretty good." I
refrained from telling her that they had such a good reputation that a few of my brides had asked Little Joe to do their
makeup for their weddings. Let's keep that as one of Ramble's dirty little secrets.

"Want some shots of him?" Marco asked. "I could take
my still cam . . ."

Gigi glared at Marco until he shouldered the camera and headed to the front door.

I gave her directions to Jans and Son Funeral Home, which, like the directions to most businesses in Ramble, consisted of "Walk down Main Street until you come to it."

When the door shut behind her, I sank down into our pew.

It wasn't really our pew in that it was marked and we paid rent like they did in the old days. But it was the pew Grandma Mae used to usher Liv and me into—and then sit between us so we weren't "carrying on," as she put it, during the preaching.

"What a place to go, indeed," I said. And then I got angry. This was a house of worship. It had been for at least two centuries. Folks were baptized here, married here. Little children who wailed in the nursery and sang songs in the Sunday school had grown, lived, and, yes, a few even died here. When Liv and I were kids, a ninety-year-old woman in a prim sky-blue suit in the row ahead of us nodded off during the services and never woke up. Grandma Mae had insisted that Miss Bernice would have wanted it that way, to go from Sunday meeting straight on to glory.

But now someone had turned the old place into a crime scene.

And speaking of crime scenes . . . I headed through the library and down the little hallway that held the bathrooms, and stood at the bottom of the narrow, winding staircase that led to the bell tower. No crime scene tape barred the entrance, so I started to climb.

I'd been up in the little room before, to see the bell. Well, at least that's why Brad *said* we were headed up the stairs that day. But I'd rather not revisit that thought.

I was rounding the first corner of the steps when the bell started chiming. Someone was in the tower.

I crept up the steps, rounded the second corner, and could see shoes—scuffed-up tennis shoes, white athletic socks, and hairy legs.

"Brad?" I asked, between peals of the bell. Yes, I recognized the legs.

But he wasn't alone. As I climbed the last few steps and entered the little square room, I saw Jordan, the sound mixer.

"Hey, Audrey," Brad said.

Jordan waved, and then went back to looking at the bell. The normal rope had been replaced with what looked like the clothesline on which Grandma Mae once hung her laundry. A new coil of it sat on the floor next to a knife.

"What are you doing up here?" Brad asked.

"I was about to ask you the same thing."

"Jordan wanted to hear the bells, maybe get some tape of them to add to the footage, but the police must have removed all of the rope."

I shivered. It was gruesome to think of Brad cutting Gary's lifeless body down. But it also made sense that the police would want to preserve any evidence found on the rest of the rope.

"And you were fixing the rope," I said.

"Well, jerry-rigging it, really. They're going to have to call in a professional, I think, to do the job right. Maybe this would be a good time to automate. Then all they'd have to do is press a button, or even program it to go off at certain times. But this should get us through the wedding well enough."

I turned to Jordan. "Had either of you been up here to check it out since you came to town?"

Jordan shook his head. "I was going to the afternoon they found Gary. But Brad convinced me to wait until dark. Good thing, too. I could have been the one to find him."

I turned to Brad. "Why would you tell him to wait until after dark?"

"I'd like to know that, too," came a stern voice from behind me.

I whipped around to see Chief Bixby leaning on the doorpost.

"Why, Brad? Why tell him not to come with you? Didn't you want Jordan to see what was happening to Gary?" Bixby moved closer. "Did you want to eliminate a witness?"

Brad's color blanched. "No, that's . . ."

Jordan also shook his head. "No, sir. He told me that it would be more pleasant here at night, cooler. And"—Jordan used a dangling shirttail to wipe his sweaty brow—"I'll have to admit he's right. I would have waited until after dark today, but we're running out of time."

"And you're here to . . ." Bixby said.

"Check the sound levels on the bells," Brad said. "Are you following me? How did you know I was here?"

Bixby only smirked. "Didn't have to follow you." He pointed up. "Clear as a bell." He glared at Brad before he turned and headed down the steps.

"What did you do to irk that man?" Jordan asked, after the sound of footsteps faded.

"He and I may have had a few skirmishes when I was younger," Brad said. "And maybe he suspected me for a few more minor infractions he never caught me at. But, boy, can he hold a grudge."

"Did any of them involve garden gnomes?" I asked. One summer when I was staying with Grandma Mae, the *Ramble On* had reported a number of thefts of garden gnomes. The gnome-napping continued unsolved for over a month, until one day, they were discovered in the soccer fields, lined up for a kickoff against a team of pink plastic flamingoes.

"That depends," Brad said. "Any idea what the statute of limitations is on the theft of lawn ornaments?"

I gave him a look.

"But I'm a reformed man." He smiled his cherubic grin, which I'm sure kept him out of juvenile detention when he was younger. "*You* were very good for me."

Jordan cleared his throat. "I think that's my signal to go."

"No, wait," I said.

"Three's a crowd." He swung his equipment bag over his shoulder.

"I wanted to ask you," I said, before he could escape down the stairs, "did Gary say he was coming to the church the day he was killed? I mean, would he normally have asked you to come along?"

Jordan studied the hanging rope. "You know, he never did mention it. He might have been there when Brad suggested that I go at night. In fact, I think he was. Come to think of it, the whole crew was there."

"So Gary wouldn't have expected any of the cast and crew to be in the tower when he came, since Brad warned them off."

"But someone was here with him," Brad said.

"What a perfect place to have a meeting," I said. "Private."

Jordan waved as he started his march down the stairs.

"But how . . . ?" I began.

"How what?" Brad asked.

"You said you got a text from Gary, then drove up to the church and heard the bells starting to ring."

"Yes."

"And you ran right in and up to the bell tower?"

"Well, *run* might be stretching the truth a little. It was hot, remember. I figured Gary was messing with the bell rope."

"So you got out of the car and walked into the church, through the library, and up the stairs to the bell tower. And saw Gary, swinging on the rope, the bell still ringing. Any idea how long it would take for Gary's weight to stop the bell?"

"No idea. The momentum would have kept it going for a while."

"Taking Gary with it. But the bells started ringing when you pulled up?"

"Yes, I . . ." Brad paled, then sat on the floor as if he were dizzy. "I never thought of that. No wonder Bixby seems sure I did it. *Audrey, where was the killer?*"

I looked around the little room. Only one door in. No windows. "He couldn't have climbed the bell rope. Nothing to hide behind." I opened the door to a small closet. It was packed with dusty old Sunday school books. "No room in here."

"He must have run down the stairs," Brad said. "But why didn't I see him leaving the church?"

I ran down the staircase. Again, running was an exaggeration, because it was stifling in that bell tower. At the base of the stairs, I saw the only two options. One marked "Men," the other "Women."

"The men's room?" Brad asked.

"Or the ladies', possibly," I said.

"You think the killer could have been a woman?"

I shrugged. "I don't think the killer cared which door. You know, from here he could have seen the front door of the church open up." I pointed down the hall, through the library, to the two large wood entry doors.

"But I didn't see anybody when I came in."

"Was it dark in the church?"

"Yes, but . . ."

"It would have taken a while for your eyes to adjust. The cameraman was just mentioning how little natural light there is in the church."

I knocked on the men's room door. "Anybody in there?"

"What are you doing?"

"Do you think Bixby would have bothered to check the bathrooms?"

"I'm sure they checked the whole building to see if anyone else was about."

"Not for someone who was there—but someone who had been there."

"I don't understand," he said.

"Okay, the killer sets Gary pealing the bells. Maybe he thought he could convince people that Gary committed suicide. I don't know. But then the guy runs down the stairs. He thinks he has a few minutes to get out, since there's nobody in the church. But as soon as he hits the bottom of the stairs, the door to the church opens."

"That would be me."

"He's trapped. He can't get past you, so he ducks into one of the bathrooms. Maybe he leaves the door open a crack and watches you."

"Audrey, it's scary that he could have been that close."

"It gets scarier. He wouldn't have known if you saw him or not. But when you walk past the restrooms and up the stairs, he figures that you haven't."

"So he runs out and makes a clean getaway before the police arrive."

I turned the door handle to the men's room and stepped inside. The bathroom was small—too small to be practical—shoehorned in before there was such a thing as building codes and handicapped access laws. And there was no room to expand them. And since there were much larger, nicer bathrooms in the fellowship hall addition, nobody bothered to maintain these much. The men's room consisted of one small, cracked vanity, a tarnished mirror mounted above it, one urinal, and a single narrow stall with the door hanging askew. I scratched my chin as I looked around, especially around the walls. But the most suspicious thing I found was a rolled-up pill bug.

When I straightened myself, I caught a reflection in the mirror. There were dark smudges on my chin. "Why didn't you tell me I had a smudge on my face? How long has it been there?"

Brad looked up and chuckled. "Must have just happened. Look, it's on your hand."

I wetted a paper towel then washed my hands. Then I took another clean towel to the door handle. Both the inside and outside still bore remnants of a black powder. I showed the towel to Brad.

"What does that mean?" he asked.

"Good news for you. Bixby's not so sure you killed Gary. He checked the door handles for prints."

The ladies' room yielded more black powder on the door handles and a larger assortment of insects dead in the corner, but nothing in the way of evidence—unless Bixby managed to discover a print on the handles.

As Brad begged off to get back to work, I was on my way out, too, when I noticed light streaming from under the door to the pastor's office.

I knocked.

Shirley, Pastor Seymour's girl Friday, swung open the door and pressed a finger to her lips. Behind her I could see our octogenarian pastor slumped back in his leather chair.

"Nap?" I whispered.

She nodded. "He's worn out. Fell asleep in the middle of writing his sermon. I hope that doesn't mean it's a snoozer on Sunday."

"I'll make sure I have an extra cup of coffee before I leave the house."

"I heard that," he growled, lifting his head. "Just resting my eyes. Contemplating mainly. Audrey," he said, with a hint of pleasure in his voice. "Nice to see you. What brings you to church today?"

"I had to meet with Gigi to discuss the flowers for the wedding, and decided to stop by and say hello."

Pastor Seymour grimaced.

"Something I said?" A grimace from the good-natured old man would translate to a swearing fit in almost anybody else.

"It's that wedding." Shirley winced. "Sour subject around here."

"I wish I'd never agreed to that whole arrangement," he said. "Brad's the one who called me about it, you know. And the way he talked, it sounded like a way to get some good exposure for the old church. Such a beautiful and historic place."

"It is a lovely church," I started.

"But it's a church, not just a lovely building. It's God's house—not a place for me to take pride in. I've lived a long time, Audrey. Nothing good comes of pride, trust me on that. God gives us all wonderful, beautiful things to enjoy and talents beyond measure. But they're to use to enrich the lives of others. Not to get all puffed up and make ourselves the center of attention." He shook his head. "Pride stirs up all kinds of trouble—jealousies, envies, murders."

"You can't think Gary was killed because you had pride in the church."

"No, I'm not that foolish. But if I hadn't been so easily flattered into letting them film here, then he would have been killed somewhere else." He shuddered. "Look at me. That was a terribly insensitive thing to say."

"Nonsense," I said. "You care about this place, and I don't think there's a prideful bone in your body."

"That's what I've been telling him for days." Shirley turned and fed paper into the copy machine.

"And if I keep listening to you two," he said, "I'm going to end up proud of my humility."

"But you naturally care more about the reputation of the church than a man you just met," I said.

"And he didn't even meet him," Shirley said.

"Talked on the phone once," Pastor Seymour said. "Everything else, Brad handled."

"When did you talk with Gary?" I asked.

"The day he was killed." Shirley bent to clear a jam from the copier. I'd used the machine in the past. I think it jammed after every three copies. It was the perfect machine for a church. It required the patience of a saint.

"He called to ask if the church would be open," Pastor Seymour said. "Claimed he needed to check something out."

"But you didn't actually see him arrive?" I asked. "Know if he came alone or with someone?"

Pastor Seymour shook his head.

"I took Pastor to the doctor's that afternoon," Shirley volunteered. "Prostate exam," she mouthed.

Pastor Seymour sent her a dirty look. "Now, don't go airing my personal business all around town."

Shirley ran a pretend zipper across her lips. Her lack of verbal control almost got me killed once, and apparently she was slow in learning the lesson.

"I told him we'd leave the church open for him." Pastor Seymour scrubbed his face with his hands. "After all, I thought, this is Ramble. What could happen?"

Chapter 16

❧

Instead of heading back to the shop, I found myself cruising up Old Hill Road. I needed a few minutes to think, and there was no better aid to thinking than pulling weeds. And I knew an old cottage that had plenty of them.

Of course, I couldn't pull *all* the weeds. The yard was almost nothing but. Still, I could pull or cut the tallest and strongest of them that were trying to strangle what remained of the perennials that Liv, Grandma Mae, and I had planted and tended over the years.

I sat back on my heels. The weeds *strangled* the flowers. And I couldn't help but think of Gary.

Of course, the weeds aren't *trying* to strangle the flowers. There's nothing malevolent in their nature. They're just trying to get their own light and water and space. The flowers are simply in the way.

Did Gary get in someone's way? Did he block someone's goals or ambitions? Or was he hogging something that someone else wanted? His job? Henry Easton had made it clear he was thrilled to take Gary's place. His wife? Gigi had admirers: Pinkleman and that Swedish Adonis of a lighting guy.

I'd cleared most of the tall weeds away from a yellow rosebush, but really could do nothing about the aphids. I fingered a half-eaten yellow rose. *Departure of love. Jealousy.*

I sat back in the overgrown grass and studied the cottage, trying to revive the happy memories. Only today they would not come. The roofline seemed more bowed than ever, the peeling paint duller, the windows, even those that Eric had recently replaced, dirtier and grayer.

I shouldn't be here, waging battle with the weeds. I should be at the shop, working on flowers for Suzy's wedding—or at the inn, trying to ferret out a killer. The safety of our little town might depend on it.

My hand clenched around the rose I was deadheading. I didn't realize a thorn in the stem had drawn blood until I pulled back my hand and stared at the red dripping down my palm.

Thorns meant *severity.* Gary was a hard taskmaster. Might his severity, his threats, have caused one of the crew to want him dead? But thorns on a rose also represent *fear.* Incidentally, the leaves represent *hope,* so when I prepare roses, I like to strip the thorns but leave as much of the foliage as I can. Why strip away hope when you remove fear? What are you left with?

And then there I was, in that cold, clinical emergency room, with the white floor tiles and white ceiling tiles, making me feel like I was sandwiched between ice cubes. I felt a shiver as I remembered.

"You're only there as an observer," my advisor had told me. "You stand in the corner and stay out of the way. No exceptions. No heroics. You're not insured."

It sounded like a cushy assignment. Pull the tags off my first pair of scrubs and stand in the corner for a few hours. For this I was getting credit?

The first few nights were just that. Oh, it wasn't as fun or as exciting as the TV shows make out. Instead of *General Hospital* or *Grey's Anatomy*, I got stuck with the old man with the rash who kept dropping his trousers to show people.

But then came the bus accident.

They came in, teenagers, just a little younger than I was at the time. Bloody, bruised, concussed. More than one broken bone. All around the room, staff hustled from place to place. I should have taken the opportunity to sneak out in the confusion, to get out of the way.

But I was still standing in the corner as a med student worked on the driver. It didn't look good. Studying the monitors, I suspected the compound fracture of his femur might not be the worst of his injuries. The med student barked out an order, but nobody seemed to follow it. Then I realized he was yelling at me. Monitors were beeping, alarms were flashing. Feet raced past in the halls.

I shook my head, both in memory and in real life, refusing to relive any more of that experience. The driver had died a few minutes later. The med student had taken it out on me, blasting me with accusations, recriminations, and grim forecasts of my career, until I slid down in my corner in tears.

My advisor later took him to task, and a formal apology was sent in writing to the nursing school.

But the damage was done. I couldn't go back to that hospital without seeing the dying man, or hearing the recriminating words. I finished out my semester with an incomplete in the internship. And never went back.

I never planned to drop out. I'd packed up all my clothes and supplies and my mini-fridge, waved good-bye to my mother, and backed out the driveway, planning to go to my dorm room. But a few miles out of town, I changed course. Instead of driving to the college, I ended up here, at Grandma Mae's.

She'd stood on the front porch—now missing—and

waved at me, that worried look in her eyes. Half an hour and two cups of coffee later—instant, lots of sugar—I knew that I was not a failure. That sometimes it is the right thing to face your fears, as my mother insisted I needed to do. But it was something else entirely to change your course when your current one wasn't making you happy.

Nursing had been more my mother's idea. A solid career, she said. But I didn't want to be responsible for the lives of others. Didn't want to? Couldn't? The terminology really didn't matter. So what *did* I want to do? Grandma Mae asked as we weeded her fall mums.

More than anything, I simply wanted to weed the fall mums.

Mom was livid when she discovered that I'd enrolled in a fledgling floral design school sponsored by a large florist. The school didn't survive long enough for me to claim a certificate, but I developed enough skills to be hired by a small florist shop. There was something magical as arrangements took shape in the vases, a fulfilling sense of creative endeavor.

And nobody yelled at me. And nobody died.

Then how did I get here? Trying to play detective and keep Brad out of jail and protect the town from a killer? I'd say deranged killer, but I suspected that was redundant.

I'd let people flatter me into thinking I could do this, in the same way Pastor Seymour was flattered into volunteering the church for filming. And, as he said, nothing good ever came of pride.

I'd made a mistake to get involved. Bixby could handle it. He wasn't some bumbling hayseed. He'd interrogated suspects, run tests on the supposed bloodstains, and had the presence of mind to check for prints on the restroom doors.

I stretched out on the cooler ground in the space that I'd cleared, leaning on my elbow and watching a few bees as they darted among the flowers and wildflowers and flowering weeds, making no distinction between them.

Yes, the thing to do was to be the bee—go about my own business. Finish the flowers for the wedding, collect my check, hopefully have enough to buy this place.

A rumble of tires hit the gravel drive next door. Through the weeds I could see Mrs. June's car. Maybe she wouldn't see me.

"Audrey?" she called. "Are you all right, child?"

I pushed myself up off the ground and waved.

She put a hand to her chest. "Don't scare me like that. Are you here to see me? Come and have some cake and visit a while."

"I . . . sure." I found a path through the remaining weeds and wound my way to Mrs. June's house. She was already in her kitchen, so I pulled open the screen door.

She flipped on a window air conditioner right by the table. "Could you get the lemonade?"

Grandma Mae always used to wrinkle her nose at the combination of citrus and chocolate, but Mrs. June seemed to thrive on it, serving lemonade with orange chocolate cake. Both were homemade from long-since-memorized recipes, no boxes or cans allowed. And both were superb.

She kicked off her shoes on a mat by the door, grabbed plates and silverware from the cupboard, and sank into a chair at the table.

I pulled the glass pitcher from her refrigerator and two glasses from the dish drainer before joining her.

"I take it you're here to pump me for information," she said. "I figured once you heard the body had been released, you'd be looking for details on the coroner's report. Turns out the rope didn't kill him. Said death was caused by asphyxiation due to manual strangulation, so the killer must have strung him up after—"

"That's good news for Brad, then." I pulled out my phone and started to text Brad the good news, then recalled that Bixby still had his cell phone.

"It won't clear him in Bixby's eyes," Mrs. June said.

"But Brad was afraid he might have accidentally killed Gary while trying to help cut him down. Now I can tell him that wasn't the case. That will help ease his conscience. At least I accomplished something before I quit."

"Quit?"

"I didn't come to pump you for information. Actually, I came for a few minutes alone to think. I've decided to quit playing amateur detective and concentrate on what I do best."

Mrs. June's smile dimmed ever so slightly. "What made you decide that?"

"I figured Bixby's more qualified to handle the investigation anyway. I was over at the church today, and happened to wonder if the killer might have darted into one of the bathrooms, and do you know what I discovered?"

"Did you find something?"

"Fingerprint powder on the door handles. See, Bixby thought about checking that days before I did."

"He also had access to the scene of the crime earlier."

"He's not incompetent."

"No, dear. No, he's not." She leaned back in her chair and let her fork fall onto her plate. "You know, my dad was the one who recruited him. He always spoke kindly of him. He used to say, 'Watch that Kane Bixby. He's going to be a great cop someday.' I even dated him a couple of times."

"Really? You and Bixby? I didn't know that."

"A long time ago. And it never amounted to much. I think, in the end, he was reluctant to date the boss's daughter. Wanted to prove he could do the job and rise in the ranks without any untoward help. And he did."

I nodded. "This is why I should bow out and let him do his job."

"I can't see where you're getting in his way. Everyone benefits from an extra set of eyes."

"But I'm not trained or qualified. I think it would be best for all concerned if I stay out of the way."

"I see. And where does that leave Brad? You know Bixby's never been a fan of his."

"But that was when Brad was a kid. And the powder on the door handles tells me that Bixby's still looking in other directions."

Mrs. June sat stony-faced.

"What?"

"They didn't find any prints on the door handles."

"Neither of them?"

"Well, there was a partial on the women's room. Turned out to be Shirley's. Nothing at all on the men's room. Bixby's sure it proves that there wasn't an unknown assailant."

"And that Brad was the killer." Suddenly the cake turned bitter in my mouth. I shook my head. "If there were no prints on the door handle at all, it means the opposite. Think about it. I'm sure Pastor Seymour uses that men's room. His prints at least should have been on the door handle. And whoever else used it since the women's auxiliary cleaned last. No prints means the killer wiped the handle clean."

"Same as the ketchup bottle they found in the Dumpster behind the Ashbury."

"They found it? I told Bixby he should look for one."

She nodded slowly. "See, another set of eyes."

"Not that Bixby would want another set of eyes."

"What men want, what they *say* they want, and what they *need* are often three different things. Haven't you learned that yet?"

I groaned and rubbed my head. "Doesn't it matter what I want? All I want right now is to finish this wedding, cash that final check, and get my offer in on Grandma's cottage."

"Still have your mind set on being my neighbor, huh?"

I smiled. "Absolutely."

She set her fork on her plate, empty except for a few crumbs. "All alone?"

"Yes. Is there a problem with that?" I said it a bit too quickly, and with what Grandma Mae would have called too much sass. I tried to cover with a gulp of lemonade and a forced smile.

She reached over and patted my hand. "Child, I know more about your growing up than you think I do. I know, for example, that when other kids thought you were quiet, you were hurting. I had many long talks with your Grandma Mae the summer your daddy left."

"I . . ."

"Now, don't go getting angry. Your grandma was a wonderful woman, and she cared for you so much that she wanted to make sure she was doing the right thing. I guess you can say she wanted another set of eyes on the problem. But she opened up her house and her love to you. She made a safe place, a place where you didn't have to hear the yelling and the fighting before he finally took off. Or stare at his empty chair after he did."

Tears came. I had no idea Mrs. June knew so much about me. I brushed a tear back and stared at the table.

"Mae created a place where you could be loved, cherished, and protected. All children deserve that."

I nodded. "And I loved her for it. Loved that cottage. Loved Ramble."

She nodded. "But you're an adult now. You need to leave the cocoon and find your life."

"Leave Ramble?"

"Not necessarily. But you're too old to run away to the country and hide from your problems."

"But how is the murder my problem? Why can't I stay out of it?"

"And let Brad rot in jail? Or that Pinkleman kid?"

"Of course not. But it's not my problem. I'm not trained or qualified."

"Maybe not trained, but you proved something—even that observation about the door handles. Maybe you're gifted, somehow. I don't know. But I listened to my father for a lot of years, and the way you talk—the way you think—it reminds me of him. Promise me you'll keep your eyes open."

"Fine," I said, resisting the urge to salute. "Yes, ma'am. I'll keep my eyes open."

From my corner.

Chapter 17

❧

Liv popped another videotape into the VCR. "Last one," she trilled.

It was only the third since I'd started watching while cranking out bridesmaid bouquets, and I don't know how Liv managed to keep watching Gary preen across the screen. His investigative reports quickly careened from dramatic to melodramatic, as if he were saving the world through his bulldog reporting, his grim expression, and his perfect teeth. That and the vintage hair and clothing styles drew more than a chuckle, especially from our younger interns.

Despite my spending the day "poking around town," as Grandma Mae would say—including a stop at the Ashbury to tell Brad the good news that he had in no way contributed to Gary's death, even accidentally—we really were in good shape as far as the flowers were concerned. We had no other weddings. Most people in town had the sense to avoid the hottest months, which also meant we had no anniversary flowers to do. Everyone in town was so abuzz about the TV

show and the murder, not always in that order, that we had
very little business besides.

A few more hours with our extended crew and we'd be
finished. Good thing, since the rehearsal was tomorrow, and
then we'd be free to place the flowers in the church and
reception hall, which we'd been contracted to do, while Suzy
would be sequestered with the hair and makeup people so
she could be duly surprised at the final reveals.

So as I prepared more barely opening calla lilies, my
attention was drawn to the tiny TV screen. Gary's videos
consisted of only his reports—and sometimes the introduction by the news anchor, especially if they had something
flattering to say. This time, the subject wasn't fraud or polit-
ical corruption. It was a missing child.

"For several days now," Gary said into his microphone,
"volunteers have been combing the area searching for any
signs of the missing child. Prayer vigils were held, and flowers and stuffed animals placed here, at the front gate of the
home little Paige Logan shared with her parents. You may
have seen the tearful pleas, aired right here on our station,
of Paige's parents, Evan and Deborah Logan, asking for the
safe return of their little girl.

"Did a stranger find a way past this fence, to that window"—the camera zoomed to the pulled curtains of a
second-story window—"to abduct the sleeping towheaded
toddler from her crib? Or does the answer lie closer to
home?"

Liv pressed pause. "I remember the Logan kidnapping.
All over the national news. Scary stuff to hear about when
you're little. On TV they made it sound like there was a
boogeyman waiting around every corner. That's when Mom
took me to get fingerprinted. I'm surprised she didn't put
me on a leash. Remember that?"

I shook my head.

"Well, kiddo, you were a couple of years younger."

"I remember," Amber Lee said. "For some reason the

media really played up that case. Maybe because the Logans were so wealthy—or little Paige so photogenic. Hard to shield the kids from the coverage. They came to class with all kinds of fears and questions. We had to go through the whole drill with them. 'Don't go anywhere with a stranger, even if they say they know your mom and dad. Don't take candy. Don't help anyone look for a lost puppy.' Makes me mad. Kids today can't even have a childhood without worrying about some nut-job off the street." Amber Lee set down her knife and rested two fists on the table. She looked like a revival preacher about to launch a fiery sermon.

"When I was little we used to leave the house at sunup, run around town all day on our bikes, and come home for meals and bedtime. Today kids are cooped up in the house all day for their own safety. And doctors blame the parents' bad examples when the kids end up obese."

"Did they ever find Paige Logan?" I asked.

"That, I don't remember," Amber Lee said.

"Let's find out." Liv pressed the play button.

"This investigative reporter has come into information regarding *this man*"—a shot of Evan Logan was panned across the screen—"wealthy business owner, paragon of the community, and trusted father of the missing child. We sat down with Evan Logan earlier today to ask him about what we learned."

"Thanks for meeting with us," Gary said.

"Anything to get my precious baby girl back," Evan said.

"You're convinced the child was kidnapped?"

"What else could it be? She's too young to wander far, and the police say they found evidence her window was pried open from the outside."

"But still no ransom demands?"

"No," Evan Logan said. "Not a word." He turned to the screen. "Listen, if you have my daughter, contact me somehow. We'll do whatever it takes to get her back. Just don't harm her. Baby, if you see this, Daddy loves you."

"But there won't be a ransom demand, will there, Mr. Logan?" The ruthless Gary we'd seen in other reports was starting to come out.

Evan looked dumbstruck.

"I'd like you to take a look at something." The on-screen Gary pulled out a manila folder and opened it in front of Evan Logan.

"I . . . I don't understand. What are you doing with this?"

"By 'this' do you mean this police report, alleging that you were guilty of sexual assault?"

"None of that ever happened. In fact, she had to drop the charges. They were all made up. It didn't take long for the police to figure that out. That has to be in your little folder, too."

"Would you like to tell your side of the story?"

"There's nothing to tell. I dated this girl in high school, oh, maybe two or three times. She seemed nice at first, but a little off. I thought she was shy. Quiet. But we really didn't hit it off."

"Is that why you raped her? This underage girl?"

"I . . . I didn't touch her. Look, she got all riled up because I never called, so she made up this wild accusation to try to get me in trouble. Nobody ever pressed charges. Where'd you get this information in the first place? It should have been all sealed. I was cleared."

"Cleared? Or did your father pay her off?"

"Is that what she's saying now? Then she's just as nuts as she was back in high school. And none of this has anything to do with my daughter's disappearance."

"Doesn't it?" On-screen Gary stared into the camera as the corner of his mouth rose in an almost imperceptible, sly smile.

Evan jumped out of his chair, which fell back to the floor with a clatter. "I don't have time for these allegations. My child is missing, do you get that? My baby. And you're here dragging up all this old garbage." He pushed the folder off the table, sending papers flying, then stormed out of the room. The handheld camera followed him until the door slammed.

The interview feed ended, and the video cut to a shot of Gary looking directly into the camera.

"Is that the reaction of an innocent man?" Gary asked. "A man with nothing to hide? Our subsequent calls to Evan Logan were not returned, but his lawyer issued a statement saying the Logan family continues to cooperate with authorities. He asks that if you have any information, you contact the numbers on your screen."

Gary followed with a pledge to keep investigating. Liv pressed pause.

"I guess Evan Logan goes on our list." Opie left the corsage she was making on the table while she crossed to our bulletin board—usually reserved for notes about jobs—and scrawled a name onto a half-full page.

"You have a list?" I said. "Of suspects from Gary's old reporting job?"

Liv nodded.

I joined Opie at the bulletin board. The list spanned half of a page, although some of the names had since been crossed off. "You change your mind?"

"Not exactly," Opie said. "We've been Googling. Some of these people are dead, and others are out of the country or in prison."

Melanie walked over to the computer. "E-V-A-N, right?"

I joined Melanie behind the screen as she did a search for Evan Logan. Up came a Wikipedia page and YouTube videos snatched from *Dateline* and *America's Most Wanted*. I pointed to a short news article from several years back, written on the twentieth anniversary of little Paige's disappearance.

I skimmed the article. "No, they never found her, and no one was charged. Evan Logan was taken in briefly for questioning. The ransom was never recovered." I looked up at

Liv, who caught on about the same time I did. "Wait, didn't the report say there was no ransom demand?"

"I wonder if Gary covered the story again." Liv picked up the remote. "Ready?"

The next segment featured Evan Logan making his way through a crowd of reporters. Microphones from local and national news outlets were shoved in his direction, cameras flashed, and larger boom mics hovered overhead.

Disembodied voices shouted questions.

"Is it true you paid the ransom demands?"

"Has Paige been returned to you?"

"What were the terms of the ransom agreement?"

Gary's question was different. "Is this a smoke screen to divert attention?"

When Evan had made his way into the building, Gary turned to the camera. "While Evan Logan again refuses to answer questions, we did learn this from a confidential source: authorities are in possession of a ransom note, asking for one million dollars for the safe return of Paige Logan. No word yet if any ransom has been paid or even if the note has been authenticated. Back to you."

Liv paused the recorder again, freezing Gary's face as he pronounced the last word, giving him fishlike lips.

"So there *was* a note," Amber Lee said.

"Gary seems to be hinting that Evan Logan is behind it," Liv said.

"He'd better do it more carefully," Opie said. "Those kinds of allegations can make or break your career." Since Opie's father was a lawyer, she'd become our unofficial legal consultant. "The station might fire him just to avoid a lawsuit."

Liv pressed play to go to the next segment. But the rest of the tape was blank.

"Apparently it broke his career," Melanie said.

Liv removed the videotape and returned it to the box.

"The only other thing in here is the DVD. Should I pop it in?"

We murmured agreement as she switched cables, removing the VCR and attaching the small DVD player. I took the time to wrap the hand-tied bridesmaid bouquet with the silver ribbon we'd bought.

"That's funny." Liv pointed to the blue screen, which featured only the words, "Disk not found."

"Are you sure it's a DVD?" Amber Lee asked.

"Maybe you should try it in the computer," Melanie said.

I set the stems of the bouquet into a small jar with about an inch of conditioned water and carried the completed bouquet into the walk-in cooler before joining the group clustered around the computer.

"Yeah, it's a data disk." Melanie pointed to the screen. "Looks like PDFs, a few saved HTMLs, MP3s, and a few MPEGS."

"Translate that," Amber Lee said.

"Text, pictures, and a few audio and video files."

"It's a mishmash of stuff." I scanned the list of files. "Look, there's old news reports, newspaper articles, and . . . oh, boy."

"What?" Liv squeezed in next to me.

"These audio files say Suzy Weber. These are interviews with the bride."

Liv leaned in closer to the screen. "Let's listen to them."

"Wait." I bit my lip. This wasn't information we were supposed to have. "We're not supposed to talk with the bride about what she wants."

"Who's talking to her?" Shelby said. "We'd just be listening."

I turned to Opie. "What would your dad say?"

"Well, I could call him, but he'd bill you for it. But if you want me to imagine what my dad might say—mind you, I'm not licensed . . ."

"Your best guess."

"I'd say it's possible you might violate your contract if you listened to it, at least before you delivered the flowers."

"Oh, come on," Liv said. "We've already designed the flowers. We're not going to change them at the last minute because of something we hear. Are we?"

"To make her happy? I would," I said.

"Me, too," Amber Lee said.

Liv sighed. "Okay, fine. But as soon as we deliver the flowers, I'm listening to them. Why don't we take turns reading the rest of what's on here? I could probably use some sitting-down time."

Liv heaved herself onto the stool in front of the computer and let her shoes fall to the floor.

I looked at her swollen feet. "You okay?"

"Hormones do it, I hear. I'll be okay after I sit down for a while."

"You should be home in bed," I said.

"Now you're sounding like Eric."

"Probably because Eric and I have something in common."

"A desire to see me become an invalid?"

"No," I said. "We both love you."

"Aw, thanks, Audrey. But don't go playing mother hen with me. That's my job. And I am really curious what Gary has saved on here. You know, watching all those hours of footage made me see a different side of him. Sad, really."

"He was so young and ambitious," Amber Lee said. "For the most part, he seemed to have good instincts."

"Not sure I like how the Logan case went down," I said.

"No," Liv said. "I think Gary jumped the gun on that one. Found a bit of evidence and thought he'd hit on something. Maybe he was right. Maybe Evan Logan was guilty and nobody has been able to prove it."

"Or find Paige."

"Or find Paige," Liv repeated. "But think about having your promising career struck down, all of a sudden like that. Losing everything you ever wanted to do."

"That's not as bad as having your child taken," Amber Lee said, "and then being accused of staging the kidnapping to cover up some kind of abuse."

"And if Evan Logan were seen in town, I'd say he'd have a clear motive to kill Gary." I hesitated. After all of the group's hard work, I hated to burst their bubbles. "But not necessarily stop the show. All of those people on your list, the ones Gary exposed, might have wanted him dead. But what about the threats afterward?"

"A smoke screen?" Liv said, then swallowed.

"Why go to so much trouble just to spread suspicion around?" I said. "It's a lot of risk. He or she could have been caught delivering the threat or messing with the dresses. If you've gotten away with murder, why increase the chance of your getting caught?" I shook my head. "No, I think the killer must really want to get the show canceled—and unfortunately for Brad, that's the very thing that points to him."

"*If* the killer is the same person that's sending these warnings," Liv said.

I nodded. Were the notes and the vandalism of the dresses out of character for Brad? No, he wouldn't have killed anybody, I was sure of that. But were the subsequent notes that much different from the shenanigans he was involved in as a youth? "I suppose the notes could have been written by some kind of sick copycat. But we have no evidence of any of those people on those tapes being in town."

"But if they were, Gary would have recognized them. Which could be why he's dead," Liv said hopefully.

I conceded that one to her. "Can we get copies of images of these people to show to Bixby, you think?"

"I've got them," Liv said, brightening. "I took pictures of the screen with my cell phone."

"Let's send them to him. We still have his business card?"

Liv pulled his rumpled business card out of the drawer and began composing a text, reading aloud as she typed.

"Chief Bixby: This image and the ones following are all people who might have had a motive to kill Gary. During his early career as a news reporter he exposed or accused them of various crimes. Some served time. Thought you might like to know in case any of these people were seen in Ramble."

"Sounds good," I said, as Liv's fingers flew across her phone.

"Full sentences. No chat speak or crazy abbreviations."

"Grandma Mae would be proud," I said.

"More importantly, Bixby will be able to understand it," she said. "Sincerely, Liv and Audrey." She hit send.

"You signed it Liv and Audrey?" I said.

"He respects you more. And I can't exactly sign it as the Rose in Bloom Detective Agency, can I?"

"You got me there. Now they're Bixby's problem, I guess."

"But you don't think it's likely that any of these people could be the killer."

I watched over Liv's shoulder as she sent the rest of the images to Bixby.

"I've met all the cast and crew and most of the fans that came from out of town. None of those people look familiar."

Liv's phone beeped. "Oh, I got a message back."

"What did he say?" Amber Lee asked.

Liv rolled her eyes and showed around her phone. "Thx."

"There's a man of few words," Shelby said.

"Not even a smiley face," Amber Lee added.

"You know," I said, "Gary thought he had a way back into the business. He must have been working on a story. Something new. Do you think that's in those data files?"

"Only one way to find out." Liv turned back to the computer screen.

Chapter 18

I took a seat in the back row of the church next to where Shirley sat folding bulletins for Sunday.

"I thought they'd be done with the rehearsal by now," I whispered. I'd been sent to make sure the church was all clear before we headed over with the flowers. I texted Liv, "Not yet."

On the platform, Pastor Seymour stood flanked by the wedding party. He'd barely uttered three words before Gigi stopped him. She repositioned the wedding party closer together, then walked back to the cameraman.

"Slow process," Shirley said. "They just finished up the groom's vows. Suzy's up next."

"Can we hurry this up?" Suzy whined. "It's hot in here." She was dressed in shorts and a low-scooped tank top with the word "BRIDE" printed in glitter across her bosom. Sweat glistened on her exposed skin. Which was considerable. If she was this warm in the evening, when a cooler breeze was starting to trickle in the open windows, she was in for a surprise when she stood there tomorrow in the heat of the day wearing a full-length gown. Possibly that vintage one with the long bell sleeves.

I stifled an amused snort.

Shirley hit me in the thigh. I looked up to see her lip quiver, then she disguised a laugh with a cough.

I studied a small pull in the knee of my jeans while I regained my composure.

As I looked up, Suzy plucked a small, folded paper out of her bra, unfolded it, and began to read her personalized vows.

"Are you going to read them or memorize them?" Gigi asked.

"Read them," Suzy said. "I don't want to forget anything."

"Fine," Gigi said. "But let's get them printed on a card and not a trashy piece of paper. And don't stick it in your cleavage."

"We could always use the more traditional vows," Pastor Seymour suggested. "My Martha and I used the traditional vows, and we had a most lovely wedding."

"Is Martha your wife?" Suzy asked. "Where is she?" Suzy peered around the church.

"Gone, child. She went over Jordan with Emmanuel, the lover of her soul," Pastor Seymour said.

"Well, that explains it. If you don't mind my saying so, Reverend, maybe if you'd have told her how you felt, in your own words, she'd be with you instead of with this Emmanuel dude."

I should not have looked at Shirley. The moment I did, we both lost it. I could barely breathe, with the combined efforts of laughing and trying not to laugh. I swiped at my nose, and when I looked up through the tears, Suzy was staring at us, hands on her hips.

"What's so funny?"

Suzy's groom leaned forward and whispered in her ear.

"Dead? Well, why didn't he just say so?"

He whispered in her ear again, and she turned bright red. Suzy turned to Pastor Seymour. "I'm sorry, Reverend. For both your loss and my misunderstanding."

Pastor Seymour patted her arm. "That's all right, my dear."

Shirley looked at me and raised her eyebrows.

Suzy went on with her vows. "I promise, from this day forth, to be your best fan, to cheer you on when the road gets long, to help you bear the burden when life gets tough. I want to be the first thing you see in the morning when you get up, the last thing you see at night, and never give you cause to regret that decision. You are the love of my life, and more . . . Ten thousand lives would not be worth living if I didn't have you by my side. I promise to love you with everything I am and have."

Stunned silence reigned in the church.

"Did you write that?" Gigi asked.

Suzy nodded.

"All by yourself?"

"Yes. Is it all right?"

"It's . . . lovely."

Shirley turned to me, and I shrugged. There was more to Suzy than most people gave her credit for.

"Are we done, then?" Suzy asked.

"As ready as we'll ever be," Gigi said.

"Well then . . ." Suzy leaned into her groom (Melvin? Micah?) for a hug, then turned to her bridesmaids. "Let's party!"

I finished my text to Liv, letting her know the rehearsal was over so our crew, ready and waiting at the flower shop, could deploy.

Brad hopped into the pew in front of Shirley and me. "Just who I wanted to see."

"I was just leaving." Shirley gave me a wink.

"No, wait," Brad said. "Actually, I need to talk with both of you. We've had a few emergencies come up, and I need

a couple of favors." Brad put his hands together in a gesture
that resembled prayer. He wore his most beatific expression.

Shirley slapped him on the arm. "What do you need?"

"First," he said to Shirley, "we need to fill the church for
tomorrow. With the distance from the bride's hometown—
and the murder—our attendance is way down. And Gigi likes
a full church. We're low on the reception, too. So could you
call around town? Another fifty or sixty people should do it."

"Just invite people? Anybody off the street?"

"Well, make sure they're not homeless or would cause
trouble or anything. You know, good old typical Ramble
folks."

"Okay, I'm there." Shirley tapped my arm. "You want to
come? How many?"

"Liv would love it. Liv and Eric. Amber Lee . . ."

"Who else?" Shirley said. "You're doing me a favor,
remember."

"I guess I could ask the whole crew. Shelby, Darnell,
Melanie, Opie. Oh, and Jenny—and maybe her mom."

"Is she back on the wagon?"

"Yes, very much so. She should be fine. And Nick." I
could see Brad's jaw tighten—or was that my imagination?
"Oh, and there are a couple of other young men from the
college that help us."

"Oh, that's thirteen right there. You made my job a lot
easier."

"You know, you might want to talk to Bixby next. I'm
sure he'd want to be there with a contingent from the police."

"Good idea," she said. "And with them and their wives,
and probably the mayor and Rita . . . I should go hit the
phones."

"Thanks, Shirley." Brad kissed her on the cheek. "You're
an angel."

"Don't bet on that."

Brad watched as Shirley walked away.

I cleared my throat. "And you wanted something from me, too?"

"Yeah, and this is going to be tougher."

"What is it?"

"It's the bachelorette party."

"What about the bachelorette party?"

"Well, ever since our problems with Jackie, a member of our staff has gone along to make sure the bride stays out of trouble. Gigi used to do it. Joked she was taking one for the team."

I wasn't sure I liked where this was going. "Please tell me you're not about to ask what I think you're going to ask."

"Gigi's not up to it. After all, her husband was just murdered. And as you may have noticed, we're low on female staffers. Gigi's planners are busy with last-minute preparations. I can't exactly send Nevena. And I couldn't trust Gwyneth to keep them in line. And you're one of the few women in town Suzy's met. Besides, you know where the restaurants and bars are and all. You could show them around town."

"I have flowers to do. This church isn't going to decorate itself. And you know how I feel about the whole bar scene."

"Yeah, but it's Ramble, so it's not like they're hitting strip joints or some sleazy nightclub. Just dinner and a few drinks. How bad could it be? But, Audrey, this would really help me out." He resumed his prayerful expression. "Please?"

"What are we doing?" Liv slid in next to me.

"Brad is trying to convince me to play den mother to Suzy and her bridesmaids. Bachelorette party. I was telling him that we had flowers to do."

"They can spare us. After all, we're basically doing the same setup that we did for the mayor's daughter. Amber Lee can handle it."

"I don't know . . . *us*?"

"I could go, too, right?" Liv looked at Brad, wearing the

same fake prayer expression. "I'd be a good den mother. And Eric has been telling me I need to get out more."

"I think he meant with him," I told Liv. "You just want to go along to snoop."

"I don't have a problem with Liv going," Brad said.

"Are you ready?" Suzy had sneaked up behind Brad and directed the question to me.

I sent a glare in Brad's direction. "Pretty sure of yourself, aren't you?"

He winked at me, then kissed Suzy on the cheek. "Have a good time—but not too good. Back at one at the latest, mind you. Even the best makeup can do only so much against those black circles."

"Yes, *Dad*." She turned to me. "Let's boogie."

I gathered my purse, and Liv stood up, too. Suzy gasped at Liv's pregnant belly.

"Don't worry," Liv said. "It's not contagious." With a broad smile, she turned to the rest of the group. "Who's up for Mexican?"

Suzy's bridesmaids seemed excited over the prospect, which was good, because Olé was one of three restaurants in Ramble that had a liquor license—one of them being the Ashbury, which was closed for the filming. And the groom (Mitchell?) and his party were sure to head out to the sports bar. And leaving Ramble would make it difficult to get back before curfew.

We walked out of the church to the chants of Tacky Jackie and her crew. "Stop the madness. Stop the wedding." I could understand Jackie being upset with how she was portrayed on TV, but I didn't quite understand why she'd want to cancel Suzy's wedding. Could she be so bitter that she didn't want anyone to be happy? And could she go as far as killing Gary?

As Liv loaded a few of the bridesmaids into one of the black Range Rovers and took charge of the keys, Suzy and one of her bridesmaids, followed by Marco, the cameraman, climbed into our CR-V.

"Oh, it smells like flowers in here," Suzy said.

"I'm allergic," the bridesmaid said. "I hope it's not far."

"A few blocks." I turned back to Marco. "I thought it was girls-only tonight."

"Pretend I'm not here. I just have to go along to film in case anything interesting happens."

As I pulled away from the curb, I glanced back in the rearview mirror and spotted Jackie and her entourage climb into a beat-up blue van.

"Uh-oh," I said.

"What?" Suzy said.

I pointed to the car behind us. "Jackie."

Suzy rubbed her hands together. "Oh, this ought to be good."

Marco turned toward the window with a small handheld camera and started shooting.

"Good? She's following us," I said.

"How good is any party without crashers?" she said.

"You do remember that there's a murderer still in town. And that Jackie hated what Gary did to her wedding. She would have had motive to kill him. Not the kind of person I'd want to party with."

Suzy reached into a large handbag and pulled out a crumpled mesh veil and hairpins. "Jackie *claims* she hated what they did to her wedding. Personally, I think she just wants more attention. Duh. Why else would she be here?" She pulled down the mirror to check if her party veil was straight.

"And what if she wants to mess up your wedding?" I said. "To attract more attention to herself."

"I don't think I'd like that," she said, then smiled broadly. "But she can't do that without drawing attention to me, can she?" Suzy and her bridesmaid high-fived carefully and in slow motion. Protecting their nails.

I shook my head. "And here I thought the show was about making wedding dreams come true."

Suzy touched my arm. "You think that's bad, don't you? Understand that I do love Michael, and we would have gotten married anyway. Heaven knows my dad's been trying to talk me out of the show for months now. But the chance to be on television. That fifteen minutes of fame? It's a pretty big draw."

"You play dumb, don't you?"

Suzy shrugged. "I have my moments. But if it's more entertaining for the camera, why not?"

By this time we were parked in front of the Mexican restaurant and Liv was tapping on the car window.

The hostess saw our entourage and the camera and clutched her stack of menus closer to her chest. "I don't know that I can seat you all together, but . . . I can ask the manager about the private room. It's not being used tonight."

She scurried off. The girls chatted quietly among themselves, while Suzy and Jackie seemed like old friends. And then it dawned on me. They weren't enemies. They were kindred spirits, each using the show, and now each other, to garner just a little more attention. But what if Gary had stood in their way? Or what if killing Gary was a way to get even more attention?

I turned to Liv. "This was a bad idea. On every level."

"Why? I think this gives us a perfect opportunity to spend more time with more possible suspects."

"Exactly. Possibly dangerous suspects. Does Eric know you're here?"

"I texted him."

"And he's okay with that?"

"Sure."

But she didn't look me in the eye when she said it. "Liv?"

"Okay, I told him I was out having tacos with you . . . which is true."

The waitress and her manager returned and escorted us

back, loudly informing us that there would be a 30 percent gratuity added for use of the private room.

Suzy waved him off. "Sure. No sweat."

The manager leaned toward me. "The cameraman. Is he filming? Is the restaurant going to be on television?"

I shrugged. "We're supposed to pretend he's not there."

"If I'd known, I would have redecorated. Cake. There should be a cake. Let me see if I can get one." He hustled off.

The room was cool after being outside. I'd never been in the back room of Olé. It was kitschy Mexico, in a somewhat charming way. The staff had pushed together the tables to make one long one, and had already lit the flickering candles placed between bud vases holding red roses (their weekly Rose in Bloom purchase) that charmed the dim room. Acoustic guitar music streamed through the speakers. Bright serapes and red clay pots decorated the burlap-covered walls. A big-eyed glass lizard sat on a high shelf. And thankfully there were no jalapeño pepper lights, inflatable cacti, or bleached bull skulls.

The waitress dropped baskets of homemade chips and three kinds of salsa onto the long table. Suzy sat at the head, with Jackie and her crew at the other end. Marco took a spot opposite Liv and me near the middle of the table, probably hopeful like we were that from there he could hear conversations at either end.

"Aren't you filming?" I asked him.

He shook his head. "I'm not here, remember."

But the only word we were hearing was "margarita," repeated enthusiastically around the table. When the waitress got to us, Liv patted her belly and said, "Virgin. Frozen."

I said the same, feeling the need to inform the waitress that I was a designated driver.

"Relax," Liv said. "She doesn't care what you drink or don't drink. Only that she gets her tips at the end of the night."

Within minutes, the waitress was carrying in a huge tray

of colorful citrus drinks. I took a sip. I wasn't so sure about
the salt around the rim of the glass, but the frozen margarita itself was crisp and refreshing, especially after the
time I'd spent sitting in the hot church.

As the rest of the women chatted happily, I leaned closer
to Liv. "I'm not sure I'm all that comfortable with Jackie
being here."

"Oh," Liv said, "I've been meaning to tell you. I did look
her up on that FMW message board."

"And?"

"I suppose she has a right to be a little bitter. Fans were
so cruel. I guess they don't realize that the people they see
on the screen are real people."

"How did she respond?"

"At first, loud and clear. Lately, not so much. Maybe
pretending that she wasn't reading it."

"Maybe she wasn't."

"But I checked her screen name, and she still logs in
regularly, even if she doesn't post."

"That doesn't reassure me." I glanced around the rest of
the table. "I don't suppose any of the bridesmaids surfaced
in your research of Gary's investigative reports."

Liv scanned the faces in the room. "They would all be
too young. Remember, those tapes of Gary's were over
twenty years old."

I nodded.

"But I did find something interesting. Most of the files
on that disc had to do with the Logan kidnapping."

"The case that got him fired."

"Yep. He seemed to be a bit obsessed."

"What about the interviews with Suzy?"

"I promised you I wouldn't listen to them until the flowers were complete."

I stared at her.

"Okay, you know me too well. They were pretty in-depth.

But you didn't have to worry. Nothing in there would have changed our design on the flowers."

"What kinds of things did Gary ask her?"

"Some basic stuff about the kind of wedding she wanted. I'm not even sure she knew there was a recorder running. Kept telling her that he found her to be a fascinating person."

"I believe it."

"Suzy?" Liv said.

I nodded and brushed some of the salt from the side of the glass before sipping my margarita. "Suzy is not exactly what she appears to be. She's an admitted attention hog who plays dumb because she thinks that will make the show more entertaining."

"Well, if she's playing at it, that's how she played the interview, too. Spent half the time almost flirting with Gary, asking him what kind of dress he thought would best show off her assets—my words, not hers."

"How did Gary respond to that?"

"He seemed taken with her. They spent hours together while he just kind of schmoozed her whole life story out of her."

"Could Gary have been interested in Suzy romantically?"

"I guess. Or maybe he treated all the brides that way." Liv set down her menu.

I leaned across the table to where Jackie and her bridesmaids sat. "Hey, Jackie," I said. "I have a quick question for you."

"I'm not doing questions." She threw back the rest of her margarita and raised her empty glass to attract the waitress.

A new round of margaritas soon followed. Only then did we order food.

The videographer looked satisfied as he sipped his Coke. "This should loosen things up." He pulled his camera out of the bag.

Down at Suzy's end, gift bags were ripped open and loud cackling giggles erupted.

Jackie banged the table. "Hey, let's see that."

Soon lingerie and naughty toys were being passed back and forth down the table.

"Yep, I was right," I said. "Bad idea." I passed the latest novelty item from the giggling bride and bridesmaids to the old regime, tossing it like the hot potato in the game we used to play in elementary school. Only then we used a chalk-board eraser, and the boys liked to whip it at you, sending clouds of chalk dust into the air.

"You're blushing," Liv said. "You need to loosen up. Have more of your margarita."

"There's no alcohol in it."

"Yeah, but the sugar might do you some good."

I dutifully tilted my head back and downed the rest of my drink in one gulp. Then I closed my eyes and exhaled as the ice hit the roof of my mouth, causing that brief but excruciating headache. When I looked up, the camera across the table was not only running, but focused on me.

I squinted at Marco. "I thought you weren't here."

He chuckled.

Heaping platters of food arrived, along with more drinks. The girls at the bachelorette party doused their spicy food with still more alcohol. Marco looked even more pleased.

"Shouldn't we try to slow down the booze?" I asked him. "Brad told me I was here to keep them out of trouble."

He shook his head. "Just get them back to the inn within an hour of curfew. That's all Gigi ever did. Besides, I think we have some good footage coming up." He pointed to Suzy, who was swaying to the Latin beat coming over the sound system.

I wondered if Jackie was similarly primed and ready to talk. I turned to her.

She belched. "I have to hit the little girls' room."

"I'll go with you," I said.

I followed a wobblier Jackie back into the main part of the restaurant, passing the manager, who was removing the glass lizard from his perch in the room. "It's his bedtime," he quipped. I couldn't blame him. The room had gotten louder, mostly with laughter at this point, but you never knew.

While Jackie was in the bathroom stall, I texted Brad. "You are so dead."

When she came out, she washed her hands, then splashed cold water on her face. She addressed her reflection in the mirror. "I swore I would never do this again."

"Must bring back memories."

"I don't know if I even remember my bachelorette party, except for what I saw on the video. Japanese food? I don't even like Japanese food. And I don't know if I would have drunk as much of that sake stuff if I knew how much of a kick it had."

"You didn't mention you liked Japanese on your preshow interviews with Gary?"

"What interviews? All I did was fill out a bunch of forms and send in a brief home video."

"You didn't sit down with Gary and discuss your wedding at length?"

"No, why should I?"

"I know Suzy did. I was wondering if it was typical."

"No, I barely talked to the man. I don't know why he would have spent so much time with her . . . Wait. Do you think Gary was hitting on Suzy? Maybe she knocked him off?"

The question took me aback. Could Gary have brought Suzy up to the bell tower for a romantic tryst? An old dusty bell tower that had to be more than a hundred degrees? I wouldn't do it, but I could picture her enthralled with the bells, Gary playing on her fascination. And then he'd make a move. But what if Suzy wasn't willing? I couldn't imagine her overpowering him, but what if Gary got tangled in the ropes somehow? Could his death have been accidental after all?

I quickly dismissed that idea. Mrs. June had said that the rope was tied after Gary's death. Was Suzy strong enough to strangle Gary with her hands? And why would Gary have texted Brad to come to the bell tower—if indeed the text did come from Gary—if he were there for a romantic tryst? Or did someone kill Gary, text Brad to lure him to the bell tower to frame him, then string Gary up?

By the time I exited the bathroom, the party had heated up even more. Someone had cranked up the music, and Suzy was dancing around the room with a rose in her teeth, doing what looked like a strange cross between a tango, a flamenco, and a line dance as her bridesmaids imitated her movements.

Liv had collected our purses and was standing out of harm's way, leaning against the door frame. Smart woman.

As the intensity of the music increased, the dance degenerated into lots of foot-pounding. Most of the women wore stilettos, and I hoped the spiky heels weren't puncturing holes into the wood floor.

Suzy hopped onto a chair, and the foot-pounding continued as she ripped off her veil and ran her hands through her hair in the same sultry manner used to sell shampoo on television.

Marco had his camera trained on her.

The other women hopped onto their chairs, which swayed as the pounding continued.

Then Suzy moved to the table, dancing across it. Glasses tipped over, and silverware and plates vibrated, as she crossed the long table in her impromptu flamenco. Her bridesmaids followed, shouting out Spanglish exclamations probably learned from watching Speedy Gonzales cartoons. Jackie and her crew pulled up the rear.

The waitress rushed in and rescued an overturned candle, then extinguished the rest, causing swirls of candle smoke to dance around the women. "Someone, stop it."

"No, don't stop!" Marco had moved to the end of the table to film them coming toward him.

"Hey, what's going on?" Nick asked, just behind me.

I whirled around. "What are you doing here?"

"Someone ordered an emergency cake for a Latin-themed party. I take emergency cake orders very seriously." He opened the lid of a white bakery box. "Tres leches cake. Muy auténtico." He looked at the group of women dancing on the table. "Not that any of them will notice or remember it in the morning."

"No! No!" The manager pushed past us and rushed into the room. "My insurance!"

But he pushed a little too hard, sending me off balance. I refused to fall into Liv, so I clutched at Nick's sleeve. The next thing I knew, Nick and I were on the floor, the cake smooshed between us.

The music stopped, and I could hear Suzy over them all. "Oooh, kinky. Way to go, Audrey!"

I looked up to find her still standing on the table, but pointing at me. As was the camera.

A loud creak sounded, then the table collapsed, sending all the women into a heap of long legs, short dresses, nachos, salsa, and margaritas.

Marco focused his camera on the aftermath, a huge smile on his face.

Chapter 19

❧

·

Warm flesh kneaded the taut muscles of my back. I pulled my pillow closer and moaned. It wasn't often I got a massage, and I was determined to enjoy it. I opened one eye partway to glance at the alarm clock.

Five a.m. Just a few scant hours since I'd delivered the bride and her party safe and sound, although smelling like a bag of Doritos, back to the Ashbury.

And today was wedding day. Yes, there were still reception flowers to place and a wedding and reception to attend.

And a killer still roamed the town, but would leave soon. Tonight? Tomorrow? And according to Bixby's dire prediction, that would mean he would likely never be brought to justice.

Chester stopped his kneading, curling into a ball in the small of my back. "Sorry, bud," I said. Despite his contented purrs, I had more pressing matters that precluded me from functioning as a heated kitty bed for the day, as pleasant as that sounded. Was I really only a few hours ago rolling around on the floor with Nick Maxwell, both of us covered in cake? Talk about bringing fantasies to life—but I had no time to go there, either.

I slowly rolled to the side, giving Chester an opportunity to jump off. Instead, claws dug in.

"Yow!" I think the same sound came from both of us. I jumped up to get his claws out of my skin. Startled, he started running, but he only made it to the edge of the bed—his claws tangled in my hair. Which, I have to admit, was still matted with tres leches. I'd been too exhausted to wash it out when I'd finally made it home.

Every attempt he made to free himself from my hair only caused me to scream louder—which made him pull more furiously. Ears back, he hissed at the hair lodged in his paws. Some of it, but not all, was still attached to my scalp.

Pounding came from the wall next door.

I clamped my mouth shut, to stop the screaming.

Chester's ears slowly went back into place.

"It's all right, bud," I said, in that high-pitched, syrupy voice reserved for pets, small children, and complete idiots. Using soothing tones and slow, deliberate motions, I was able to disentangle myself from Chester's claws, while he only scratched my hand once. As he hopped to the edge of the bed to lick the remains of tres leches and a clump of my hair from his paws, I rubbed my scalp and headed to the shower.

The steamy shower smelled faintly of sour milk as the hot water loosened the remnants of frosting and started pulling my mind back to fully functioning mode. There were a wealth of suspects to choose from, for sure. Gigi had motive to kill Gary, financial and otherwise, if their secret marriage was on the rocks. The grief-stricken Nevena and Gigi's personal lighting guy could be added to those who might have been spurred on by jealousy. Brad wanted out of his contract—and maybe he wasn't the only one—while Henry Easton wanted in. All of these people had ready access to the Ashbury to deliver the threatening notes and damage the wedding dresses.

And after my conversations at the bachelorette party, I added Suzy to the list. If Gary's interests toward her were more than those of a wedding consultant, might she have resented his attentions? Fought him?

Other candidates included Tacky Jackie and ultimate fan Dennis Pinkleman. Both struck me as unstable enough to have killed Gary, and I guess, in their own minds, each would have had motive. But did they have access to the Ashbury to deliver the threats? Still, since it couldn't be proven that the threats were sent by the same person who'd strung up Gary, they remained on the suspect list.

And what about the files that Gary had kept? And the tapes of his reports and his statement that he had found a way back into the world of serious journalism? Was Gary onto some kind of story? Still, none of the bridal party would have been old enough to feature in his twenty-year-old investigative reports. And Liv had said nothing about a new story on the disk, only more files relating to old cases. But why the facination with Suzy Weber?

I slammed my shampoo bottle back onto the ledge, sending tiny bubbles aloft, carried by the steamy air. I sure hoped Chief Bixby had more than a wad of tissues to pull out of his sleeve, because except for those who were seen at the Ashbury at the time of Gary's death, I'd not been able to eliminate anybody. Gary's killer could have been anyone in the cast and crew who came to town to film the wedding.

I drove by the church first, relieved to see no sign of Jackie's group and their protest signs. Probably back in their rooms sleeping off those margaritas.

Amber Lee and our crew had finished putting the flowers in place last night, leaving time this morning for us to concentrate on delivering and placing the arrangements for the reception space. Festoons surrounded the door, and cheerful swags of bellflowers and calla lilies hung from the wrought iron railings. The door was locked, but like most residents of Ramble, at least those who attend church, I had a key.

Liv had been right. Amber Lee could handle the church. The flowers were all placed perfectly, from the pew markers to the large altar piece to the swags hanging from the rafters to the small arrangements sitting in each window. And the smell—I should say fragrance. A brief explosion of floral scent intermingled with the steady, moldering smell of an old church. Bixby was going to have a cow.

I locked the church as I left, then drove the slowly wakening Main Street to the Rose in Bloom. The air had not yet grown hot, but it was sticky nonetheless, warning of soaring temperatures to follow. It was a good idea to have placed the flowers in the old church late at night. The reception flowers were done and ready for transport, and the Ashbury would be air-conditioned and comfortable to work in. I mentally patted myself on the back that at least I had planned something right.

I pulled down the alley to the shop just behind Larry's truck, here for our morning delivery.

The weathered older gentleman climbed out of the cab, greeting me with his Kewpie-doll smile.

"I didn't know Liv had ordered anything," I said.

"She called me last night. Said you used up about everything you had and wanted me to replenish the coolers."

I placed my key in the door to unlock it, but it already was unlocked. "That's odd." There were no other cars in the alley. "Maybe Amber Lee walked in today." I pulled open the door, but only a thin opening showed that the person to open up the shop wasn't Amber Lee.

I rushed inside. Petals and ribbon were strewn everywhere. Floral foam was ripped to bits. Vases were in shards on the floor. The cooler door was left open and hanging at an odd angle, as if some gorilla had tried to tear it off.

"No, no, no!" I cried. "Who would do . . ." And then I saw the note, not on paper, but scrawled with spray glitter on the door to the cooler. The word "wedding," crossed through and with a circle around it.

Larry followed me in. He grabbed a stool, holding it over his head. "They're not still here, are they?"

A thought that hadn't occurred to me. I followed as he made his way through the shop, checking in the cooler and behind the furniture we used as display pieces.

He shook his head when our search turned up nothing. "Better call Bixby."

"Oh, he's going to love this."

"Who would do such a thing?" Larry said. "Kids?"

I shook my head and, with trembling fingers, speed-dialed the Ramble Police Department. I had no idea which emotion was fueling the trembling. Fear? Anger? Panic? But I had enough adrenaline flowing through me to keep me up for about a week. A week and a half if I added coffee.

Liv was the next to arrive. She walked in the back door and stared, the color drained from her face.

"The police are on the way," I said.

Amber Lee opened the door a minute later. Her ready smile transformed immediately to shocked seriousness. "Good heavens!"

Bixby was next to arrive. "You had a break-in, you said? Was anything taken?"

I looked around the shop. Crushed and bent flowers, loose petals, pottery shards. "No idea. Hundreds of dollars of damage, though. Maybe thousands."

Amber Lee crossed over to the cash register and opened it. "Money's still here."

Bixby pulled a handkerchief out of his pocket and started wiping his nose while he stared at the message scrawled on the cooler door. "So whoever broke in wanted to stop the wedding."

"The TV's gone," Liv said. "And the videotapes."

"Videotapes?" Bixby sniffled. "Who steals videotapes?"

I bit my bottom lip.

"Gary's videotapes," Amber Lee said. "Old news footage,

from back when he was a serious reporter in Boston. We sent you the pictures . . ."

Bixby nodded, then sniffed. "And you'd have those because . . ."

"Gigi told us we could take a look at them," Liv said. "Call it curiosity."

"Snooping," Bixby said. "So that muddies this up. Whoever did this—who may or may not be the killer—came to get the videotapes and decided to tear up the place for good measure. Or they came to tear up the place, hoping to stop the wedding, and happened upon the videotapes. Who knew you had them?"

"Gigi," I said. "And everyone who works at the shop. And whomever they might have told."

Bixby looked at Amber Lee. "Which could be half the town. Don't touch anything else. I'll get someone down here to take photos and prints."

"But we've got a wedding to do." Liv raked her hand through her hair.

"I'm sorry," Bixby said. "I don't see how that's going to happen."

"Then the killer wins," I said. "Or whoever is trying to stop the wedding."

"Surely they can have a wedding without flowers," Bixby said.

"Yes, and the church is all ready. These are only for the reception. But without the flowers, they'd have a hard time filming the reception. It's supposed to be a wonderland, Gigi's masterpiece, and without the flowers . . ."

Bixby sniffed, then ran a tissue under his nose. "So what you're saying is, if there are no flowers for the wedding reception, the wedding may go on, but the show will likely never air."

"Unless they decide to delay the wedding," I said. "I don't know. But someone is still desperate to stop the filming or stop the wedding. And the best chance of catching him—"

"Would be to let the wedding take place as scheduled," Bixby said, "hoping to draw him out."

"If nobody gets killed in the process," Amber Lee added.

Bixby put his hands on his hips and scanned the room."If I get the prints and pics done in the next hour, can you still pull off the flowers?"

"Can we?" I turned to Liv.

I could practically see the numbers crunching in Liv's eyeballs. "If I called in a few favors. Maybe we could get some of the centerpieces made in nearby shops and rushed in."

"I took pictures of the completed ones," Amber Lee said. "They're still on my phone."

Liv picked up a calla lily that looked undamaged. "And if we can salvage anything in here."

Bixby hit his radio about the same time Liv hit her cell phone, the former rushing one of his men to come with a print kit, the latter calling all the neighboring florists on her speed dial.

Bixby ushered us out when his man arrived, and Liv, Amber Lee, and I walked down to the Brew-Ha-Ha. Amber Lee forwarded her cell phone photographs to the handful of florists that Liv had subcontracted. Before my coffee was cold, Liv set the cell phone down and sighed.

"Done. And the rest of the crew is on their way in, but it's going to set us back a pretty penny. We're going to have to file an insurance claim against the damages from the break-in if we're going to come out ahead on this thing."

I nodded. I had a down payment for a certain cottage riding on this wedding, and no killer or vandal was going to stop me.

Chapter 20

We decided the most effective plan was to have the subcontracted centerpieces delivered directly to the Ashbury. Eric brought in a few members of his construction crew to handle the task of cleaning up the shop. Darnell and his friends stayed there, too, tasked with rescuing any usable blooms and running them down to us at the Ashbury.

The reception space itself was waiting only for flowers. The linens on the tables were fresh and pressed. The up-lighting was in place, filtered through gossamer draping that softened the rough edges of the room. Every few minutes, the colors changed. The effect was ethereal, but I couldn't imagine Kathleen Randolph was all that pleased. She'd hoped the reception would showcase the charm of her historic inn, but you couldn't see more than a few square inches of it. Gigi, however, as she rushed about overseeing details for the reception, heaped more than a few praises on her lighting guy.

On the other hand, she sent a few sideways glances our way as we draped new shower curtains we'd purchased at

the dollar store over a couple of her perfectly covered tables
and started using them as impromptu workstations.

Meanwhile, the baker with the national reputation was
placing the cake on a gigantic wheeled cart so it could be
unveiled at just the right moment. It was lovely, yes—tier
after tier of fondant, festooned with edible bells dusted with
edible glitter. I couldn't help but think that Nick could have
done just as good a job.

Fortunately the bell-shaped vases we'd special-ordered
for the table centerpieces were metal and not smashed along
with our other containers. A couple were dinged up a bit—
not much we could do about it—but if we placed them away
from the camera, maybe dangled a few ribbons over the
sides . . .

Gigi winced as we explained our plan. "I can't believe
you're doing this to me."

"We're so sorry," Liv said, a model of diplomacy. It
wasn't our fault that someone broke into our store and vandalized it.

"We're doing everything in our power to make it right,"
I added. Yes, I was a fellow graduate of Grandma Mae's
School of Diplomacy for Girls.

Gigi let out one last frustrated huff. "Will there be one
or two that will be perfect enough for a close-up?"

"Absolutely," I said sweetly. "More than that. We'll place
any that are lacking at the tables farthest away from the
VIPs and the camera. They will still look gorgeous."

"Flowers are very forgiving." Liv's tone implied that Gigi
ought to be, too.

"We can film the venue just before the bride and groom
come in, after we restage the wedding at the church to shoot
the close-ups," Brad said. "There's a good three hours
between the end of the wedding and the reception, so there
shouldn't be a problem."

"There'd better not be." Gigi glared at Brad. "We've had
enough of those."

When she marched off, Brad turned to us, placing a firm hand on my arm. "Please tell me you really can pull this off."

Liv sighed. "As long as all our flowers come in."

Liv's contacts proved amazing. Within three hours of her emergency call, arrangements started to arrive, roughly approximating Amber Lee's pictures. Liv placed the plastic containers they were constructed in into the large bell-shaped vases, draping greenery and ribbons over any dings and scratches.

I had a strong sense of déjà vu as I reproduced the bride's bouquet using the flowers salvaged from the shop and from Larry's morning delivery. Amber Lee worked beside me, helping to re-create the bridesmaids' bouquets—although a little smaller and differently composed than the originals. Then again, the bride hadn't seen those.

Shelby arrived with Melanie and Opal in tow, escorted by Ken Lafferty. "What happened over at the shop?" Shelby said. "Eric just told us to meet you over here."

Liv explained about the break-in to our interns, then set them to work. Melanie met with the baker to arrange some of the rescued flowers around the cake. Opie began making new boutonnieres, mumbling about what she was going to tell her dad, while Shelby joined Liv in tweaking the newly arrived centerpieces.

Henry Easton bustled in with Nevena in tow as I was setting the completed bridal bouquet in its holder.

"Why are you doing this at the last minute?" he asked, but never waited for an answer. He roughly lobbed the completed bridesmaids' bouquets into a box with the boutonnieres and corsages. "It's bad enough to have to use all that makeup to cover bruises on all the bridesmaids . . . because *somebody* wasn't adequately supervising the bachelorette party."

Somebody had thrown me under the bus. When was that ever my responsibility? I was failing in an attempt to bite back a snarky remark when Easton handed the box to

Nevena. "You. Carry. Church," he said, slowly and loudly, as if volume were the key to understanding.

Nevena nodded, but looked slightly confused. I expected her English lessons involved sentences with more parts of speech in them, rather than Easton's Tarzan-esque variety.

Easton cradled the bride's bouquet, popped the stand into his suit pocket, and nodded to me. He left without another word, but somehow I translated the nod as "Bouquet good." Still in Tanzan-speech.

With the bouquets and boutonnieres for the wedding party completed and out of the building, we turned our full attention to the reception flowers. When a half dozen arrangements came in from another florist with bluebells instead of bellflowers, I closed my eyes and exhaled.

"What should we do?" Shelby asked. "We don't have enough of the white and pink bellflowers to replace them all."

"I think they look lovely," Liv said. "The question is, do we want to keep them as they are? Or pull some of the bluebells and mingle them with the bellflowers in the other arrangements?"

I was staring at the bluebells when Liv put her hand on my arm. "What?" she said. "You look disappointed."

"The meaning of bluebells. Well, they can have two meanings, so I guess it's okay. They can mean *constancy*, like any other bellflower."

"I take it that the other meaning isn't as positive," Liv said.

"*Sorrowful regret*. Not the best wedding flower. But in a way, it fits. I know I'm sorry I ever got involved in this wedding."

Liv pulled me into a hug. "No one but you will know that." She then gestured at the room. Three quarters of the tables held their arrangements, and I had to admit, the reception space looked almost as spectacular as I had envisioned it. "You know, with all the shops we called—and them having to call in extra workers to help them—half the florists in Virginia had a hand in this wedding."

"Flower power," Opie called out, fist raised, and the rest of us chuckled.

It was a good, cleansing laugh. And it helped to have my hands working with the flowers. A couple more hours of work, and all the tables bore their gorgeous calla lily and campanula—or bluebell—centerpieces in the metal bell vases, albeit with a little extra greenery and a few festoons of ribbon draped "randomly" over the sides. We'd even managed flowers for the buffet stations for the cocktail hour. The dinner itself would be strictly sit-down. We could have done more, but we were simply out of flowers.

Liv pulled out her cell phone and glanced at the time. "I wouldn't have guessed it this morning, but I think we can still make it."

"Make what?" I asked.

"The wedding, of course."

Shelby and the girls bounded around us.

"I'd given up on the idea that we'd have time," I said.

Liv shrugged. "Nothing more we can do here. Why not?"

When I rushed in my door to change, Chester hinted strongly that he needed to eat again. I scooped a little soft food into his dish before staring into my closet, wondering what would hold up best in that overheated church. I pulled out a lightweight maxi dress with a geometric print in teal. Its open back was a good choice for the warm church, but the drop waist was easy and breezy enough to wear in case I ended up having to work.

And then I eyed shoes. I'd picked up the high teal pumps I had bought to go with the dress, then shoved them back into the closet, opting rather for the thong sandals that could play dressy, but were much more comfortable for standing, walking, dancing, and stalking killers. Plus a good choice when I didn't want to tower over a date. Not that I had a date.

I pulled into the church parking lot as Eric was helping Liv out of the car—and Liv was complaining that she wasn't an invalid.

"How's the shop?" I asked him.

"Not too bad," he said. "Little damage to the fixtures, and we were able to straighten the hinges on the cooler and get most of the spray glitter off the door."

"I can see that," I said, picking a bit of glitter from his suit jacket.

"How did that get there?" he said. "I showered and changed."

"It's glitter. It's insidious." Liv pulled another speck from his beard.

One of Bixby's retirees stood, wearing his dress uniform and holding a clipboard, just outside a newly erected police barrier. I doubted the barrier or the elderly man guarding it would keep out anyone truly determined to get in. But the small crowd outside the barrier seemed well behaved, at least at the moment. Jackie and her bridesmaids were sitting on the curb, drinking iced coffee from disposable cups from the Brew-Ha-Ha.

"There's Audrey Bloom, the florist!" Dennis Pinkleman shouted, his camera phone in the air and focused on me. "Say hi to the fans!"

I sent him a tiny wave.

"Audrey Bloom . . . Olivia Meyer . . . Eric Meyer . . ." The retired officer peered at us over his reading glasses, and then highlighted our names on his list. We must have passed muster, because he let us pass.

As we walked into the church, Shirley and Pastor Seymour were pacing the foyer—Pastor Seymour probably pacing out of nerves, and Shirley there to make sure he didn't fall down.

"Good afternoon," he said, coming over to shake our hands with his still-firm grip.

"How does it look in there?" I asked.

"How am I to know? That woman won't even let me in."

"Gigi?" I asked.

"Said I can't even keep my water glass by the podium. And on a hot day like this."

"She meant that it wouldn't look nice on camera," Shirley said. "But I've got a water bottle right here for you." She pulled a plastic bottle out of her purse. "You can keep it in your pocket."

"Confounded plastic." He shook his head, like a diver shaking water out of his ears. "Listen to me, sounding like a crotchety old man."

"Like?" Shirley said.

He glared at her, but then resumed a playful smile. "I guess I don't like being put out of my own church. But soon the wedding will be over, and they will all scatter to wherever they came from, and we can get back to normal."

A huge sneeze punctuated his last sentence, followed by Bixby and Brad walking out of the auditorium. At first I thought Bixby was escorting Brad—as in Brad being arrested. But then I realized that Brad was leading.

"I'm sorry," he said, "but the microphones are picking up all that sneezing and sniffling. You can't stay."

"But I have a murder to investigate."

"Then take some Benadryl," Brad said.

"I did take some Benadryl." Bixby sneezed again. "I've been doing nothing all day except taking Benadryl."

Brad waited until the chief wiped his nose and eyes. "Sorry, but until it kicks in, you'll have to wait here."

"Hi, Audrey, Liv," Brad said. "Gigi loved the flowers in the church. I have to . . ." He pointed in the direction of the church and ducked back inside.

Pastor Seymour laughed. "Welcome to the doghouse," he said to Bixby.

"You all can go in," Shirley said, gesturing to us. "The ushers are seating guests now. Make sure you check out their cool guestbook."

Liv, Eric, and I walked up the stairs, and as soon as we rounded the corner, stopped at a long table covered with a poster and ink pads. The poster was of a large tree, with branches curling into hearts in various places. A few bells hung from the tree, almost as an afterthought, and they were already mostly obscured by the inked fingerprints of the wedding guests, which resembled the leaves and blossoms of the tree. Brad was manning the station, handing little packets of hand cleaner to the couple who had just signed.

"You'd think there'd be more bells," I told Brad. I scanned the signatures and recognized the bride's, next to the groom's illegible scrawl at the center, surrounded by those of some of the bridesmaids I'd met at the bachelorette party, then some townsfolk, too.

"Not my idea," he said. "This was one of Gary's pet projects."

I pressed my finger onto a light green ink pad, dabbed my digit on an empty spot on the poster, and signed my name above it with one of the fine-point Sharpies there for that purpose.

Instead of handing me the towelette, Brad opened the package and took my hand. "We've been to a lot of weddings in this place," he said, stroking the cloth over my finger.

I swallowed. Where was he going with this?

Another couple filed into line behind me at the table.

"Look," he said, finally releasing my hand and handing me a fan with the wedding program printed on it. "I have to work, but save a dance for me at the reception?"

Little did he know that since the last wedding I'd attended, I'd given up dancing. But I nodded just the same.

I barely had time to reach into a basket to pull out a beribboned silver bell—"Ring the bell for the first kiss"—before Liv took my arm, nothing gentle about her grasp. "What are you doing?" she whispered, as we made our way to the usher standing near the doors.

Before I could answer, we were being escorted to our seats. From the end of an otherwise empty pew, Nick Maxwell stood waving in our direction.

"Tag team?" Eric said, looking mildly amused, at least until Liv socked him in the arm.

She pushed me ahead of her so I'd be next to Nick, who was looking dapper in a dress shirt and tie, if not a bit sweaty in the warm room.

"You look hot," I said, then wanted to do an instant face-palm.

He chuckled. "It is a bit warm in here, if that's what you meant." He winked. "But you look hot, too."

Liv had slid close next to me, making sure there was little room between Nick and me. No hiding where her sympathies lay.

I glanced around the church. Most wedding guests, upon arrival, would probably be looking at the people. Newcomers to Ramble might check out the architecture. I looked first at the flowers. Except for two standing altar arrangements that had each been moved a foot closer in, all the other flowers remained just how we'd placed them. They looked fine at the moment, all in full bloom, but I could tell some of the more fragile varieties would start drooping and turning brown around the edges as early as tonight due to the excessive heat.

Only after I was satisfied the flowers would make a good showing did I notice the robed bell choir overflowing the choir loft with their lushly draped tables covered with gleaming bronze bells. The bells ranged from tiny ones, a little over an inch, to some with diameters of over a foot. Mallets rested next to the largest ones.

Then I looked at the guests. Except for maybe a dozen strangers near the front, the rest of the church was filled with Ramble residents, dressed in their Sunday best and sitting with their finest postures. Shirley's invites. The police were there in force with their families, sans Bixby, but an empty space next to his wife indicated the spot from whence he had been removed. Lafferty was also missing, but I knew he still had guard duty over at the Ashbury. I waved across the aisle to Mrs. June.

"The police presence should make it safe," Nick said.

I nodded. "As safe as it can be with a killer still out there." I got a chill thinking that this would be the killer's last chance to stop the wedding.

"Any ideas yet?"

"Too many," I said. "Narrowing it down is the hard part. Too many people had some kind of motive. I can't see any of them going to such an extreme."

"Including your friend Brad."

"Yes, including Brad, but—"

"Listen, Audrey, I've been thinking." He took my hand in his. "I've been a bit foolish. I was jealous when Brad came back into town, and I'm sorry for that. I trust your instincts, and if you say he isn't the killer, then I believe you."

I nodded, and he squeezed my hand a little tighter. The bell choir started playing Beethoven's "Moonlight Sonata." I swallowed. I'm a sucker for the "Moonlight Sonata."

"And I was wrong when I said that we should date other people," he said. "It's true that I have no claim on you—and I can't even think about . . . taking our relationship to the next level until I have the means of supporting . . . Well, it sounds so old-fashioned, but it was how I was raised."

I nodded again.

"But I'm not sure I was being completely honest with you."

"Not honest?"

"Well, while I said those words, I knew that the last thing in the world I wanted was to date other people, and I hoped you'd feel the same."

I squeezed his hand as the doors opened and the ushers escorted family members to the front.

"Who are they?" Nick followed my gaze.

"My guess would be the groom's parents." As a smiling older couple took a seat on the right-hand side, I added, "Yep."

"How do you know?"

"Grandma Mae used to always say, 'The groom insisted

he was right, so the bride left,' to help us remember which side was which at weddings. At least that's the case with traditional Christian weddings. I think Jewish weddings are the opposite."

"The bride is always right?" Nick said. "Sounds like a safer plan."

"His parents look pretty happy."

"You had them on your suspect list?"

"Briefly," I said. "If for some reason they didn't like Suzy, they'd have motive. But they weren't staying at the Ashbury. In fact, I haven't seen them around at all."

I turned to Liv, who was rubbernecking the crowd in the church. "Looking for suspects?" I asked.

"That man," she said. "Third row." She pulled out her phone and flipped through the images of the people from Gary's exposés. "Does he look like . . . ?"

I looked at the picture on the phone first. It was a grainy picture. "Who is this guy?"

"Alderman. Took bribes."

I looked up at the third row. There was some resemblance in hair color and profile, but then *she* turned around.

"Never mind," Liv said as she snatched back her phone.

No family was escorted to the bride's side, probably because Suzy's father would be walking her down the aisle, and he was a widower.

The next person in the room was Marco, the cameraman. Nathan, covered in camera gear, looked like a foreign legion soldier who had just crossed the desert. Sweat beaded on his forehead and soaked through the back of his shirt. Brad also carried a camera, smaller, but more portable. And the sound guy had his boom mic.

And when the cameras were set, Gigi and Henry Easton came in next, arm in arm. The cameras focused on them as they pointed and looked dreamily at the empty stage. I recalled watching the show and seeing Gary and Gigi commenting on how nice the wedding was turning out. But of course, with limited cameras, this was not taking place at the same time as the wedding, as the viewer was led to believe. All staged and scripted and edited to look like it was happening in real time.

The music changed to "Canon in D" as Pastor Seymour, followed by the groom and the groomsmen all wearing their campanula boutonnieres, entered through a side door. The groom (Michael or Martin, or whatever his name was) strode to his marked spot at the front of the church. I could tell it was marked because he stopped, looked down, then shuffled three inches to the right. He sent a brief, nervous smile to his parents, then fixed his eyes on the back door, his Adam's apple bobbing up and down.

The bridesmaids seemed to race down the aisle, wobbling a bit on their stiletto heels. As they did, I could have sworn I heard sleigh bells, their random tintinnabulation clashing with the clear tones of the bell choir. As the bridesmaids took their places at the front of the church, I began to figure out where all those tinkling sounds were coming from. Bell earrings. Bells woven into their hair ornaments. Bells on the sashes of their dresses. Bells on their shoes. Wasn't that an old nursery rhyme—rings on her fingers and bells on her toes?

And here I was worried that bellflowers would be too literal.

When the bride and her father appeared in the doorway, the room hushed. Except for the bells. The bride was wearing the vintage bell-sleeved gown, but they had at least altered it to remove the high neck. The sleeves started just below her bare shoulders. They were fitted until they reached the elbow, then flared out into a fluttery bell shape that no longer quite reached the floor. Seed pearls sewn in bell shapes decorated the bodice and the train, and more seed pearls repeated the same pattern on the veil. The effect was striking. Nevena must not have slept in days.

As the bell choir started the next tune, Suzy's father

rubbed his trimmed beard. Apparently Suzy failed in her bid to get him to shave it. She held her bouquet low, probably as Easton had directed her so that the camera could pick up the dress. The muted colors of the campanula mixed well with the white of the calla lilies, making the bouquet seem airy and light, as if it were in soft focus. And although you couldn't see much of the bell design on the silver bouquet holder, I knew that Suzy knew it was there. And by the smile on her face, I imagined she was pleased.

Max looked shell-shocked as he made his way past the cameras with Suzy tugging his arm as she half-walked, half-danced down the aisle to the bell choir playing a rocking tune. I checked the program.

" 'You Can Ring My Bell'?" I whispered to Nick.

"I think it's an old disco tune," he said with an amused smile.

In fact, all of the *uses* were with us. Pastor Seymour looked a bit *bemused* at the bell choir. Most of the audience looked *amused* as the bride sashayed down the aisle to the beat of the music with her evidently *confused* father in tow. And my eye caught Bixby, standing near the back door leaning on the frame, the silhouette of his gun in its holster evident under his suit coat as he *mused* over the situation.

Butterflies in my stomach discoed to the rocking processional tune. Would the wedding go on as planned? Or would the killer make one more attempt to stop it?

I think I daydreamed through much of the rest of the wedding. Well, not quite daydreamed. When younger, I'd let my mind wander during weddings, thinking about the day I'd march down the aisle. I'd planned my dress, my flowers, and my cake. That seemed less likely to happen all the time, but those were the silly daydreams of a young girl. Today, however, my eyes darted back and forth among the various suspects. I could see why the Secret Service wear those dark glasses—it not only cuts down glare, but it hides the direction in which they're looking. If anyone was looking at me that day, they probably thought I had some kind of spastic eye disease.

When the groom began his vows, I breathed deeply and tried to focus.

"Suzy, you bring joy and laughter into my life. I promise that I'll be true to you, cherish you, and take out the garbage. I will never take you for granted, or ask you to be quiet because I've had a long day at the office. I'll be ready to listen, ready to share all of life with you, to the sound of the tinkling of hundreds of bells. I won't even complain if you keep your Tinker Bell doll on the bed, because I know it reminds you of your mother. And I love her without even meeting her because she's the one who gave you to me."

At this point, Suzy's eyes welled up, and she pulled a small handkerchief from the middle of her bouquet. I don't necessarily recommend brides store them there, but it happens.

I didn't pay much attention to Suzy's vows, since I'd heard them at the rehearsal. Until she left her script and started winging it.

"And at the beginning, I didn't know whether you'd end up being my best friend or something more. Until that first kiss . . . Then I knew we weren't destined to remain friends."

I couldn't help the snort that escaped. I tried to mask it with a sniffle and prayed that it didn't make its way to the front of the church or the running microphones.

An intake of breath from Nick made me look in his direction. He was studying the floor with a jaw so tight I could tell he was stifling laughter. I didn't dare look at Liv.

Then, nothing . . .

Nothing happened. When I looked up, the bride and groom were staring at each other. Members of the wedding party were looking around. Pastor Seymour's head was bowed, as if he were in deep prayer. Only townsfolk had seen him do this before.

Shirley left her seat near the front of the church and climbed the podium, squeezing in behind the bridesmaids before coming up to the pastor and simply laying her hand on his arm.

He awoke with a start, cleared his throat, and said, "Let us pray."

I have no idea if a prayer was supposed to go there, but while Pastor Seymour offered a quick prayer for the happiness of the new couple, I peeked under my lashes to watch Shirley creep off the stage and the wedding party share a few smiles.

Shortly after the "Amen," the couple exchanged rings, kissed, and walked down the aisle. The bell choir remained silent, but up from the belfry came the deep peals of the church's historic bell. I hadn't heard it since it had marked Gary's death, and it gave me a thrill of victory, that the killer hadn't been able to stop the wedding.

Then again, the killer had not yet been caught, so the victory wasn't complete.

The bell choir played another tune, and then another, and I was grateful when the ushers finally released our row to stand in the reception line. Not that the choir wasn't good, but I think I was starting on a heat-induced headache. Good thing we had three hours before the start of the reception. I'd need a shower and a change of clothing.

We stopped and briefly chatted with Pastor Seymour and Shirley. The bell choir filed past us, whipping off their robes at the earliest convenience to reveal sweat-soaked T-shirts, and the bridal party went back into the church with their photographer to re-create scenes they'd missed the first time.

I watched them for a few minutes, relieved that the wedding went off—and without a hitch. And the flowers lasted, even in the heat. Nick, Liv, Eric, and I exited the church to observe an animated exchange between Bixby and Brad. I rushed over.

"Some security," Brad said, shaking his head.

Just when everything seemed to be going right. Had the killer struck again? "What happened?" I asked.

"You shouldn't have left the keys in it," Bixby said, ignoring me and answering Brad. "My men were watching the entrance, not the parking lot. But I'll file the report."

Brad ran a hand through his hair. "File a report. What good is that going to do?"

"Maybe someone will find it. Or try to sell it. I can interview the crowd, ask if they saw anything."

"I already did that," Brad practically whined. "Everybody was watching the building, waiting for the bride and groom and the cast to come out."

I put my hand on Brad's shoulder. "What happened?" I asked again, only this time a little louder.

"Somebody stole the Range Rover," he said.

Bixby took Brad by the arm and gestured to a spot in the churchyard farther away from the throng behind the barriers and we followed him there. Dennis Pinkleman had his cell phone camera focused in our direction. I didn't see Jackie and her crew among the group of onlookers, but they could have headed out for more coffee. Or more margaritas, for that matter. Hopefully not in the Range Rover.

"And you're sure it's stolen?" Bixby asked. "Maybe someone else from the show needed to use it."

Brad shook his head. "That was my first thought, too. But I checked already."

"When did you last see it?" I asked.

"I didn't misplace it, Audrey," Brad barked back. "It was stolen."

"I didn't say you misplaced it," I said. "I simply asked when you had last seen it."

Bixby crossed his arms and looked amused. "I'd answer the lady. It's a good question. In fact, it was the next one I was going to ask."

"I carried the guestbook and supplies out just before the wedding began."

"That's a big window," Bixby said. "Could have been taken during the wedding, or after." Bixby scanned the crowd and sighed. "I should try to establish a time frame for who left and when. I don't suppose the Pinkleman kid would relinquish that cell phone voluntarily, would he?"

"You might be better off waiting until he posts his pictures on the fan site. I suspect he's not your number one fan. Wait!" I turned to Brad. "Did you say the guestbook was in there? What else?"

"Odds and ends, mostly. The street clothes for the whole wedding party. They changed here. An extra outfit for Gigi, just in case. Thread, ribbon, emergency supplies."

"No expensive video equipment or anything like that?" Bixby asked.

Brad shook his head. "Anything valuable is either locked up or being used. I was going to run this stuff back to the inn, unload, and come back for some of the cast and crew." Brad froze for a moment, the blood draining from his face.

"What is it?" I asked.

"The marriage license," he said. "It was in the van, signed, but not filed yet."

"But that means . . ." Bixby started. Nobody finished the sentence.

Someone had managed to stop the wedding after all.

Chapter 21

※

I sent a group text to Liv and all the Rose in
Bloom employees. "Meet me at the shop in twenty."

I showered quickly, dried off in front of the air conditioner in the bedroom, and slipped into a jade dress. I pulled
into the alley behind the shop just before Amber Lee.

When I unlocked the back door, I was amazed at how
clean the place looked—and how incorrectly Eric and his
crew had managed to put all the salvageable supplies away.
It would take us weeks to find everything and straighten it
all out after his straightening.

I turned the thermostat down to bump on the air conditioning.

"Do we have a floral emergency?" Amber Lee said.

"No, I just—"

Darnell was the next to peek his head in the door. Followed by Shelby. I hadn't bothered texting our irregular
interns. When Liv and Eric arrived, looking every bit as
confused as the others, I started.

"I think you all have heard that a *Fix My Wedding* Range Rover was stolen," I said.

"With the wedding license," Liv added.

Amber Lee raised her hand. "But I heard Bixby got the county clerk to issue a replacement. They got it signed and filed, so the wedding *was* valid."

Our little group applauded that, and since Amber Lee's gossip sources were generally reliable, I was happy for the couple.

"But someone did try hard to stop the wedding from being official," Shelby said.

"Maybe," I said. "Or maybe they were after something else."

"Like what?" Liv asked.

"Range Rovers go for a chunk of change," Eric said.

"True," I said. "But how coincidental that someone would steal that particular vehicle, even if the keys were left in the ignition."

"The theft of the Range Rover has to be tied in with the other things," Liv said. "The break-in here. The damage of the wedding dresses. And maybe Gary's murder."

"All to stop the wedding?" Amber Lee asked. "Then he failed. Or do you think there's another angle?"

"Suzy's wedding does seem to be the focus of it all, doesn't it?" I said. "Liv, you mentioned there were a bunch of interviews that Gary did with Suzy on the computer disk. Was that disc taken during the break-in?"

"No," Liv said. "It was still in the computer."

"Good. Then we still have access to it."

"But whoever vandalized the shop was interested in those old videotapes of Gary's," Shelby said.

"Which is why I'd like you and Darnell to head to the library. Take a copy of the list of Gary's news stories, and see what you can dig up. Ask for Mrs. McGregor, the research librarian. Those stories are over twenty years old, so not all the information might be available on the Internet."

"Mrs. McGregor is like seventy," Shelby said.

"Who better to know how to find something that's not on the Internet?" Amber Lee said. "Now shoo. It takes longer with microfiche."

As our two part-time employees made their way out the back door debating what microfiche might be, Liv squinted at me. "You know more than you're telling us."

"It's not something I know. Just . . . what if the person who took the Range Rover wasn't after the marriage license?"

"What would they be after?" Amber Lee said.

Liv's eyes grew wide. "The guest book . . . or poster . . . or whatever they want to call it."

I nodded. "With all the fingerprints on it. It's a cute keepsake, but it caught my attention because it really didn't have much to do with the theme of the wedding. Yes, there were a few bells hanging from the tree, but not enough to stand out. Yet Brad told me that Gary had specifically chosen it."

"Gary was investigating—trying to get someone's fingerprints," Liv said. "Maybe someone with a record? Someone who was at the wedding."

"The story that was going to relaunch his career," I said.

"His last story," Amber Lee said.

"And it's not finished," I said. "But what put Gary onto this new investigation that was going to relaunch his career? Does it tie in with an old story he worked on as a reporter? Or something he came across in his interviews with Suzy?"

Liv gnawed on a cuticle. "Gary must have had some suspicions prior to his interviews with Suzy."

"Why's that?" Eric asked.

"Because we learned from Jackie that Gary normally doesn't . . . didn't . . . do such in-depth interviews with the brides," Liv said.

"At least he didn't then," I added. "It is possible that he started that later. Although Gigi did tell me that Gary seemed especially fascinated with Suzy. Maybe you could talk to Gigi? See if she knows more about Gary's interviews and why Suzy was chosen." I turned to Eric. "Is that okay?"

"Only if I can go with her," he said. "We'll be at the reception anyway."

"Do I have an assignment?" Amber Lee asked.

"Could you go over the computer files again, maybe jot down some notes? Try to follow what Gary was asking. You've seen all the videotapes. See if you can draw any correlations."

Amber Lee saluted and made her way to the computer.

"And where will you be?" Liv asked. "So if I hear sirens, I know whether or not to panic."

"Not going anywhere dangerous. I'm checking in with the police to see how the investigation is going."

"Bixby's not going to tell you anything," Eric said.

"Who said I was going to talk to Bixby?"

Mrs. June ushered me into the conference room of the police station. Her normal chair was occupied by another retired member of the police force, a red-cheeked man with a shiny bald head and a beer gut that looked like he'd swallowed a Clydesdale.

"In case any unrelated emergencies happen today," she said, gesturing to her normal chair as we passed it. "Not that I think the miscreants will venture out in this heat—at least not until after dark."

"So Bixby has you going to the wedding and the reception," I said.

"Not as an investigator, I'm afraid. More of an errand boy, I think." She quirked her face into a half smile. "Unless he's trying to keep me in sight so I don't participate in the *informal* investigation."

I gave her my most innocent look and batted my eyelashes.

"If you want to know what Bixby's come up with, it

amounts to a lot of data that doesn't add up to anything. We did get word of a torched vehicle over behind the high school. He's headed there now to see if it's our missing Range Rover."

"That proves someone was after something inside the SUV, doesn't it?"

"Or a malicious prank," Mrs. June said. "He sent a couple of men out to verify the whereabouts of Jackie and her crew. And he's got someone bringing in that poor Pinkleman kid again."

"Probably for his cell phone."

"And he's already talked to Brad."

"Rounding up the usual suspects." I bit my lip. My next question would be harder to ask. And possibly more dangerous to Mrs. June's employment if Bixby found out.

"What do you need, child?"

"Gary had told more than one person that he was leaving the show to break back into serious journalism."

"So he was working on a new story."

"But was it a new story? Or was it an old one?" I said. "Gary was fixated on the case that ended his journalism career. Can you get official police records? From other departments? Quickly?"

Mrs. June exhaled through pursed lips. "Maybe. Depends on which departments, how old the case, how sweetly I ask them, and how cooperative they're feeling. What are you looking for?"

"Boston. The Paige Logan kidnapping."

Kathleen Randolph was probably right about the show being good for business. Most of Ramble was just outside the police barriers in front of the Ashbury. I recognized Tacky Jackie and her cohorts by their protest signs as they were being interviewed by a local news reporter. And more than one of our local teens were walking behind them, probably trying to get their faces on camera. That's what this whole thing was about, wasn't it?

I entered the Ashbury as Kathleen's white-gloved crew was placing the hors d'oeuvres into steam trays, a task probably not made easier with the white gloves. I couldn't help but ogle the food first. There were soft cheeses under bell-shaped glass canopies, hard cheeses on bell-shaped cutting boards—surrounded by fruits and vegetables, including plenty of bell peppers. Baskets of bell-shaped pretzels. Other foods were cut with bell-shaped cookie cutters or shaped in large molds to resemble bells. And the bell-shaped croquettes made my mouth water, even if they were looking a little droopy.

I was staring at a tray of mac and cheese when Kathleen came up behind me.

"Campanelle," she said. "The bell-shaped pasta. I thought of you when I ordered it." She pointed to the bluebell arrangement we'd placed on the serving table, and then down to the pasta. "To me it looks more like the flowers. Sure soaks up the cheese, though."

The anteroom was mostly empty still, with plenty of space at the high cocktail tables to set down drinks and food. I looked over the small crowd, waved to a few townsfolk, claimed a glass of punch, and set it on an unoccupied table.

My head was spinning and my stomach so stressed that the punch felt like pure acid as it worked its way down my esophagus. Just a few more hours of reception, and the cast and crew would leave town, and someone would literally get away with murder.

And I had no idea why that bothered me so much.

It wasn't my job. The flowers were finished and looked lovely. Since the wedding took place, we would get paid. And if the episode ever aired, it should help our business. And since the killer was undoubtedly part of the cast or crew, once they left town, Ramble streets would be safe

again. And although that meant not catching whoever broke
into our shop, either way, it wouldn't happen again.

And it's not as if Gary and I were best buds. Our brief
meeting left me a bit ambivalent to him, personally. I thought
of the sprig of foxglove he had placed in his lapel. *Insincere*.
And it fit, which was why investigating his murder turned
out to be so difficult. He represented himself as a sweet,
caring wedding planner, a fairy godfather who only desired
to make nuptial dreams come true. But instead, he tended
to be ambitious, self-centered, and definitely not sweet. At
one time, he was a very good reporter. And when he was
murdered, he was apparently on the heels of some breaking
news. Had he kept better notes on what he was working on,
the killer would probably be in jail already. Did he have
more secrets that we'd never discover?

Still, Gary didn't deserve to die. He'd done a lot of good,
too. Like stopping that Balkan adoption ring scandal. I drained
the rest of my punch, wincing at the burn in my throat.

"I sure hope that's not spiked." Brad set his phone and a
small leather notebook on the table. "And if it is spiked, I'll
get you another if you let me take you home tonight." He
snapped his fingers. "But we have to take your car. Mine is
still smoldering behind the high school."

"So that was the Range Rover they found."

"Yes, but if someone was trying to stop the wedding, they
messed up."

"I heard Bixby helped expedite the new marriage
license."

"Didn't know the man could be so helpful. I still don't
think he trusts me."

"He doesn't get paid to trust anybody. And you do have
a history."

"The record of all of my youthful misdeeds has been
sealed since I turned nineteen. Expunged is the word I think
they used. And nothing after that has ever been proven. Not
that Bixby would forget."

"Someone called?" Bixby sidled up behind Brad, and I could see Brad's posture straighten.

"I was saying how helpful you were in replacing the wedding license."

Bixby set his punch down at the table, then removed the small floral centerpiece to a neighboring table before returning. "When do the cast and crew plan to head out?"

Brad inhaled audibly. "First thing in the morning. The first stop is the funeral, to show our support for Gigi. Without the Range Rover, we'll just squeeze in a little tighter. We'll ship ahead everything we need for the next wedding—and we've one less person. Oh, that sounded insensitive. I just meant that Easton has his own ride."

"So the show goes on," I said.

He nodded, reaching over to take one of the new couple's signature cocktails from the tray of a server, a pink concoction called a spiced silver bell. "At least until the network says otherwise." He sipped cautiously at his drink.

I glanced at Bixby. The departure time would give him a few more hours to work on the case, but how much investigation could he reasonably accomplish when most of his suspects would be snoring under their down duvets?

"Anything new in the investigation?" I asked sweetly.

He gave me his condescending Mr. Rogers smile. "Nice try, Audrey. But word gets out—both ways, you know. You need to stop this snooping of yours. I know it was your shop that was broken into, your business reputation on the line, so I can see where you feel you have a personal stake in this. But you could impede our investigation. And meddling with murder could end up being dangerous."

Darnell slid up to the table, plopping a heaping plate of mac and cheese on top of a manila folder. "Hey there."

Bixby focused on the folder, then on Darnell, then gave me a stern look. "Dangerous . . . for everybody." And then he left the table.

Darnell exhaled. "Something I said?"

"Well, I need to get back to work, too," Brad said. "I have to make sure the new bride is ready for her big entrance. See you later, Audrey."

Shelby walked up and took Brad's spot, setting down a well-balanced plate filled with fruits and vegetables. "Mrs. McGregor sends her regards. Says you still owe her a dollar eighty in fines."

Darnell pulled out the folder and looked around the room before he opened it. "We thought this might be helpful. Found it using something called *The Readers' Guide to Periodical Literature*." He shoved over a photocopied article about the kidnapping.

"This is recent," I said.

"A where-are-they-now story," Shelby said.

I scanned the photo that accompanied the article. Evan Logan—the prime suspect in the case, at least according to the younger version of Gary—was standing next to his wife. The couple had never stopped looking for their daughter. Most of their savings had gone to pay the ransom, and the rest of their assets over the years to pay private investigators and lawyer fees. Their marriage suffered. They divorced a few years after the kidnapping, then remarried each other a couple of years after that.

"We lost our daughter. We only had each other to lean on, to cling to . . . to keep searching." I squinted at the picture of them taken in front of a more modest home than the McMansion I'd seen on Gary's videos. The new Logan home was a lackluster ranch with peeling gray clapboards and weeds growing where flowers should be.

"We're encouraged," the father was quoted as saying, "by the recent recovery of other victims of child abduction. We rejoice with the families reunited with their now-grown children."

"Our daughter likely wouldn't remember us," the mother added. "But we won't give up hope."

"Hope," I said.

"We figured the dad's gotta have a motive," Shelby said. "Gary accused him, and instead of focusing only on finding the child, he had to deal with all the accusations. It took a toll on his marriage."

"But he's not someone we've seen in town. Have you?" I stared at the picture. "But the mother looks . . . I know I've never seen her before, but she looks oddly familiar."

I hate assigned tables at wedding receptions. It always seemed like all the interesting conversations were taking place elsewhere while I was seated with the guy with the dripping sinuses, the woman detailing her food allergies, the silent and sullen couple on the verge of divorce, and the snarky woman explaining why Emily Post would be appalled at the most recent wedding faux pas. At least the last one was entertaining.

I was relieved when my card directed me to table thirteen—not an omen, I hoped—to find Liv and Eric already seated there.

The room looked absolutely gorgeous and ethereal, probably as a result of all that draping and up-lighting. Near the side door stood a large ice sculpture, towering about five feet above the height of the table it rested upon. It was carved to look like two beribboned wedding bells. "Just shy of five hundred pounds," I'd heard Gigi say to the camera as we passed her coming in. Guests encircled it, watching it dispense more of that pink cocktail. Ramblers were easily entertained.

Liv waved me to the seat next to hers. "I just had a talk with Gigi."

"*We* just had a talk with Gigi," Eric said.

"About how Gary chose Suzy," Liv added, waving Eric off. "And all those interviews. It seems he was extremely secretive and kept Gigi pretty much in the dark about it."

"I'm sure that must have raised her suspicions," I said.

"I guess she drew her own conclusions." Liv shrugged. "She was a little more open this time. Said she figured her marriage was pretty much over anyway at that point. But they figured a secret divorce would be even harder to carry off than a secret marriage."

"Hence her taking up with Sven the lighting guy," I said.

"Well, hey, y'all." Mrs. June set her punch on the table and scooted in next to me. More guests had arrived, and the room filled with the chatter of conversation. "Wasn't that a lovely wedding? But I think I need to run to the little girls' room." She hoisted her pocketbook onto her lap and tapped it meaningfully. If taps can have meanings. These did.

"Let me join you," I added.

"How many women does it take to go to the bathroom?" Eric said.

"Me, too, I'm afraid." Liv hoisted herself up. "Baby pushing on the bladder and all."

Mrs. June led the way to the ladies' room like a woman on a mission. Cue the *Mission Impossible* soundtrack. The crowd that was milling about the tables parted before her like she was Moses crossing the Red Sea. After we pushed our way into the restroom, she put a finger to her lips while she checked under each stall, then pointed to one that was occupied.

I turned to the mirror and pretended to primp.

Mrs. June plopped onto the upholstered chair near the door and kicked off a shoe, examining it like something was stabbing her support hose.

Liv ducked into an empty stall. "I wasn't joking when I said the baby was pushing on my bladder."

And then we waited. And waited. I'd done as much primping as I could. Liv had finished her business and was washing her hands. And still, whoever had occupied that last stall hadn't budged.

"We can't stay in the bathroom all day," Liv whispered.

I looked to Mrs. June, who shrugged.

"Are you all right in there?" I called.

No answer.

And suddenly, my mind filled with everything that could go wrong that could keep someone locked in a ladies' bathroom stall—from stomach disorders to wardrobe malfunctions to childbirth (Hey, I saw it once on *I Didn't Know I Was Pregnant*) to murder. Was there another corpse attached to those feet I could see under the stall door?

"Can I get you anything?" I asked, softening my voice. Finally I went to the stall and knocked on the door.

Moments later the toilet flushed and Nevena exited, rubbing the back of her hand under her running nose and then across her mascara-stained cheeks.

I stood back as she went to the sink, washed her hands, and splashed cold water on her face. I handed her a few towels from the dispenser.

"Are you okay?" I asked. Stupid question. Obviously she was far from okay. "Here, sit." I guided her to a chair opposite Mrs. June and handed her a tissue box from the counter.

She sighed and closed her eyes. "It's so hard. The wedding . . . without Gary."

"I didn't realize you and Gary were so . . . close," I said.

Nevena nodded, then gasped. "No! Not close. Not like that."

Liv reached over and held her hand. "How were you close, then?"

Nevena sniffed and reached a hand toward Liv's belly, stopping inches short. "May I?"

Liv nodded and Nevena rubbed Liv's belly.

"In Bulgaria," she said, "there's old tradition of putting dried honeysuckle into cup of water, and drinking it to speed on labor; something about hand of the Virgin."

"In the language of flowers," I said, "honeysuckle means *generous* and *devoted affection*. Of course, the variety matters."

"Don't think about it," Liv said. "I'm not nearly ready to deliver yet."

This was a nice Hallmark moment, but it really didn't answer any questions. "About Gary," I said.

Nevena bit her lip and nodded.

"If you weren't involved with him romantically," I said, "what exactly . . ."

"He was helping me. Ever since I come to country, he helps with immigration."

"He was helping you become a citizen?" I asked.

She shook her head. "I am citizen. I was born in country."

Chapter 22

❧❀

I wasn't sure how you tactfully asked a U.S.-born citizen how it was that she knew so little English. But I didn't need to.

"I grew up in Bulgaria. Gary helped that. He was very good to me and Mother. That's why I am so sad to think he is dead . . ."

"Gary saw to it that you grew up in Bulgaria?" Liv asked. "How did that happen?"

"Is long story," she said. "My mother, she was young. So young. And not married. She could not stay with parents, and my father, he was . . . as you call, rat." She smiled in triumph at her word choice. "People tell her, go to America. Work and have baby there. So she goes . . ."

"The adoption mill," Liv said. "The one luring Balkan girls to the U.S. to have their babies. Did your mother know Gary from the story?"

Nevena nodded. "You've seen story? Mother was so proud of what she did. They tell her no one would believe her. That she has to leave baby and go home, but Mother, she doesn't listen. She talks to Gary."

"She was the whistle-blower," I said.

Nevena knit her eyebrows in puzzlement.

"To blow the whistle means to turn them in to the police," I said. "She must have testified against them."

Nevena nodded. "She blow whistle many times in court. Many threats against her, but bad men go to jail. Then we go back to Bulgaria. The government does not help, like here. It was still hard for us, but better to be together. She work in dress shop. I helped."

"So why all the calls to immigration?" I asked.

"Since I am American citizen, I can live here. And ask that Mother be allowed to immigrate as well. The new people don't know what she did, how she helped them. So they don't want to give her visa. Gary was helping me bring her over. He said he wants to hire her. We both work on the show. But now . . ."

"Have you talked to Henry Easton about your mother?" Liv asked.

"Easton, he only scream at me. Talk like I a child. I don't know what will happen if Mother comes and she has no job. She very good seamstress. Better than me, and I'm hot stuff."

"Would you like us to talk to Henry?" I said. "Or maybe Brad can."

"Brad, he is nice. Handsome man, too. Yes, I think Brad can help. I think Henry might like to talk to handsome, young man like Brad."

Mrs. June snorted, then smiled at Nevena.

Nevena stood. "I have to go to work now. See if bride need anything pressed."

As the door swung behind her, I shrugged. "So much for my theory that she was having an affair with Gary. Another confirmation that Gary wasn't a total jerk."

"But that doesn't mean that Gigi didn't think he was

having an affair with her," Liv said. "So I wouldn't cross her off the list just yet."

"Of course not," I said. "We'll keep adding people until the whole world could have killed Gary."

"Now, now, girls." Mrs. June opened her purse. "Maybe I can help."

"What did you find?" I positioned myself next to her chair so I could read the papers on her lap. Liv took a position on the other side.

"What I found was more details on an old kidnapping. All of this is pretty much public record, so it wasn't much trouble to get."

"Oh, you got pictures." Liv leaned over Mrs. June's shoulder.

I was fascinated with the pictures as well. This was Paige Logan's nursery, shot shortly after the kidnapping. The crib was lined with a lacy bumper, and a mobile was dancing in the sunlight. "I recall the story. Deborah Logan put one-and-a-half-year-old Paige to bed that night and turned on the mobile. And never saw her again."

Liv put an unconscious hand on her stomach. "I can't imagine," she said, her voice cracked with emotion . . . or hormones . . . or hormone-induced emotion.

I leaned in closer. "What's that?" I pointed to the objects dangling from the mobile. "And that?" I pointed to another shadow in the window.

"I think those are wind chimes in the window," Mrs. June said.

"And that's a little bell on the mobile," Liv said.

"Is there a police report detailing the scene?" I asked.

"What is it?" Mrs. June shuffled through her papers. "You've got the 'eureka' look on your face again. I don't think I've seen it this strong since you discovered those tadpoles in the creek with the frog legs half grown on them."

I snatched up the police report. "There was a good set of prints found at the scene."

"Unfortunately, there was nothing to compare them to," Mrs. June said. "Whoever left it wasn't in the system. Never in the military. Never arrested."

"But wouldn't that have been enough to clear Evan Logan?" I asked.

"I'm afraid not. When they start taking fingerprints, they can be found anywhere—and anyone can leave them. Police fingerprint the family to eliminate most of the prints. The few they can't identify could lead to a suspect. Even then, it's a long shot. More often than not, they're left innocently. The uncle that visited once, and the family forgot to mention it. The babysitter. The babysitter's boyfriend the family never knew was in the house. Even the person in the department store who assembled the crib."

I read a little more of the report and my hands started shaking. "There was a Tinker Bell doll missing. The parents believe it was taken from her crib."

"Where's the picture of the baby?" Liv asked. "Little Paige."

Mrs. June handed it over. "You've got the same look," she told Liv.

"Is it her?" I asked.

"I can't tell. Might be."

"Who are you talking about, dagnabbit?" Mrs. June said.

"Suzy," Liv and I both said together.

"The bride?" Mrs. June asked. "How do you figure? She has a father."

"But is her father really her father?" I said.

"Oh," Liv said, practically jumping up and down, "That's why the fingerprint guest book thingy was stolen."

"And why Gary wanted it in the first place," I added. "It would be odd for the father of the bride not to participate. Then all Gary had to do was compare the signed fingerprint to the one on file."

Liv inhaled. "That explains the interviews and all the background information Gary wanted. He even had a copy of her birth certificate."

"Wait," I said. "He had Suzy's birth certificate? Was Max listed as her father?"

Liv nodded.

I rubbed by chin. "Are we jumping the gun here?"

"Maybe the certificate was forged," Liv suggested.

"There's a fingerprint for Paige in here, too." Mrs. June shuffled through the papers again. "Is that enough to go to Bixby with? What if Suzy isn't Paige Logan, all grown up?"

"Then we do what Gary was planning on doing," Liv said. "We collect fingerprints for him to compare. I mean, even if Bixby doesn't believe us, he'll check them just for the satisfaction of telling us we're wrong, right?"

"Don't go doing nothing dangerous," Mrs. June said.

"Nothing dangerous at all," I said. "This is a wedding. They are going to be touching things. All we"—I glared at Liv—"*I* . . . need to do is discreetly collect things they touch. Then Bixby can compare the fingerprints to the ones on file and decide what to do."

A knock sounded at the outer door. "Is everything okay in there?" Eric said. "You've been in there a long time."

"Just peachy," Liv yelled back. "We'll be right out." She rolled her eyes. "Men. He's probably worried I've gone into labor in here."

"If you're going to collect things they've touched," Mrs. June said, "try to get smooth and shiny things, like a glass."

"And put them where?" I held up my miniscule clutch purse, which would only be helpful if the thing they touched were a pack of gum. And not a very large pack, at that.

Mrs. June patted her gigantic handbag. "Right here."

We took our seats as the wedding party started to file in. A gigantic bell was projected onto the floor, and the couple was introduced and took their first dance . . . to a pleasant acoustical—but totally inappropriate—version of Bob Dylan's "Ring Them Bells."

Amber Lee, Shelby, and Darnell had made their way to our table. Mrs. June joined what I learned was her official table, over with the police presence.

And Nick waved as he wandered around with his place card still in its little bell holder, before taking a seat on the opposite side of the room. No, I didn't need to worry that bellflowers were too literal. Not in the least. But I did wonder if Brad had anything to do with Nick being seated at the farthest point possible from my table. I smiled. The cad.

Amber Lee leaned in closer. "I went over those computer files again."

"Anything?"

"Not really. Gary seemed equally obsessed with both Suzy Weber and the Paige Logan kidnapping. He had both their birth certificates, if you can believe that. And guess what he was doing with them."

"Checking to see if one was forged?"

Amber Lee's jaw dropped. "You take the fun out of everything. But, yes. He had notes on both certificates, checking the markings and signatures."

"Did he reach any conclusions?"

"He apparently decided they were both genuine."

The emcee picked that moment to start the program. Toasts followed, and I eyed the table where Max Weber sat drinking from a tall champagne flute. The perfect object from which to get a fingerprint.

After the newly-married couple danced, they sat at a small sweetheart table and rang a little bell. The servers started serving food, first for the couple, and then for the rest of us. I kept rubbernecking the table where Max sat with the groom's parents. But I couldn't exactly go over there and steal the champagne glass right out of his hand.

I barely tasted dinner, which consisted of stuffed bell peppers with a really nice cut of steak that had no apparent connection to bells. (The horror!) After dinner, the DJ announced the father-daughter dance.

I watched it for a few moments. Marco had his camera trained on Suzy and Max, but I couldn't help notice how Max seemed to swirl in a way to ensure that the camera focused on Suzy. Or was he trying to keep from being on camera?

But I excused myself, sent a look to Liv, and carried my untouched champagne glass over to the place where the groom's parents sat. And where Max's champagne flute stood unguarded.

"Well, hello, there," I said, setting my glass coolly on the table near where Max's glass stood unguarded and waiting. I proffered my hand to the groom's mother. "I've so wanted to meet the groom's parents. I'm Audrey Bloom, the florist." They introduced themselves with names, I must admit, just as unmemorable as their son's, and then proceeded to tell me how lovely the flowers were.

I thanked them profusely, chattered inanely, and, as the dance was coming to a close, bid them adieu. I picked up Max's champagne flute by the stem, leaving mine in its place, and headed over to Mrs. June's table. My flute was full since I didn't want to drink, and his was empty, but I hoped nobody else would notice the switch and that he'd assume some waiter refilled it while he was dancing.

"But it's empty," she tried to say, when I set the flute next to her spot.

I cleared my throat.

"Oh!" She then picked up her napkin and wrapped it around the glass before turning to her colleagues at the table.

The one problem with using Mrs. June's purse as a collection vessel for our fingerprints is that how do you explain to a table full of cops why you're absconding with the Ashbury's glassware.

"Evidence," she said.

They shrugged but then were distracted as a multitiered tray of desserts arrived at the table. Little cheesecakes and cookies shaped like . . . You guessed it. I was saved by the bell.

I'd walked three feet from the table when I felt a hand close around my forearm.

"What do you think you're doing?" Brad pulled me to the side of the room. "We paid a deposit on that glassware. If any of it goes missing, the show is liable to pay."

I shushed him. "Listen, it's not what you're thinking, and I'll make sure I clear it with Kathleen."

"What is going on?" he said.

"Fingerprints."

"Whose fingerprints?"

"Max Weber's," I whispered.

"Why would you want Max's fingerprints?" he said, a little too loudly for my taste. I took Brad's arm and led him into the cloakroom.

"Will you be quiet?" I said. "It could be dangerous if anyone finds out."

"But I don't understand. I know you've been poking around Gary's death, but I also know that Bixby didn't find any stray fingerprints in the belfry or church to compare. Did he find some at the shop?"

"No, nothing to do with what happened in town. Well, it does, but the fingerprint is old. Over twenty years old."

"Will you make sense, woman?" Brad said.

"She'd probably make more sense if you'd let her talk," Nick said, sliding in next to us.

"What are you doing here?" Brad asked.

"I saw your discussion across the room, and I wanted to make sure Audrey was okay."

"I'm fine," I said.

Nick's brown eyes flashed with concern.

"Really," I said. "Brad saw me take one of the Ashbury's glasses and give it to Mrs. June."

"Who put it into her purse," Brad said. "I was concerned."

"Well, if a whole table full of cops had no problem with it," I said, "I don't see why you should."

Nick turned an inquisitive eye back to me.

"Okay, but try to keep quiet about this." And then I explained to them our whole theory about Suzy being the missing Logan baby. "Crazy?" I asked.

"Yes," Brad said.

"No," Nick said.

"Well, not a crazy theory," Brad amended, "but you have no proof."

"Which is why she was taking the glass." *You lunkhead.* Nick didn't say that last part, but my Spidey sense picked it up loud and clear. Or maybe it was his eye roll when Brad wasn't looking.

"So you're going to give the glass to Bixby?" Brad said. "To compare it to the prints found at the scene of the Logan kidnapping?"

"As soon as I get one more set of prints."

"A backup?" Nick asked.

"No. The police also had Paige Logan's fingerprints on file."

"So you want Suzy's," Brad said. "Just be careful."

"We will be," Nick said.

"We?" Brad said. "You're going with her?"

Right at that moment, Mrs. June pulled open the door. "Audrey, are you okay? Did you get . . . ?" She looked at Brad, and then Nick, then back to me. "Did I interrupt something?"

"No. I was about to get Suzy's glass. *Alone.*" I fixed a look at Nick and then at Brad. "Anything else might be too suspicious. Don't move. Wait here until I get back."

I walked out of the coatroom without another look back and focused on the sweetheart table where Suzy and (Michael? Mark?) fed each other bell-shaped desserts. Then rinsed them down with champagne. From the same glass. Ugh. And by the look of the pastry grease smeared on the outside of the flute, I doubted—even if I could somehow switch glasses without anyone noticing—whether it would yield a clean print.

But her bouquet, still in the silver reproduction holder, sat at the front of their table. I hadn't seen anyone else handle it since their arrival, and the shiny metal surface that she had grasped should yield a clear print. I headed in that direction, almost reaching their table when the bells started ringing—a signal for the bride and groom to kiss. Which they did, with a lip-lock that felt like it lasted a good fifteen minutes, at least when I was standing there towering over them.

"Congratulations to the happy couple!" I said, when they finally came up for air.

Suzy stood and gave me an air kiss, missing my cheek by about eight inches. "Oh, Audrey! I never should have doubted you. The flowers look lovely."

"Thank you." I then shook the groom's hand. "But I know they're still filming, and I'd really like to freshen your bouquet for you." I grabbed the bouquet by the ring of embossed bells on the bottom, a place unlikely to yield many fingerprints. "I'll be back in a jiffy," I said with an exaggerated smile.

"You can't take those," Suzy said, then lowered her voice. "I'm not supposed to know it, but they have a surprise for me later. They've got confetti and balloons and streamers in the ceiling."

"Suzy, have you been snooping again?" her groom asked.

"Maybe just a little. And I need to look surprised for the camera. And I'd really love the flowers to be in the shot."

"All the more reason for me to spruce these up," I said. "Won't take a minute."

"But they look fine to me. Don't they look fine to you?" she said with a pouty lip to her new husband.

"Well, I don't know that much about flowers . . . ," he started. Then, when Suzy sent a glare in his direction, he added, "But if Suzy says they look fine . . ."

"Oh, but they must be perfect," I said. "All part of our service." And I started walking away.

"Michael, stop her," I heard, but I quickened my pace.

"I think you should put those back," a male voice said behind me. But it wasn't the groom's uncertain tenor. It was Max Weber.

Chapter 23

❧

"Smile, pet," Max said, gripping my arm. "Weddings are such happy occasions." Then I knew what all those mystery novels meant by "a viselike grip." Already I felt my fingers growing numb from lack of blood flow.

"Of course I'm going to smile." I tried for nonchalance, but my cracking voice betrayed me. I cleared my throat and tried again. "Lovely wedding. I was going to freshen up these flowers."

"Don't play dumb," he whispered, then laughed, as if we were having a perfectly normal conversation. "Mr. Glock doesn't like it when people play dumb." He patted a lump in his suit coat pocket. "Set those flowers on the table. You and I are going to take a little walk."

"But I have to—"

"Leave them." His face held the oddest contradiction I'd ever seen. Angry gray eyes, but a huge fake smile. Across the room when you couldn't see his eyes, it would look like we were best buds shooting the breeze.

"You can't do this. Someone is going to notice."

But right at that moment, the emcee announced the cake cutting, and all eyes—and the camera—focused on the opposite corner of the room as the nationally known baker, dressed all in white, wheeled out his huge cake, surrounded by sparklers.

"Like I was saying," Max said, "you and I are going to take a little walk outside so we can have a nice quiet chat."

"You can't get away with this. I know that Suzy is not your daughter. And I'm not the only one."

If possible, his grip tightened. "Who else? Who else knows?"

I thought of Liv and the baby and everyone else who could be put at risk if Max knew who they were. I bit my lip. Had my boast escalated the situation? After all, he'd proven his propensity to kill anyone who could expose his secret. If I forced his hand, involved more people, who could predict what he would do? Would he fire into the wedding guests? Sure, the police would eventually take him down, but how many of my friends and neighbors could he take out with one Glock?

I shook my head. "No one," I said. "No one knows."

"That's what I thought. I'm not a bad man," he said. "I'm not a bad father."

"But you're not Suzy's father."

"Yes, I am," he rasped into my ear. "I raised her. Changed her diapers. Told her bedtime stories. Comforted her when her mama died. Drove her to school on the first day of kindergarten. Paid for her braces. *I* raised her."

"Her mama died?" Since Paige Logan's real mother was still alive, this must have been a Mrs. Weber. Was she in on the kidnapping with her husband?

We walked about five feet toward the side door, pushing through townsfolk who were still rushing toward the cake. I guess Max was smart enough to avoid the main entrance, where the whole town, the police, and the TV reporters would see us leave. Since the side door led only to Kathleen's

back garden and could only be opened from the inside, it
was likely to be unguarded. And if we made it that far . . .
My best chances were to get help before we made it outside.
With Max to my side but slightly behind me, I made odd
faces at my neighbors, trying to get their attention. But I
suppose the draw of cake, or perhaps being on camera, made
them not raise an eyebrow.

"Come gather round to see the cake cutting," the emcee
said again.

"What happened to your wife?" I asked, trying to inject
as much sympathy in my tone as I could.

Max shook his head. "She was sick. Ever since the birth
of our daughter."

"Your daughter? Suzy?" I remembered that Liv and
Amber Lee had both remarked on finding Suzy's birth certificate in Gary's research. "Something happened to Suzy."

"Margaret had given Suzy a bath. When I came home,
they were both asleep in the tub. The drugs they gave Margaret did that sometimes. It wasn't her fault."

"Suzy drowned?"

"Suzy was *asleep*," he said, his voice cracking with emotion. "I put Margaret to bed. Told her Suzy was sleeping.
But I couldn't . . . I couldn't bear to see what would happen . . ." He let out a shaky breath. "When Margaret woke
up, Suzy needed to be there."

"So you found another Suzy."

"I'd done some landscaping work for the Logan's neighbors. When I saw the little girl next door, I thought right off
that she looked like our Suzy."

"And your wife never noticed the difference?"

"If she did, she never said. She just picked up where she'd
left off, and everything was fine. It was a mistake, you see.
An accident. Why should Margaret have to pay for an
accident?"

"But Gary had to?"

"Gary was about to destroy my family. I could tell by the

questions he was asking Suzy. Asking me. He was thinking he was so smart. Just because I work with my hands doesn't make me stupid, you know. I caught on to what he was doing. So I told him that I had something I needed to get off my chest. I mentioned the church. When he got there, I told him I wanted to check out the old bell tower."

Finally the last cluster of cake groupies separated to rush past us, and Brad stood in front of the door, arms folded across his chest. "Audrey, you can't leave now," he said with a teasing voice while he wagged a finger at me. "You promised me that dance."

"I did," I said to Max. "I did promise him a dance."

Max squinted at Brad, then smiled that disturbing grin of his. Or maybe it wasn't the grin so much as the context. "Of course. Why don't you join us outside for a breath of fresh air first? There's something I'd like to discuss with you, too."

Brad's Adam's apple bobbed, but his friendly facial expression didn't change. "Sure," he said, with even a semblance of enthusiasm. And then he took my other hand and gave it a little squeeze.

Max let go of my arm. "Okay, you two head toward the door." He put his hand in his pocket. His Glock pocket. "I'll be right behind you," he said in a creepy singsong.

"He's got a gun," I mouthed to Brad.

"Quiet," Max whispered.

I balled up my hand, trying to get feeling back in my fingers. No one was watching our little drama. All attention was still on the cake as the national baker gave a little speech saying how honored and humbled he felt to be included. There was maybe fifteen feet left before we reached the door. I exhaled. Not a lot of time or opportunity to get away, and no way to hatch a plan with Brad. If I survived this situation, I vowed to learn Morse code, because then I could at least tap a message in Brad's hand. Not that even that would be practical in the short time we had left walking to the door. And it would only help if Brad knew Morse code, too.

We were right in front of the ice sculpture when Nick jogged over and laid a hand on Brad's shoulder. "Where do you think you're going?"

"Nick, no," I said.

"I'm talking to Brad." Nick gave Brad a little push to the shoulder. "Where are you going with my girl?"

My girl? What was Nick playing at? Did he not see Max Weber behind us?

Brad gave a little push back. And then I figured it out. An element of surprise, and they had Max's attention on them. Now, if I could only sneak away and maybe get to the table of cops. Any second and Max could pull out Mr. Glock and start a massacre.

I inched backward. My closest path to the table where Bixby sat with some of his officers would be right through the spot where Brad and Nick were staging their little fight, but if I could sneak behind the ice sculpture . . .

"Stop it," Max said. "Let's discuss this outside."

Nick and Brad scuffled right in front of the ice sculpture, unfortunately drawing Max's attention to where I was trying to make my escape to get help. I crouched behind the satin-draped table, then shifted so that the massive ice sculpture was between Max and me.

One of them—Brad, I think—fell against the table with a thud, and I watched as the sculpture started to wobble. It would be just like me to escape a deranged killer only to be crushed by five hundred pounds of ice in the shape of two wedding bells. And at the Ashbury, of course.

But then Nick shouted, "No you don't, you coward." I felt the table move, and soon Brad crawled out from underneath, followed seconds later by Nick.

Through the clear parts of the sculpture I could see an angry Max approach the table, his features distorted by the curves of the ice, taking on the appearance of a fun-house mirror. He drew the gun out of his pocket and pointed in our direction. Gasps went up in the crowd.

"Now!" Brad said, and he and Nick pushed on the table. When I saw what they were doing, I helped.

Max stopped suddenly, looking googly-eyed at the wobbling bells. The legs of the table gave way, sending the mound of ice in Weber's direction. A single shot rang out, but his arm was directed straight up as he tried to shield himself from the mountain of ice. Then the bells crashed on top of him, sending chunks of ice, and thankfully Mr. Glock, sliding in a huge arc, like an exploding sun, across the newly polished floor.

"Daddykins!" I heard over the gasps of the crowd. And all around us, bell-shaped confetti and ribbons rained down from the ceiling from where Mr. Glock had released it early.

Chapter 24

❦

Most of the guests had gone home, with Bixby's blessing. And the last time I peeked out the front window, the only ones left standing under a streetlight were Dennis Pinkleman and Ken Lafferty. Even the news truck was gone, leaving shortly after Bixby had gone out to give them a brief statement in time for the ten o'clock news. I suspect Jackie left after the news truck did.

Gigi sat at a table, her heels kicked off and her bare feet resting in the lap of her lighting guy. He massaged her arches while she murmured into a glass of champagne.

Henry Easton, disheveled and working on a ten o'clock shadow, busied himself with his cell phone. Most of the film crew were sleeping, heads down on tables, except for Marco, who had stretched out on top of a table, hands folded across his chest like a corpse. Only his snores reassured us that he was alive. I'd been tempted to put a lily in his arms.

Eric had already insisted on taking Liv home to get some rest, under Liv's protests, of course. But even Bixby hadn't been able to resist Eric's protective instincts. "You know where to reach us," he'd said. Liv's wide eyes were focused backward on the scene of the wedding-turned-crime-scene as he practically dragged her out of the room. I'd imagined she would have been a good model for a painting on Lot's wife as he dragged her out of Sodom. Grandma Mae had often told us that old Bible story. If it contained a cautionary tale about looking back, I never quite got it, but Liv and I did spend a delightful afternoon trying to figure out how to make salt stand up in a pillar.

A red-eyed Suzy, still in her wedding dress with the bell sleeves, shredded a tissue in her hands as she sat between Mrs. June and her new groom. He untied his tie and unbuttoned the top button of his shirt as Mrs. June patted Suzy's hand and tried to explain to her why her father had been handcuffed before being placed on the gurney when the ambulance came. I was certain Mrs. June would hit up Bixby for overtime. She deserved it.

Speaking of Bixby, he cleared his throat to regain my attention. "So you suspect that Gary discovered that Max Weber was the Logan kidnapper. Gary planned to expose the whole story to reboot his journalism career, which is why Max killed him. Allegedly."

"And if I'm right, the fingerprints should prove it. Max's and Suzy's."

He nodded. "I've already gotten a print from Suzy and compared it to the one in the file found conveniently in my receptionist's purse. The one for the missing Logan baby."

"And?" I leaned forward in my seat.

"I'll send it to a qualified expert, but I suspect it won't even take him ten seconds to verify that they're a match. And we'll take Max's when we book him to compare."

"It also explains the beard."

"Okaaay."

"Sorry. It's not really a non sequitur. I was just thinking about the full beard Max Weber came to town with. Suzy wanted him to shave it off, but they compromised on a trim."

"I don't see what the man's choice of facial hair has to do with anything," Bixby said.

"Don't you see? It's why Weber wanted to stop the show, and why he seemed so camera shy. He must have started growing that beard as soon as Suzy signed up for *Fix My Wedding*. He'd been trying to convince her to drop out of the show all along. He must have been terrified that the Logans would see him and recognize him as one of their neighbor's gardeners—and see Suzy as the spitting image of Deborah Logan."

"So we have him for the kidnapping. Compiling enough evidence to charge him for Gary's murder might be a little harder, but we'll have your testimony and we've got time to pull everything else together."

He looked across the room at Suzy. "Perhaps Suzy . . . or Paige . . . whatever she decides to call herself . . . can place him at or near the scenes of the crimes."

"Someone needs to look into what happened to the real Suzy."

Bixby inclined his head.

"Suzy Weber has a real birth certificate. From what Weber told me, she died in his wife's care, but he said Mrs. Weber wasn't all that *healthy* at the time. It was really unclear to me whether it was an accident or the wife killed her."

"But he's at least an accessory." Bixby pulled out his handkerchief and wiped his raw nose. Poor guy. All these crimes happening in rooms full of allergens. I was beginning to have a little sympathy.

"They must have hid the body. Dang. Those are more charges there. Another municipality. And we found those missing videotapes still in Max's room. So we have him on the B and E. But you really should have come to me. Going after those fingerprints was a dangerous thing to do."

"It didn't seem very dangerous at the time," I said. "I thought you would have wanted more proof. I was trying to bring you that. What would you have done if I'd told you earlier?"

He worked his jaw for a minute. "Probably pass on the information to the appropriate jurisdiction, since the Logan kidnapping is way out of ours. And maybe they'd have taken me seriously."

"But this way, it's solved here. If you were worried about the town's reputation—"

"And what about the town's citizens?" he shot back, but then calmed his tone. "Please, don't put yourself in that kind of danger again. And I promise, I will listen to whatever wild, crazy theories you come up with."

I flashed him my most innocent smile. "Pinky swear?"

He shook his head and laughed. "Get out of here."

When I rose from the table, I spotted Brad and Nick on the other side of the room, sampling the uneaten cake.

"Have you no shame?" I said.

"We were hungry," Brad said.

Nick scrunched up his nose and tossed his plate back onto the table. "Not *that* hungry. Dry as anything. Probably because he had to transport it here. That's the problem with not buying local."

"Well, don't worry, my friend," Brad said. "The baker won't get any accolades for this one. This episode is definitely kaput. *Although* we might be able to sell a good chunk of the footage to the news services. The kidnapping and all."

My friend? When did Brad and Nick get so chummy?

Brad turned to me. "Sorry, Audrey. That means the Rose in Bloom doesn't get the exposure, either, but we will honor our contract to make sure you get paid as originally agreed."

Nick cleared his throat.

"And maybe a little extra," Brad said, "if I can swing it. You deserve it. Here I thought I was doing you a favor, getting them to do the show in Ramble."

"It's not your fault," I said. "Besides, I really appreciate you two saving my life. Did you conspire to—?"

Nick shook his head. "There wasn't time."

"All I told him was that I was going in," Brad said.

"And when he couldn't get you away from Max," Nick said, "I knew that something was up. My first idea was to stage the fight and draw some attention."

"When he pushed me toward the ice sculpture, I saw it wobble," Brad said.

"And then I came up with the idea," Brad and Nick both said, almost in unison.

I chuckled. "Well, thanks for saving my life, no matter who figured it out first."

Brad and Nick eyed each other in a way to suggest that it did matter, and that they were going to settle it, one way or another.

"Well, thanks again," I said, "and good night."

"Audrey?" I froze for a moment, afraid to turn around when I recognized Suzy's voice. On what was supposed to be the happiest day of her life, she'd had her whole life turned around, and I wasn't sure if she was going to thank me or blame me for my part in it.

"Yes?" I would say that I tried to inject sympathy into my voice, but this time it oozed out naturally.

"Don't go yet. I wanted to . . . I know you could have been killed, and that you were only trying to help. I wish I could thank you, but please understand, I'm not there yet. Part of me is grateful. But Da . . . Max Weber was always good to me. Part of me doesn't believe it and hates you for messing up my life. It's too much to process."

"I understand," I said. Not that anyone could. I'd lost a father, but I'd never had one stripped away from me and branded a killer—only to then find out he wasn't really my father to begin with. "I suspect you have new parents to meet."

"They're on their way. Should be here by morning." Suzy closed her eyes and exhaled a shaky breath. "I hope I can pull myself together for them. I'm afraid I won't know how to react. The woman with the police"—she pointed toward

Mrs. June, who smiled and nodded encouragingly—"said they'd been searching for me all my life, but I don't remember them."

"Maybe you remember more than you think." I leaned in to hug her. "I saw the pictures of your nursery. Bells everywhere. And the Tinker Bell doll you loved—it was given to you by your real parents. So maybe . . ."

"Maybe I remember more than I think? But they'll want me to love them."

"But they love you, so I'm sure it will come. And they'll be patient."

Suzy nodded and turned back toward her groom, who threw his coat around her shoulders and pulled her into a long embrace.

"I'm glad she has somebody to care for her," I said.

"That's going to put a kink in the honeymoon," Brad said.

"Can I take you home?" Nick offered.

"No." I watched Michael comfort his bride. "I have the CR-V here—and a very hungry cat waiting for me."

Chester was curled up on the back of my living room couch, one of his favorite perches, as evidenced by the gray and white hair always collecting on it and the pronounced sag visible even when he wasn't there. Instead of getting up and running for the door, he lifted one eyelid, identified who I was, then curled up tighter into his ball.

"Sorry to be so late, old man," I said, slipping off my shoes and curling up next to him. I rubbed his ears, and soon I could feel rather than hear his gentle purring. I tufted the fur on his head into a spiky fauxhawk.

"This apartment living isn't good for you. You need to be out in the country, chasing birds and butterflies." I then thought of the hawks, coyotes, and even bears. "Or maybe you can just stalk them from the window. But as soon as the money comes in . . ."

Chester meowed at me. Not sure if he was making conversation or if his new hairdo rubbed him the wrong way.

"Don't get a hair ball. You'll love it out there. So quiet." I leaned back and rested my head for a moment. And before long I was dreaming of Liv and me as children, running in with dirty clothes and faces. And Grandma Mae standing at the door, her arms crossed in front of her flowered apron while she tried to maintain a stern look. But the smile radiated from her eyes.

After a few days the Ashbury reopened, but the film crew was slow to leave town. I'm not sure they were on the clock, but they seemed to be filming a documentary about the finding of Paige Logan. I guess it was a case of being at the right place at the right time.

Gigi and Henry left first, driving a small caravan, which consisted only of the wedding planners, makeup artist, seamstress, and, of course, Gigi's lighting guy. Where they were headed after the funeral was anyone's guess. Even Brad didn't know if the next wedding was going to be filmed. The town that had welcomed the mass caravan in with a fanfare barely gave a nod to the limo and deluxe RV as they skulked out of town. It seemed Ramble had had its fifteen minutes of fame, but was glad it was over.

So was I. Although I have to admit I did take some pride in looking over Dennis Pinkleman's viral posts on the *Fix My Wedding* fan site and on Pinterest, all of which he'd entitled "The Episode That Wasn't." His pictures of the bouquets and centerpieces were truly gorgeous, and he had heaped all kinds of praise on the flowers, calling me the "florist to the stars and a genuinely nice person." I guess it was better than "Dr. Dolittle."

The fan site was also a magnet for Jackie, who'd decided to get with the program and posted a careful apology for her rants against Gigi and the now-deceased Gary. "Mistakes were made . . ." (She had a career in politics.) She'd also posted that she and her husband—I guess he was now her ex-husband—were in couple's counseling and considering reconciling. Poor guy.

Meanwhile the show appeared back in the tabloids when an enterprising member of the paparazzi captured a photograph of Henry Easton in Boston with a family alleged to be his wife and five kids. Easton neither confirmed nor denied . . . yada, yada, yada.

Life at the shop resumed a sense of normalcy, even if we were still putting things back to rights after Eric's reorganization. On Monday, which was my day to start late, I poked my head into the back room where Liv was up to her elbows in gladioli.

Then the shop bell rang, and I headed to the front to greet the latest customer. "Suzy?"

She looked much more somber and, frankly, older since I'd seen her last. She was flanked by a couple I recognized from the news footage as the Logans.

"Actually," she said, "I think I've decided to go by Paige."

Deborah Logan smiled at that, and Evan Logan looked ready to shed a tear or two.

"I wanted to come by and say thank you," Paige continued. "Without you I might have never known my parents."

And with that, they all rushed me, and we passed the next few minutes in a massive hug-fest. Liv soon joined us.

"Another reason I'm here," Paige said, "is that I've decided to get married again. Under my real name. And with my parents—my real father—to walk me down the aisle."

"Congratulations!" I said.

"Even if it means I have to go through life as Paige Turner. I think I'm going to be Paige Logan-Turner. But I still want to get married in the old church. Not a big deal this time. No huge reception. No camera. Just my new family and a few people we met here. So, one more time, could you make me a bouquet? And we'd love to have you and your friends join us at the wedding."

Paige and her parents followed me to the consulting nook, where we designed a new bouquet. And yes, she still wanted bell-shaped flowers. "Now I realize that my love of bells was almost like a light," she said, "guiding my way home."

This was clearly not the shallow, bubble-headed woman she'd tried to portray on camera.

I explained we'd cornered the market on bellflowers and might have difficulty obtaining more.

"What about the blue flowers that were at the reception?" she asked. "I thought those were pretty. What do they mean?"

"Bluebells can mean *constancy*—but also *sorrowful regret*. That's why I chose other colors of bellflowers originally."

"But that's perfect," she said. "Sorrowful regret will always be a part of my life. I loved the Webers. I'll always regret what happened here, what Max did. Part of me will always think of him as my father, and I know he cared for me. And all that time the Logans were constantly looking for me. I regret that we were not able to share my childhood."

She sniffed. "Yes, let's use the bluebells."

Chapter 25

❧

While Suzy Weber's wedding day had been hot and sticky and almost unbearable, Paige Logan's day started out with a bang, as a brief band of thunderstorms ushered in a cold front that brought much relief. By the time I was walking into the church, a light, refreshing breeze was drying the pavement and the sun was playing peekaboo with scattered clouds.

I shuffled into a pew behind Mrs. June as the pianist began to play. I put my hand on the older woman's shoulder. "You're here early."

She swiveled in her seat to face me. "I had some news for the family. Just decided to stay."

"News?"

"Mixed news, really. They found Suzy Weber's body—the real Suzy Weber—buried not far from where the Webers lived at the time. The forensic accounting guys also dug up . . ." She shook her head. "Sorry, bad choice of words, but they discovered a money trail. Weber was smart about the money."

"Money?"

"The ransom money he demanded and collected from the Logans. He sat on it for a long time."

"I never got why he sent that ransom note, anyway. Why take the risk of being caught claiming the money? From what he told me, he just wanted another Suzy." I shuddered. Replaceable children.

"Well, Max is talking now. And I might just have seen a transcript of one of the questioning sessions . . ." Mrs. June paused and fanned herself, even though the church was untypically cool for the season. "Apparently he convinced himself that he did it for Suzy, so he could give her all the advantages the Logans would have. Like child support."

"There's a demented logic in that."

"I guess he also used the note as an opportunity to misdirect the investigation. I just caught a glimpse of a copy of the analysis of the original ransom note, and he deliberately threw them a few curveballs. Used a special paper he'd gotten from another state. He's ambidextrous, and he wrote the note using block letters in mechanical pencil with his left hand. Profilers were looking for a bankrupt engineer from Idaho."

"Still very risky."

"I'm not so sure he didn't want to be caught. Anyway, his plan must have worked, because Weber wasn't even on their radar. When it appeared he had gotten away with it, he still had all that cash to deal with. He slowly began adding it to his landscaping business—padding the money he received from clients and then inventing fictional accounts. To the whole world it looked like he was just doing really well in the landscaping business. Which in turn brought him more clients. He probably tripled the ransom money in profits."

"Nothing breeds success like success. Any chance that the Logans will get any of it back?"

"A good chance they'll get all of it. In time. And with a

good lawyer. Meanwhile, the FBI has frozen all of Weber's assets. He can't move his accounts. He can't even use them in his defense."

"How's the homicide case coming?"

"Wrapping up nicely, especially since Weber's spilling his guts to anyone who will listen, much to the chagrin of his public defender. They've also matched Weber's handwriting on the ransom demand with the warning notes."

"At least Brad's off the hook."

"I did learn that it was Weber who sent the text from Gary's phone, asking Brad to meet him in the bell tower. At that point, Gary was already dead."

"Brad would make a decent suspect, to Max's way of thinking. He was there when Gary blew up and threatened to fire Brad. And he must have known Brad used to ring the bells. Do you suppose I'll need to testify?"

"Oh, honey. It won't be so bad. Besides, you've seen the Logans together. Isn't it a beautiful thing?"

Nick Maxwell slid in next to me before I could answer. Liv touched my shoulder as she and Eric took up the pew behind me. And soon the ceremony was under way. The tolling of the bell in the belfry marked the beginning of the processional, much shorter and more informal than before.

Pastor Seymour, his trusty water glass by his side, stood at the front with Michael Turner. (I finally got his name right.) They watched as Paige made her first appearance, in a simple, demure, knee-length white dress. She had both her parents by the arm and walked the aisle at a glacial pace, stopping to whisper to each of them along the way. I was impressed with how hard it seemed for them all to let go—giving their daughter in marriage when they so recently found her.

But Michael Turner left his spot at the altar, met them halfway, and embraced the Logans. And while the little church was nearly empty since the hoopla of the show was over, I was sure there was not a dry eye in the place.

I felt movement in the aisle, and Brad, slightly out of breath, slid into the empty space on my left. I suspect he was the one ringing the bells to mark Paige's entrance.

As the simple, heartfelt wedding commenced, Nick reached over and took my right hand, giving it a gentle squeeze.

Maybe there was a future there, if I was patient enough to wait for his business to start turning a profit. He worked hard, so that was sure to happen. Perhaps someday he'd be standing in front of the church in a spiffy rented tux, smiling at me while I walked down that aisle in a size-twelve wedding dress—not bought from one of Easton's overpriced and undersized salons.

I was relishing our closeness—and designing a new bouquet for myself—when Brad took hold of my left hand. His thumb stroked mine in that old, familiar manner, sending my heart rate into overdrive. Was it attraction? Did I still have feelings for Brad?

Or was it a sin to hold hands with two men at the same time?

And in church!

And maybe Grandma Mae's spirit was still alive in the old pew where she'd spent so many Sundays, because I could have sworn I heard her sweet voice, only this time mildly reproving.

What in tarnation? Have you got leave of your senses?

Yes'm. I think I have.

Turn the page for a preview of Beverly Allen's
next Bridal Bouquet Shop Mystery

Floral
Depravity

Coming soon from Berkley Prime Crime!

"Let me guess, Audrey." Liv pointed to my hand. "He loves you not?"

I glanced down. I'd only intended to remove the guard petals of the rose I was working on. Instead, I'd accumulated a pile of rose petals and one decimated stem. "Sorry. Distracted, I guess." I set the remnants aside on my worktable—little in the floral business was ever wasted—then picked up another gorgeous red rose. Good thing our cooler was well stocked.

My cousin Liv came over and pushed a sprig of boxwood into a bare spot in the funeral flowers I was preparing for a feisty local woman. She'd passed away at the ripe old age of one hundred and three, and the red roses were ordered by her seventy-nine-year-old husband. (Did that make her a cougar?) He claimed they were her favorites, and he wanted to give them to her one last time.

Although arranging funeral flowers tended to cast a pall over the shop, I still smiled when I incorporated a few unopened rosebuds. Not only would the arrangement

continue to grow lovelier as they opened, but the meaning
of the red rosebud, *you are young and beautiful*, was almost
delightfully ironic. This arrangement, as it aged, would play
out a slideshow of their lives together. As it barely began to
bloom, it would represent *timid love*. Then as they opened,
a *vibrant love*. I closed my eyes and swallowed the lump in
my throat.

"There's still time to get out of this, you know," Liv said.
"You don't have to go through with it."

"What, this condolence arrangement? I've made hundreds like it." Although I much preferred wedding bouquets.
Even though I specialized in wedding flowers at the Rose
in Bloom, the shop Liv and I co-owned, we all pitched in
where needed, so I'd done my fair share of funeral arrangements.

"You know what I mean."

"Uh-oh," Amber Lee said. "If it's time for *that* discussion, I'm going up front to check the self-service cooler."
Amber Lee, a retired schoolteacher, came to us with little
floral experience but loads of enthusiasm after she discovered that retirement didn't suit her. She was technically my
assistant and helped with all the wedding arrangements, but
had proved herself capable in almost every area of the shop.
She was indispensable. More than that, she was becoming
family.

"I just did that an hour ago," Liv said.

"Then . . . well, I'll figure out something else to do," she
said.

As Amber Lee hustled out of earshot, I sighed. "We've
been through this."

"I know." Liv set down her tools and stretched her back.
"And I don't want to tell you how to run your life. It's just
that it's such a big commitment."

"And what exactly is wrong with big commitments?" My
words came out sounding a bit defensive, so I forced a more
casual tone into my voice. "You've made a few of your own,

if I'm not mistaken. A husband, a house of your own"—I pointed at her burgeoning belly—"a baby due in about fifteen minutes."

She waved off my concern. "I've got weeks left, and then some. The doctor suspects the baby will be late. But don't change the subject."

"I'm not changing the subject. We're talking about responsibility. I'm twenty-nine years old. Why is it that you can run full-speed into adulthood, but when I take on one responsibility—"

"It's not just . . . " Liv rubbed the top of her stomach and breathed out, a pained expression on her face.

"What is it? A contraction?" My irritation melted away into concern. Liv and I squabbled on only the rarest of occasions, and I found staying angry with my cousin and best friend about as possible as man-powered flight, perpetual motion, or a box of chocolate remaining untouched in the shop all day.

"No, I'm fine. And you're right." She put her arm around me. "I don't know why I'm such a mother hen at times. I'll try to support you, even when I don't agree with your decisions."

"Of all people, Liv, you should understand what that cottage means to me." Liv and I had spent many happy childhood summers there with our Grandma Mae. It was she who inspired our love for flowers.

"I do. I have fond memories there, too, remember? But we're not talking about making a scrapbook. Some decisions you have to make with your head, not just your heart. Can't you treasure Grandma Mae's memory without buying her old cottage? You heard what the inspectors said."

"That last one was more positive. The bank approved the loan."

"He also said the sewer line to the road needs to be replaced."

"Well, of course I know the place is going to need some

work." All of a sudden, my stomach went a little queasy. "Are sewer lines expensive?" Most of my money would be tied up in the down payment. I'd hoped to be able to do repairs and make improvements little by little.

"Eric said there is no sewer line to the road. The cottage has a septic system in the back. What if the only reason you got the loan was because they somehow inspected the wrong house?"

"What are the odds of that?"

"Better than you think. Eric and I figured out what that scrawl on page three said. Something about the bidet on the second floor leaking."

The cottage didn't have a bidet. Come to think of it, it didn't have a second floor, either. "But maybe it's providence. Maybe I'm meant to have that house."

"Kiddo, the good Lord would never saddle you with that place . . . unless you've been a lot more wicked than you've been letting on. Besides," Liv said, laying a gentle hand on my forearm, "if you're all that confident, why do you keep stripping our roses?"

I looked down at the second bare stem in my hand and tossed it onto the worktable.

"Would you like to leave early?" Liv asked. "What time do you sign the papers?"

"Not until five," I said. "You just don't want me ruining all the stock."

Liv snapped her fingers. "You saw right through me."

I shook my head. "I have a bridal appointment in a few minutes, anyway."

"Oh, new wedding? Who's coming in?"

"Who do you think?" I rolled my eyes.

"Again?"

Amber Lee peeked her head in the back door. "Is it safe?"

"All better," I said.

"Good." She lugged in a large wrapped box and placed it in front of me. "This came for you a few minutes ago."

"For me?" I looked at Liv and she shrugged. But a twinkle in her eye and a half smile tickling her lips told me she knew something about it. I pulled off the bow and ripped open the paper. Inside the box was a tool kit and a cordless drill. "I can't say anyone has ever given me hardware before."

"Consider them a housewarming gift from all of us at the shop. From what Eric told me about the place, you're going to need them."

"I suggested we add a good man to help you with the repairs," Amber Lee said, "but we couldn't quite fit him in the box."

Liv sent her a look, which saved me the trouble. My love life was a bit complicated, since it involved friendly dates with Nick Maxwell, the local baker—who was unwilling to commit. And long phone conversations and regular texts with Brad Simmons, my ex-almost-fiancé—who seemed determined to erase the "ex" part.

"Oh," Amber Lee said, "Kathleen Randolph and her daughter are here for their bridal consultation, take three."

"Four," I said, "but who's counting?"

I propped a smile on my face as I mounted the steps to the wrought-iron gazebo we used as our consulting nook. Kathleen Randolph, owner of the Ashbury Inn and prominent—but often long-winded—local historian, had called to say she was bringing a few reference books along to this appointment to help finalize the flowers for her daughter Andrea's wedding. Since the wedding, planned to be held at a local medieval encampment, was now just two weeks away, I hoped they didn't have anything too exotic in mind. But it looked like they'd brought half their library. About fifty moldering tomes were piled in front of them.

I'd like to think my smile didn't dim, but I'm not sure I'm that good.

"We brought more reference books," Kathleen said brightly. "Found some great stuff on the Tudors."

"Nice," I said. I refrained from telling her the only things

I know about the Tudors had to do with stucco and fake wood beams.

The next two hours were steeped in history, leaving me feeling much like a cold, wet teabag, but I managed to sketch out some flower suggestions amid their rapt discussion of the Middle Ages.

"And you *must* come to the ceremony," Andrea said.

It wasn't unusual for brides to invite me to their weddings. Ramble, Virginia, was such a small town that I was likely to know the bride, anyway. And it seemed to reassure them that their flowers would be there, look lovely, and if anything happened at the last minute I could fix it.

Kathleen pulled out a sheet of folded parchment and smoothed it on the table. "I drew you a map to the encampment."

I looked at the page. It resembled a pirate's map. All it was missing was the skull and crossbones, a sea monster, and a big X. I take that back. It had an X in a clearing surrounded by woods. "I can't use my GPS?"

Kathleen and Andrea shared a snicker or two at my expense before Andrea took pity and explained. "The encampment is not accessible by roads. Having a parking lot right next to a Medieval encampment would make it look too much like a . . . a Renaissance fair." I swore they both shuddered at the words.

Did I dare ask? I dared. "What's the difference?"

"Renaissance fairs are for the . . . " Kathleen trailed off, leaving me to wonder if she was going to say "unwashed masses."

"For people who want to play with swords and speak in dreadfully awful cockney accents," Andrea finished.

"Worse than Dick van Dyke in *Mary Poppins*." This time there was no mistaking it. They both shuddered.

I happened to adore Dick van Dyke, so it took great effort to hold my tongue.

"And eat turkey legs!" they both said in unison, with distasteful grimaces on their faces.

I quirked an eyebrow.

"Turkey is a new world bird," Andrea said. "They wouldn't have had it in the Middle Ages."

"The Guardians of Chivalry Encampment is for serious-minded historians who want an authentic experience," Kathleen said. "We camp a mile from the nearest road. No electricity. No running water. Authentic dress is required. We don't just play at the Middle Ages. We live like we are in the Middle Ages."

"We hunt and gather, butcher our own animals, learn the old crafts," Andrea said.

"We have a sizeable village constructed," Kathleen said. "When we first started, oh, maybe thirty years ago, it was nothing more than a caravan of tents. We try to put up a new structure every year. But now we're working on a castle, so it's going to take longer."

"I see," I said.

I'd heard of the encampment, of course, and had seen the visitors traveling through, stopping at the local restaurants on the way in and, much grubbier looking and more foul smelling, on the way out.

"We've decided to go with the hand-fasting," Andrea said. "Although the ceremony was most usually an engagement, many historians say that if the marriage was consummated at that point, the couple were considered legally wed by the church."

"Hand-fasting?"

"We tie our hands together while we give our consent to marry," Andrea said. "Of course, to make it legal in Virginia, we'll have an officiant. We have someone licensed coming as a friar this year."

"A licensed friar?" I asked.

"No, not really a friar," she said, "any more than the knights have been dubbed by a queen. But he's licensed by the state and will be using the persona of a friar. It couldn't be better."

"So you can bring the flowers the day of the wedding,"

Kathleen said. "And stay for the grand feast. Of course, it will be too dark to go back, so you'll have to stay the night. And I suppose you might need help carrying everything."

"I . . . I guess I will. We've never made a delivery to the middle of the woods before."

"And you'll need to come in costume." Andrea gnawed at her cuticle. "I don't suppose you have a medieval dress in the back of your closet."

"She'll just have to rent something," Kathleen said. "I mean, it's not truly authentic, but it does the job for someone coming for the first time."

"Most of the regulars own their own medieval wardrobe?" I asked.

"Most of the regulars *make* their own wardrobe," Kathleen said. "Stitched by hand. Some even spin their own fibers and weave and dye their own cloth."

"That must take . . ."

"Some old-timers work on their clothing all year long," Andrea said. "A few even sew extra to sell—a truly authentic garment can go for thousands. We've been working on the wedding dress for ages. Made the pattern based on an oil painting. A lovely blue."

"That's where we get our 'something blue' tradition," Kathleen said. "And you'll bring the bachelor's buttons for the festivities later?"

"They're going to be a riot," Andrea said.

I nodded, but I could feel my cheeks turning peony pink. To the Victorians, the flower known as the bachelor's button often symbolized *celibacy* or the *blessing of being single*. Apparently in medieval time, "blessings" took on a whole new meaning as young women would hide the flowers in their clothing, and the bachelors would be tasked with finding them.

Although her order was simple—just her bouquet, a wreath for her hair, and the extra bachelor's buttons—I decided this might just prove to be the most memorable wedding yet.

"There's a nice shop that has some decent stuff," Kathleen said. "But they sell out early."

"Of course, you can add the costume charge to our bill," Andrea said.

"Andrea," Kathleen said, "I'm sure Audrey wouldn't mind renting her own. After all, we just invited her to the wedding."

Andrea shot her a look. "It's only right, Mother. It's part of the expense of getting the flowers to the venue."

She jotted down a name onto a sheet of scrap paper and handed it to me. "Just remember, they sell out fast."

I arrived at Grandma Mae's cottage with only my suitcase and a smile. Okay, I also had a sleeping bag, food in a cooler, an old Coleman lantern, and a couple of flashlights, since the power wouldn't be turned on until the morning. And carpal tunnel from signing all those documents.

Eric, as property manager for the Rawlings—the most recent owners and neglectors of my new home—had been by earlier to build some impromptu stairs, since the old ones had been torn off to ensure anyone foolish enough to try to climb them wouldn't fall through, hurt themselves, and sue the Rawlings. Not that even the Jehovah's Witnesses or the most ardent Avon lady had the dedication to climb those rickety steps.

Just getting to the stairs through the jungle of a front yard was difficult in the twilight. But I didn't stop for the burrs that were clinging to the hem of my jeans as if I were dressed in Velcro. I'd waited so long. I pulled the key from my pocket—it wouldn't go on my ring with my ordinary keys, at least not yet.

The lock turned hard. I was worried it would break the

key, but finally it yielded—just another thing to have oiled.
Eventually. Just like the hinges on the squeaky door that
announced my arrival.

Home.

The walls seemed to squeal it. I closed my eyes—
probably a good idea, because the place was truly in sham-
bles; even my enthusiasm for the cottage couldn't hide that
fact. But I paused to breathe in the memories. Grandma Mae
bustling at the old electric stove. Liv and I sitting at the table
on a rainy day with a fresh box of sixty-four Crayolas
between us. I could almost still smell them. We'd giggled
until one of us had the hiccups and we slid from our chairs
to the floor. Grandma chided us, but we could see she didn't
really mean it. The twinkle in her eye gave her away, and
her shoulders shook in quiet laughter when she turned back
to the stove.

The old stove was still there, and I had a sudden craving
for a cup of instant coffee, only that wasn't going to happen.
Not until there was electricity. Along with water. Eric had
promised to help with all of that. But not until the morning.

I lit the old lantern while I still had enough light to do so
and cleared a spot in the middle of the living room floor for
my sleeping bag. The air felt stale and foul, so despite the
coolness of the evening, I pushed open the only window that
wasn't stuck or broken and boarded up.

So, with too much energy to sleep but too little light to
do anything productive, I climbed into the sleeping bag and
planned what I would do with the little cottage. I'd give the
outside a new coat of white paint, and maybe an archway in
the front dripping with wisteria: *Welcome, fair stranger.* Of
course, it would take me weeks just to weed the old garden.
Almost easier to start new. But preserving any of Grandma
Mae's plantings was well worth the extra effort.

Nick and a few others had promised to help me move in.
I'd bring Chester over last, since I wouldn't want him to run
away from strange surroundings when the doors were open.

He hadn't been out of that apartment much since I brought him home from the SPCA, except for an occasional excursion to hide under my neighbor's truck—and the dreaded trip to the vet's office. He'd whine the whole drive, then hop on the scale and refuse to budge. Yes, he was a bit pudgy. Maybe living in the country would be good for him—all those birds and rabbits to watch from the window.

I was still thinking about Chester, so when I heard the plaintive little meow, I thought I imagined it. Old houses have strange noises—I knew that ahead of time—but when I heard it again, I could tell this was definitely an animal sound. I scooted out of the sleeping bag and grabbed the flashlight.

The little cry sounded again, followed by what cat owners recognize instantly as the sound of claws on the screen.

I swung the flashlight beam to the open window, and there, crawling halfway up the battered screen was a tiny jet-black kitten. It mewed again.

"Where's your mama?" I asked.

It answered me with the most pitiful series of mews, as if it were pouring out a tale of woe and sadness. My heart melted for the thing.

"I'd let you in, but you need your mother." The kitten was so tiny and bright-eyed, but with fur matted in spots, that I doubted if it had been fully weaned. Still, I searched in my cooler for an appropriate bit of food and decided to try a smidgen of turkey salad from my sandwich. I grabbed two foam plates and a bottle of water and went outside, half expecting it to run away. But it didn't.

I poured a bit of the water into one plate and put the turkey on another, setting both on the little temporary porch, then peeled the kitty away from the screen. I winced as the wires popped.

She trembled in my arms but didn't fight me. I put her by the food and she sniffed it. Then a little pink tongue came out and tried the turkey. She licked it to death, leaving most of it on the plate and then sniffed at the water, but wasn't even lapping it effectively.

"You're not even weaned, yet, are you?"

I scanned the flashlight across the yard, looking for the reflection of eyes, hoping to find a mama cat for this little thing. Meanwhile, the kitten started weaving around my legs and purring. I picked her up and cradled her against my shoulders, and she let out a contented sigh.

"All right, kitty. If no one in the neighborhood claims you, you can stay here with me." I mentally added buying a bottle and kitty formula to my burgeoning to-do list.

"I just hope Chester doesn't have you for breakfast."